Fallen Virtue

Of Beasts and Buzzards Series

Book 1

RJ Benson

Fallen Virtue

Of Beasts and Buzzards Series

Book 1

Copyright © 2019 by RJ Benson

Author Portrait by Pamela Pizarro-Ruiz

Cover Design by Story Wrappers

ISBN - 9781626130982

Library of Congress Control Number - 2018953961

Published by ATBOSH Media ltd.

Cleveland, Ohio, USA

http://www.atbosh.com

Dedication

To my amaze-ballz family, friends, and everyone who has supported my long struggle to find my passion in life.

To my publisher, ATBOSH Media, thank you for your help and taking a chance on me.

I'd also like to thank my alpha reader, Faith B. for all your help and beta readers, Lydia Moore (iFlow) and Katja B.

A couple of honorable mentions go out to Rachelle, Robinson, Susan and Kyle, Tim and Justin V. for being such great writing buddies, friends and my chosen family.

To my biggest fan and first patron,

Billy A. Thank you for all your support!

Thank you, Dad, for supporting me through the dark times and always encouraging my dreams, big or small.

To my Mom and Paul, for helping me out far more than I can ever repay.

Finally, to my big sister, Kristen for being my biggest inspiration and, my biggest Super Hero. You are the kindest person I've ever met, and you deserve the world.

I love you all, so much.

Dear Reader,

I'd, first off, like to thank you for choosing this novel. You have no idea the gratitude I feel towards a person who is willing to open their mind and take a chance on a new author.

I started writing as a young girl, story upon unfinished story filling my filing cabinet. I'm so happy and excited to get the chance to bring these barely begun works to fruition. I hope you will be satisfied with the following journey you're about to take. I've poured myself into this world, dragging my writer friends kicking and screaming, editing and editing until every word sounded just right. And then, editing some more.

Zane's journey is only beginning with this first novel. I hope to bring a new series to your world, one not constricted by the traditional norms of romance. A series for all to enjoy; straight, disabled, gay, bisexual, transsexual, lesbian, and so on. The series will be incorporating as many types of relationships as possible.

I've taken a chance with this new series as a novice author, but I believe it's a story worth sharing with the world. Everyone deserves a romance they can relate to. My goals, as a writer, are to do my best to provide. I hope you will stick with me.

Please enjoy the first book in my series, Of Beasts and Buzzards; Fallen Virtue, Book One.

Sincerely,

RJ Benson

Damaceous slapped two five-dollar bills on the bar and shook his head. "Thanks. Keep the change." Picking up the glass, he turned his back to the bar, leaning against it casually. He didn't intend to drink the alcohol, but he needed something to help him blend in.

He closed his eyes, let his senses reach out. There. Stronger this time. A tug…just on the edge. Almost impossible to perceive. Had Damaceous not been investigating this area, he wouldn't have bothered to find out more. But there it was…that familiarity, remnants of power just barely outside those edges.

Damaceous craned his neck forward, peering beyond the black awning above the bar area. Off to his left, further down, a metal staircase spiraled up toward an office with a balcony bordered by golden railings. On his right, back by the entrance, a line snaked around to the restrooms. Two sets of stairs led down to the dance floor, and the place was busy tonight, people crowding the stage below to watch the band. More enthusiastic patrons were seated at tables on each of the surrounding levels.

A gaggle of giggles reached Damaceous's ears. A pair of blonde women and a redhead passed by, taking their place at the bar to order drinks.

The redhead wiggled her hips and peeked around him toward the line for the bathroom. "Ugh. Guys, I *really* gotta go. Order me something?"

"Ha! Fine, bitch. Just hurry up. This night is about to be *lit*. I'm gonna' meet this hottie tonight and take him home!" the curly-haired blonde replied, whooping loudly, her dress of pink sequins sparkling under the lights. The redhead facepalmed and shot Damaceous an embarrassed smile before hurrying off.

"Ashley! Shut up. Yeesh...hey, bartender!" The other blonde wobbled forward, leaning against the bar. Both already seemed to have imbibed earlier in the night. Damaceous observed them discreetly over his glass, amused but then he turned his back, pretending to take a few sips when the bartender returned.

"What would you like tonight, ladies?" From his peripherals, Damaceous watched Ashley lean over the bar, holding out her phone.

She grabbed the bartender's collar. "Hey!" She tried to whisper but her voice was loud, and it came out more like a raspy shout. Ashley pulled the man forward. Not at all subtle.

"Ash!" the other blonde admonished her friend, yanking at the pink sparkles of the woman's dress.

Ashley waved her off with a scoff then held up the screen of her phone for the bartender to see. "Hey...my friends and I heard if we ask the bartender, we could meet him..." She cranked her body around, one hand pointing straight down to the stage. "Him, the singer! We heard it's a secret though. Can you get us in?"

The bartender glanced toward Damaceous, but he'd suddenly found himself interested in the lights above the dance floor. "Well...," the bartender continued. "I could probably help you out *if* you let go of my shirt, miss."

"Really? O.M.G., Beth! He can do it!" Ashley exclaimed. She let the man's collar go and sunk into a stool. "When can we see him? It's Zane, right? That's his name? Omigosh. He's *so* frickin' hot!"

The bartender leaned forward, glancing around again. "Yes. And, they take a break soon." He beckoned to a man who'd been walking passed. He was burly, a large scar running down his cheek and arms like watermelons. "This is Dale. One of our bouncers. He can take you back there." The bartender pointed toward a door just beyond the spiral staircase labeled; Staff Only. "It might be a little bit until the band takes their next break, but you're welcome to wait. I'm sure Dale wouldn't mind accommodating you. I can let Zane know as soon as they come off stage."

Damaceous's lips thinned, eyeing the bouncer. A distinct dark red sclera. Wrath Faction.

"Oh, thank you! Come on, Beth, let's go!" Ashley jumped up from the stool and grabbed her friend's arm.

Beth glanced back toward the line where the redhead still waited. "Maybe we should hold off until she gets back."

"She won't care. Kat' doesn't want to meet him, anyway. She's not interested in *men*, remember," Ashley loud-whispered to her.

"God, Ash', don't be such a dick," Beth said. But she sighed, giving in to the peer pressure. "Fine. Alright."

"Yay!"

"Will you tell our friend where we went? I don't want her to freak out when she comes back and sees us gone," Beth asked the bartender.

The man nodded. "Sure thing, I'll send her over. Have fun, ladies."

The bouncer, Dale, rolled his eyes, escorting the women toward the door and the bartender went to serve more drinks. Damaceous watched the women leave, suspicion rising with every step they took. His grip tightened around his glass. Surely, with a friend waiting for them, these demons would leave the girls unharmed. It wasn't usual practice to take those with loved ones who might miss them. Damaceous steeled himself and forced his eyes away when the door closed behind the women. There was nothing for him to do except observe. He had no authority to act.

Lights overhead began to strobe. Damaceous was about to step away when he glanced back one last time. Blue light flashed around the edges of the door while the music swelled. He flinched backward, sucking in a sharp breath and bumped into someone from behind. His drink slipped from his hand, the glass clattering to its side on the bar, whiskey spilling onto the countertop.

The bartender hurried over, glaring as he soaked up the alcohol with a rag. "What the hell, guy?"

"Apologies. The drink must've been too strong," Damaceous muttered. He peered around at the other patrons, none of them seemed to have noticed. If Damaceous hadn't been watching the door, he wouldn't have either. His brows scrunched together. Perhaps he'd imagined the blue light...but no, his gut told him otherwise. Something dangerous happened to those girls.

"You want another?"

Damaceous opened his mouth to refuse but hesitated when the door opened again. Dale walked out of the room and locked the door. He must have stared too long because the bartender's eyes narrowed with suspicion.

"Uh...No. No, thank you." Damaceous smiled back politely and turned, heading down the nearest staircase to the dance floor. He kept a relaxed pace but sweat beaded down his spine. His heart beat a mile a minute, and it was suddenly too hot. He shrugged off his hooded jacket, placed it on a nearby table before entering the crowded dance floor.

There was something wrong about this situation. Had he stumbled into a nest? Everywhere Damaceous turned, yellow eyes flashed from every staff member around the room; waiters, bouncers...even the band's eyes changed when he looked in their direction, but not all were yellow. Green. Black. Purple. Except for one...the lead singer.

Damaceous pushed his way farther into the crowd, swaying awkwardly while he tried to get a better look. As he moved closer, the tug on his extra senses grew stronger. But when he finally stood in the middle of the floor, Damaceous understood why there was such a familiarity with the energy signature.

His eyes traveled over the singer, taking in his multicolored hair and blue eyes. He'd witnessed those fingers pluck not guitar strings but a smaller, more refined instrument. Damaceous remembered the hypnotic rhythms of his voice. And those handsome features; chiseled jawline, deep-set eyes, full lips, high apple cheeks...the face had aged, but there was no denying its owner. Damaceous faced an angel. But why was he on Earth? Was he Fallen?

Why was he working with demons? Damaceous had so many questions, his thoughts spinning.

Blue eyes caught his gaze, the singer staring back at Damaceous. What had those girls called him...Zane? He'd had a different name before.

Zane smiled down at the investigator, singing and circling his microphone stand with a quick twist of his body. Fingers strummed a fast-paced melody, the crowd gyrating around Damaceous. The singer nodded to another band member, a blonde guitarist, and they picked up the tune. Zane kept singing without missing a beat while he placed his guitar on a stand. Damaceous's eyes stayed glued to the man as he strode to the right outer edge and descended a small set of stairs.

When Zane reached the floor, the crowd parted for him. He strolled right over to the investigator. His breath quickened. Damaceous swallowed, mouth drying out as Zane sidled closer. Long lashes fluttered over the singer's heated gaze, and the investigator about swallowed his tongue when a hand reached out. A single fingertip trailed over his shoulder, and up his neck, twisting into a lock of his brown hair. Damaceous shuddered, goosebumps rising on his skin.

Hypnotic notes washed over him while Zane sang. The other man was close enough to whisper in his ear. He couldn't make his brain work, his thoughts scattered. Damaceous had never reacted like this before.

When the song broke for an instrumental verse, Zane smiled, letting the microphone in his hand tilt to the side. "Hey, handsome," he spoke, loud enough for Damaceous to hear him over the music. "I've never seen you around here before." He snaked an arm around Damaceous's waist, pulling the other against his chest.

Unused to such intimate physical contact, Damaceous blushed, his pale white skin turning a bright shade of pink. But with the flashing lights, he was glad the other wouldn't notice. He gave a shaky smile and let one hand settle on the singer's shoulder, enjoying the feel of the soft black cotton tee.

The singer reached up, traced a fingertip over Damaceous's temple. "You have some seriously beautiful green eyes."

"And you have an amazing voice."

Zane chuckled, a low rumble vibrating from his chest. "Do you dance?" The song picked up again, and Zane motioned for the violinist on stage to take over instead. The singer swayed, a hand on Damaceous's hip, rocking both their bodies to the beat.

Damaceous was unable to stop his lips from curving into a smile while they danced as if he *had* drunk the whiskey earlier. He leaned into the singer. His fingers curled through Zane's multicolored hair; the front dark midnight, but near his nape, his hair became golden blonde. Just like Damaceous remembered.

"It is you..." he whispered. "Zhanerious."

"What...an interesting version. But it's just Zane. Are you feeling all right?" Zane asked into the crook of Damaceous's shoulder, hot breath making the investigator shiver again.

A cold, icy touch ghosted over the back of his neck. Damaceous whipped his head around, searching for the source.

"Are you okay?" the singer asked, pausing their movement when Damaceous's eyes started to dart here and there.

"I...uh...I don't know..." When his gaze landed on the balcony above the spiral staircase, Damaceous's stomach dropped. Bright golden eyes with violet irises pierced across the room. The temperature seemed to dip as a menacing aura arose from a man with long blonde hair, wearing an expensive white suit. He sat at a small round table, glass in hand, lording over the room from above.

"Culzahr..." Damaceous had gravely underestimated the situation. He needed to leave, *now*.

It was too late.

Dale stalked down the stairs towards him, the greasy haired doorman doing the same on the other staircase. Hindered by patrons going back and forth, the men kept having to stop to let the customers pass. He might have just enough time…

"Hey. Are you okay?" Zane asked. He grabbed Damaceous's arm as the investigator left the floor, searching for an escape route. Damaceous shrugged off his arm and grabbed his sweatshirt from the nearby table.

"Is there a back way out of here?" Damaceous demanded, his eyes keeping the other men in view while he pulled the hoodie back on.

Zane pointed with his thumb over his shoulder. "A side door right over there."

Damaceous looked to see a bright red exit sign hung above two double doors just beside the stage. "Thank you. You have my gratitude."

"Hey, wait!" Zane called. But Damaceous already headed toward the exit, shoving people out of the way.

Just as he had escaped through the door, Dale caught him. The bouncer snatched at his hair, wrapping one arm around Damaceous's neck in a headlock. "Come 'mere, asshole," the demon snarled.

"Get off me!"

"Carl, get his feet!" Dale ordered. The other man grabbed at Damaceous's ankles, helping Dale drag the struggling investigator to the alley between the club and the building next door. A few feet further, he was thrown to the ground, his back slammed into a dumpster.

Damaceous groaned, rolling to his side. The fog over his mind drifted away, but he still swayed when he stood, leaning against the dumpster. He wiped his scraped palms on his pants, glancing between the men. "What do you want with me?"

"Our boss doesn't take snitches kindly," Carl answered.

Damaceous played dumb. "I'm not sure what you mean."

"Oh, come on. Sneaking in on his territory...poking around where you're not wanted...Your kind is always *such* a nuisance."

Damaceous frowned. "My kind? I'm nobody. Just another person trying to have a good night, drinking and dancing with the rest."

"You can't deceive the master. He's too old, too powerful to fall for your games," Dale replied.

"And everyone knows the master's first rule," Carl added.

Damaceous's eyes narrowed. "What?"

Dale gave a menacing smile, running his hand through his hair again. He leaned in closer. "No buzzards."

Green eyes widened.

Dale slammed his skull into the dumpster. Stars burst through his head, leaving him nauseous and unguarded enough for Carl to drive a fist into his kidney. His knees gave out as he slumped to the ground, coughing blood into his hand.

Dale kicked him in the face. He felt his cheekbone shatter and his vision blurred as pain radiated through his skull.

Carl cackled. He grabbed the brunette's head and dragged him to his feet by his hair. "What? Are we too much for ya' to handle, ya' wimp?"

Damaceous growled, and jabbed him in the face, loosening Carl's hold. He stomped his foot into the side of Carl's kneecap. The demon howled, his mouth contorting in pain. A metal object smashed into the side of the investigator's temple and knocked him to the ground into another daze.

"Forget about me, stupid?" Dale bent close to his ear. "Don't worry, I'll make sure it doesn't happen again."

"He fuckin' hit me!" Carl shrieked.

Dale rolled his eyes, grip loosening on the metal pipe he'd found in the garbage further down the alley. "Shut up. Here take this."

Dale handed Carl the pipe and took a pack of cigarettes out of his pocket. He lit one, eyeing the bleeding brunette. His brows furrowed, lips puffing around the filter. Dale sucked a long drag on the cigarette then blew out a plume of smoke straight into the investigator's face. "Let's quit playing and finish with this shit. We've got jobs to get back to."

Damaceous glared through swollen eyes as Carl turned and raised the pipe, the smell of stale ash wafting to the brunette's nose. "Don't worry, man. This won't take long."

TWO

Zane scrunched his nose. A putrid smell wafted into the air as he opened the restroom door. Zane usually avoided the restrooms at his workplace. The constant turnover of patrons in and out of the stalls set up the right conditions for all kinds of nastiness. But this evening, his bladder had forced him to relieve himself.

The trip to the main level of the building took longer than he preferred. Zane kept having to extricate himself from excited fans or questions from fellow staff members. By the time he'd reached the bathroom, his step had a discrete wiggle.

Pushing the door open, he rushed across the room. He urinated, exhaling with relief while leaning forward, one hand against the tiled wall.

Compared to the club's interior, the bathroom was in poor shape. The urinal was a simple trough with ice spread across the bottom.

The toilet stalls to Zane's left had no doors; their walls covered in graffiti. The tiles were the ugliest yellow, better suited for a morgue than a public bathroom. The mirrors were in decent shape, but the overhead florescent lighting flickered, casting the already ugly room in a dismal glow.

The door to the restroom slammed open.

Zane flinched, twisting his neck around. He saw Carl and Dale shuffle through the doorway. The two men noticed him and stopped. After a moment, they plastered polite smiles on their faces. Zane gave his co-workers a nod in acknowledgment and returned to finish his business. Both men walked over to the sinks which lined the wall behind Zane and washed their hands.

Zane glanced back. He noted the bruises on Carl's face. "Rough night?"

Dale glanced over but, chose to ignore Zane's question. Carl grunted a confirmation.

Less than a minute later, the two men exited the room, muttering to themselves.

Zane frowned. He'd heard one of the men mutter words along the lines of "wingless buzzard." He rolled his eyes. The bouncer's conversations were always strange.

Finished, he went to wash his hands. A sticky sensation greeted his fingers when he grabbed the sink. Zane grimaced. He lifted his hands into the light and noted a bright red smear on his skin. The liquid was most likely blood from some random the bouncers had removed from the building. "Gross."

Zane washed his hands with gobs of soap from the dispenser, scrubbing vigorously. He wasn't a germaphobe, but blood was considered a biohazard. Between the bathroom and the blood, Zane wasn't taking any chances. He didn't want to catch some strange disease. With a shake of his hands—the towel dispenser was broken, as always—he returned to the main room.

As he passed the bar, a redhead came toward him, a worried expression on her face. She grabbed his arm, stopping him mid-stride. "Hi. I'm Katrina. I'm looking for my friends. I left them at the bar to go to the bathroom. When I came back, they were gone. Have you seen them?"

Zane shook his head. "Sorry. I have no idea who you are, much less your friends, miss."

The redhead frowned and held up her phone screen. "Ashley posted this while I was in there." Her phone showed a pair of blondes huddled over a small blue stone. "She hashtagged; 'meeting the dreamboat.'" Katrina's voice pitched upward in desperation. "You *must* know something. You're the person we were here to see."

Zane blushed but stepped away. "I'd love to help you but, I can't. If they were here, the bartender might have seen them. But, honestly? I've been on stage all night. This was the first break we've taken. I really am sorry. I hope you find them."

Katrina sighed. "Thanks, I'll ask the bartender."

"Good luck, though!" Zane waved, then headed back to the stage.

The last note ended on Zane's lips, the lights in the club faded on, and a mass of groans assaulted his ears.

"All right ladies...gentlemen." Zane smiled and waggled his eyebrows. "I appreciate you coming out on this crazy Thursday night— but we are closing. Have a good night! Please, be safe returning to your beds."

He pulled the guitar over his head. He set the instrument on a nearby stand then made his way backstage. The rest of the band was already there, busy cleaning their instruments, packing up shop for the night. Zane sat on a cushioned bench beside Maribel while she tended her violin.

"It was another good night," Garrett said, his exhaustion apparent as he wiped down his cymbals, sweat leaving a dark stain around the collar of his shirt.

Zane's lip twitched as chains rattled on Garrett's pants. Garrett liked offbeat clothes. With his wavy chestnut hair and tanned complexion, the drums suited his dark fashion.

But when it came to her looks, Maribel was on the opposite end of the spectrum from Garrett. She had white porcelain skin and ridiculously voluptuous curves, tempting enough for any man...women, too. She reminded Zane of the cartoon woman, Jessica Rabbit. Her lips were heart-shaped, her eyes a forest green. Her hair, ever-changing in color, fell to her waist in neat, clean curls; never a strand out of place. She was always perfectly...perfect.

Today, her hair was a snowy blonde, like an ice princess. Her manicured fingers moved a cloth along the strings of her violin, wiping away remnants of dust and skin oil. Zane could not tear his gaze away, mesmerized as she worked.

"What are you looking at?"

"Sorry." Zane realized Maribel had caught him staring. Color burned his cheeks. He rubbed his neck. "I must be tired...zoned out a bit."

Maribel set her violin down and jumped into Zane's lap, giggling. "Oh, no excuses. You can say you were staring, baby."

Zane pushed her back onto the bench beside him. "That's okay. I'm actually planning on heading home." He stood before Maribel reached for him again.

Across the room, Victor chuckled as he put away his guitar. "Right. Totally believable."

Zane glared daggers at him. Victor returned his glare with a wink and a knowing grin.

Victor wasn't too bad-looking either. In fact, all the band members were abnormally pretty people. Victor, with his mixed style of white frat boy and edgy punk rock, was not an exception to the rule. Even on the leaner side, his tight maroon shirt still strained to hold in his biceps and chest. He had spiky blonde locks and piercings running the edges of his ears. His blue eyes shone like the sky during a thunderstorm. With Victor's usual humor, his sculpted jaw along with full lips were occupied, a tongue sticking out in Zane's direction.

The singer shook his head with a snort. Victor was the closest thing to a best friend Zane had. But it didn't mean the guy wasn't a tool half the time...the shithead.

Zane picked up a rag someone had left on the floor and launched it at Victor's face.

As Victor caught the rag, Zane noticed Rylan's glare. Rylan's charcoal eyes were brimming with contempt. He leaned against the wall, his arms crossed. Rylan was a large, stocky man, his arms more suited to a wrestling ring than onstage with a guitar, the biceps barely contained by the sleeves of his tight white shirt. Tonight, he wore his usual studded jeans and boots, his long black hair kept in a tight ponytail tied at the base of his neck. He had a tan complexion and a sturdy jaw. Zane knew exactly how sturdy, because he'd enjoyed the satisfaction of having punched his jaw, more than once before.

Their distaste for each other was mutual. Maribel was his girlfriend, and Rylan treated her like a queen, but everyone else...less than the dirt under his shoe.

But Zane simply held up his hands, too tired to start a fight. He gathered his things and waved, heading home.

THREE

The employee exit clicked shut. The sound echoed loudly in the quiet parking lot.

Zane took a deep breath through his nose, appreciating the chill of the morning air. He hefted his guitar higher on his shoulder and made his way toward his car. It wasn't fancy; just a rusty hatchback, the forest green paint peeling off in random places.

Zane opened the trunk then set his guitar and bag into the spacious compartment. *Spacious,* he thought. *Hah. What a joke.*

Nearby, a street lamp flickered.

A shiver trailed up Zane's spine, and as he opened the car door, the twinkle of something shiny in the nearby alley caught his eye. He stepped toward the object. As Zane moved closer, he saw a hooded body laying against the brick wall, limp, still as death.

"Fuck," Zane cursed. He knelt on one knee. "Don't be dead...Please, just be drunk."

He leaned forward and pulled the hood back from the stranger's face. Hair stuck to the man's skin, matted with blood. Zane gasped as he recognized the brunette he'd danced with earlier.

"Shit." Like a mantra, he began to chant "Please, don't be dead" over and over in his mind. Zane pressed two fingers to the victim's neck, checking for a pulse. He felt an unsteady throbbing, and he let out a sigh of relief. He examined the man's face, noting the bruises. Both eyes and a cheekbone were swollen, deep purple spreading to his jaw. The man's lips were cut in several places. His nose and a gash on his forehead were bleeding.

Zane knew little about first aid and worried his lip. He pulled out his phone, searching for advice on the internet. He scanned through the instructions until he understood enough of what to do, then pocketed his phone.

Leaning over the other, Zane searched for more injuries, patting down their body. He unzipped the hoodie and pushed the brunette's shirt as high on his chest as he could without jostling him.

Tanned, ivory skin greeted him, but the bruising on the man's left side had destroyed his lean stomach. Zane reached out, examining the body with his fingers to determine if the other man had any more injuries. Zane's eyebrows scrunched when he brushed the man's ribs.

There was a pained whimper and eyes fluttered, trying to open.

"What the hell happened to you...?" Zane muttered to himself. "Dude, you need a hospital..."

He was about to take out his phone to call for an ambulance when the man grabbed his shoulder, grip weak. His bright green eyes opened, glazed over in pain. "No," he said. "No hospital."

Zane opened his mouth to answer, but the man fell limp, passing out again.

Shit, now what am I supposed to do with him?

The singer scanned his watch, the digital face showing zero four fifty-six in the morning. People all around the city would be waking up soon. But Zane couldn't leave him lying there, helpless after being assaulted.

He pulled the stranger's shirt down and rezipped the sweatshirt, tugging the hood back over the man's face. Zane dragged the injured man to his feet, his weight unexpectedly light, and hooked one of the man's arms over his shoulder. He put his other arm around the unconscious man's waist for support then headed back toward his car. The singer opened the passenger door, placing the brunette inside with the utmost care.

This early in the morning, there weren't many cars on the road. Using a shortcut to cross the river, the drive home only took Zane a few minutes.

He pulled into the parking garage beneath the Riverside Apartments. Zane found his spot and finished parking before hopping out. He walked over to the passenger side. The singer hoisted the injured man out of the car and headed toward the elevator. Each step he took echoed on the concrete of the empty garage. The low walls amplified the scrape of the man's feet as his shoes dragged on the ground, making Zane cringe.

When he had finally made it to the elevator, Zane pressed the button and waited. His nerves tensed with every second that passed. He rolled his shoulders and punched the button a few more times.

The elevator *dinged,* and the doors opened. Zane let out a breath he hadn't known he had been holding. A few moments later, still dragging the brunette, he stepped out of the elevator and onto his floor. He lived in the apartment only a few steps from the elevator, the second door on the left.

"All right," he said. "Stay right there..."

Zane propped the stranger against the wall next to his door. The man was still unconscious, but by speaking to him, it was easier for Zane to pretend he was just...groggy.

Zane fished his keys out of his pocket and opened the apartment. Just then, from somewhere down the hall, he heard another door unlocking. Moving fast, he grabbed the brunette and dumped him inside.

"Well, hello, Zane."

His neighbor walked closer, striding up to him.

Zane was caught. His inner southern courtesy demanded he turn back to his neighbor with a smile. He knew it was Remus, standing in his Friday morning biking outfit. He was an older, dark-skinned black man, his hair now a salt and pepper mix instead of its former brown. He had moved in the same week as Zane five years ago, and they'd quickly become good friends.

"How ya' doin', sir?" Zane said, holding his door shut.

"Oh," Remus responded. "Same old creaking and aching. I think once my body gets warmed up, I'll be fine." His tone dripped with sarcasm. He glanced at Zane, noting the sweat on his brow. "How 'bout you? You're playing go all right last night? I hear you're getting serious publicity these days, son."

Zane's smile became strained. Any other morning, he would have gladly conversed for a good ten minutes.

Remus raised an eyebrow, his unusual silver-blue eyes narrowed. "Is something the matter?"

"No." Zane shook his head. "I'm just…exhausted. It was a long night. Ready to hit the sack, ya' know?" Zane smacked his lips, bobbing his head. He hadn't lied. He *was* tired.

Remus's stare filled with suspicion. His gaze slid to the door, beyond Zane's shoulder. Zane tensed, inhaling a short breath, waited for the ball to drop.

After a moment spent in eternity, Remus's eyes slid back to Zane's. He opened his mouth to ask another question but hesitated. "All right," he said, surrendering to the impatience in Zane's eyes. "I'll leave you to get some rest. Sleep good, kid."

Zane waved, smiling an apology to the older man. Remus continued to the elevator as Zane slipped inside his apartment. He closed the door and leaned against it, exhaling with relief.

His focus shifted back to said injured man and Zane winced.

The brunette was lying face down, limbs were splayed out. Zane's brows scrunched. The brunette's left forearm was bent at an odd angle. Zane hadn't noticed a break earlier, and his concern mounted. With the way the man's sleeve had ridden up, the bruising was more apparent now under proper lighting.

His apartment's open kitchen was to the right of the entrance, and his bedroom was a few feet down the empty hallway. Out of sight was his living room, a balcony just beyond the typical sliding glass doors. He picked up the injured man and moved into the kitchen. He laid him across the surface of his island countertop— a.k.a., the dining table he never used. He leaned the brunette forward, removing the hoodie one arm at a time.

Zane moved into his bedroom's master bath to fetch a pair of scissors, bandages, and a washcloth; the only basic first aid elements he could think to use. Sifting through the drawers, the singer rubbed his left eye. His contact was drying out. Zane grabbed his contact solution from the top drawer.

For a moment, he stared into his mirror, the length and width of which spread from counter to ceiling, and from wall to wall. He was popular for his distinctive electric blues and oddly colored hair. An article published in a local magazine about Zane had commented on his "odd" features. To make matters worse, the reporter had played on his tattoos and scars, making him sound like a bad boy, a notoriety Zane resented. The article itself had been published months ago, but the reporter had recently decided to update it and had added his picture. The combination caused the piece to go viral within hours, and the flood of comments gave him no end of trouble.

Zane took out the contact and frowned into the mirror at his mismatched eyes.

God. I'm such a freak.

He returned to the kitchen, carrying the scissors and washcloth, but he hadn't been able to find any other first aid materials.

Hell, he couldn't remember having the sniffles, much less a paper cut.

He made quick work of cutting off the brunette's shirt then wetted the washcloth with warm water. He cleaned the bleeding wounds along the man's torso. The stranger had a lean, solid build with tanned skin, noticeable even though the bruising hid most of it. He brushed the injured man's side with the wet cloth, causing goose bumps to rise along the area. The brunette shivered silently on the countertop.

Zane rinsed out the cloth then moved to clean the man's face. He hunched over the brunette to work. Just as the singer was wiping the blood off his cheekbones, the man's eyes opened.

His gaze locked onto Zane's. His eyes glowed a piercing neon green. He raised his arm and quickly grabbed Zane crossways by the collar and pulled him close.

"What're you doing…?"

Before Zane could react, the brunette pressed his lips firmly to Zane's mouth.

With their lips pressed together, Zane felt frozen. It was merely a kiss, but something was off; Zane felt the hold on him grow stronger while his own vitality drained away.

He couldn't move. His vision dimmed, his knees gave out. The stranger was the only thing holding him up...until his fingers released his collar.

Zane crumpled to the floor but, he had already lost consciousness.

FOUR

An eyelid cracked open, revealing a violet iris which glowed in the dim light of the cavern. He inhaled sharply, letting out a long breath, and stretched his sleepy muscles. Metal pieces clinked beneath him, creating a warm, satisfying fuzziness in his chest and soothed the sharpest edges of the morning. He had been lying on his side, but now he turned over, brushing his long, midnight hair out of his face.

Culzahr leaned forward, snapping his fingers.

Candles throughout the cavern brightened slowly, letting his eyes adjust. The candles were scattered around hand-carved shelves cut into the broad, rocky ledges of the cavern, their wax melting silently onto the cold stone. A large bath had been carved into the rocky floor a few feet from where he slept.

Knocked loose from the pile as he shifted, gold coins fell into the pool's dark, quiet water.

Although not a comfortable place for a human to sleep, every Greed demon refused to slumber anywhere else, intent on safeguarding their personal hoard. Their single-minded avarice fueled the myth that dragons slept under mountains of gold in secret caves. The irony of the Demon Lord of Greed sporting horns, fangs, and claws wasn't lost on him; he was happy to fuel the rumors even further. After all, dragons were their ancestors.

Culzahr snapped his fingers a second time, his claws clicking together.

A servant demon appeared, kneeling before the demon lord. The female was hairless and nude. Her bat-like ears twitched and her large, slanted blue eyes with goat-like pupils, regarded him with reverence. Her lips were plump, her waist petite and her small breasts were perky and inviting.

Culzahr sat upright, his mind still foggy from sleep. Out of habit, he turned a golden coin between his fingers.

The servant bit her lip with the tip of her fangs, arrow-headed tail swishing behind her with an eagerness to please. Her lord's air of regality dripped off him; his every movement filled with grace and poise. She licked her lips and grabbed Culzahr's hand, placing worshipful kisses on the back. His skin reminded her of black leather which had been polished to a shine, reflecting the glow of candlelight. His hair was midnight, falling in straight waves to his waist.

Her master's body was simply delicious, lean and slender, and eyes that glowed like a nightlight; golden with a neon-violet iris. But the best part...his horns. They protruded from his forehead, curling backward, dark as onyx, golden veins running through every inch, a crown of glory. The urge to touch their terrible beauty overwhelmed her whenever she was in Culzahr's presence. But touching another demon's horns was bestowed as the highest, most intimate, honor; touching them without permission was considered severely taboo. She had never grown horns and placed with the lowliest of demons, only good enough for servitude.

"Master Culzahr," the servant said. "How may I be of service to you?"

Culzahr curled his lip and raised a single eyebrow, snatching his hand away in disdain. "Heat my bath."

The lowly demon stood and bowed. "Of course, my lord." She snapped her fingers. Immediately, a second servant, her twin sister appeared, materializing with a puff of air. "We are always honored to serve you." They moved around the cavern. She stepped into the bath, opening a flue for the heat to warm the stale, brackish water, the steam already rising, culled from lava rivers nearby. Her sister headed to the armoire and picked out Culzahr's suit for the day.

Culzahr lounged on top of his stash, admiring one piece and then another of his gorgeous, endless treasure. When steam began to rise over the water, he waded into the bath, sitting on the rocky bottom, chest deep. The sister servant came in from behind and washed his hair. The original servant sponge-washed his body.

Culzahr closed his eyes. He relaxed into the warm water. When his hair had been cleaned, the second servant set her hand on his back, helping him lean back to rinse. Unconsciously, the sister brushed against his horns. His cock stirred. He sat forward, his muscles tense.

Finished with his hair, the twin demon left the bath. She made her way over to her lord's hoard of gold and jewels and began the daily routine of counting every piece.

The original servant smiled to herself. She continued her routine with the sponge bath. As she worked her way to Culzahr's thighs, he caught her wrist.

Culzahr quickly drew her palm down to his cock. The servant wrapped her fingers around the thick member. His flesh engorged with pleasure. He leaned against the bath wall, resting while the servant continued to stroke him. His neck muscles bulged, and his mouth drew into a thin line. Pleasure overtook him.

Without warning, her tail snaked around his waist, and the servant lowered herself onto his penis. She let out a sharp, breathy moan. Culzahr lifted his head to growl in protest and reprimand her, but she wrapped her hands around his horns.

Pleasure exploded, paralyzing his mind.

He gripped the servant's waist, pounding his hips into hers while his fangs clamped down on her neck. The servant clung to him, her fingers refusing to separate from the hard bone of his horns. She screamed in pleasure as Culzahr roared with his own climax. The next moment, pleasure turned to bloodcurdling pain as he ripped out her jugular with his teeth, and plunged a hand through her chest, piercing the servant's heart while black blood dribbled from his mouth.

Culzahr lifted the other demon's body off him and stood, the water sloshing around them. She floated away, lifeless, her eyes still open in shock.

The demon lord washed the blood from his mouth and hands then stepped out of the bath. He glanced around for the twin. He found her cowering behind his pile of gold, panting in fear, her eyes wide and round.

"Come," he beckoned. "I need to finish getting ready."

Hesitantly, she came over to him, her head lowered.

Culzahr grabbed her chin. The servant whimpered. "Do *not* lay even a single filthy fingertip on my horns. Understand?"

She nodded, then fetched a towel and started drying him off. Carefully, she brushed his hair out until the midnight mass had dried. After dressing, she helped him shrug into a blazer jacket. Culzahr then waved her off; the servant returned to counting the gold.

Culzahr walked to a large curtained object across the cavern from his bed.

"Have this mess cleaned before I return," he instructed.

The servant nodded, looking with dread at where her sister lay in the bloodied water of the pool.

Satisfied, Culzahr opened the curtain to reveal a full-length cheval mirror. The glass of the mirror glowed...He ran a finger across the round edge and stepped through, the glass rippling.

Culzahr stood in an office, off to the side of a mahogany desk. Turning back to the mirror, he waved a hand over the glass. The image in the mirror turned from his cavern to his own reflection. His glowing eyes were now a chocolate brown, and his midnight hair was a stark white, which matched his suit. His horns had disappeared, his fangs had withdrawn, and his hands, now, were human. Cyrus Vasilakis was ready to continue his day.

He closed the curtains over the mirror then turned to his desk, sighing. More papers lay on top of the usual piles. Supplier receipts, schedules to sign off on, payroll, and other various paperwork required to run a nightclub. With a frown, he made himself comfortable in his desk chair. He checked to make sure the left drawer of his desk remained locked. Then he settled in to complete the tedious task of paperwork.

Sometime later, a knock sounded on his door.

Rylan stood on the other side, his frown more agitated than usual. Cyrus waved him in, still bent over the piles of paper on his desk. He paused his work to lean on his elbows, intertwining his fingers as he waited.

Rylan bowed low. "Lord Culzahr." After a moment, he straightened. "We might have a problem, sir."

Culzahr cocked an eyebrow. "Oh?"

"Zane never showed this evening for practice. It's almost nine o'clock, and we're about to open for the night."

"Has anyone tried his cell?"

"No, not yet."

"Well, Lieutenant, call him first. Perhaps Zane has been delayed."

"And if he's not here by eleven?" Rylan asked.

Cyrus glared at Rylan. "Then have the slave from Envy take over until he does."

Rylan nodded, his expression skeptical, but he left Cyrus's office the next moment.

A few hours later, Cyrus shattered the glass of whiskey in his hand. Pieces of glass fell to the floor at his feet, liquid dripping off the balcony ledge. His face was tight, his teeth grinding. The crowded line outside of the club had dissipated when news filtered out Zane wouldn't be performing. Some customers even dared to request refunds. Fortunately, the place was not dead. With the DJ still at his station and the other members of the band onstage, the remaining patrons partied per usual.

Cyrus looked at his hand. Black blood welled from his fingers. Carl, who had informed him Zane was a no-show, rushed to stanch the bleeding with a napkin.

"Si—Sire, let me he—help you."

Cyrus yanked his hand away from Carl. He stood, every movement jerky and tense, and grabbed Carl by the collar. "Inform my lieutenant; *locate* that ungrateful brat. By tomorrow night!"

Carl nodded, his eyes wide with fear.

Cyrus released the idiot. Carl fell backward, knocking over the small private table.

Cyrus's lip curled in disgust. He had had enough. He stalked past Carl. "And clean up this mess before I return!" he shouted, entering his office and slamming the door behind him.

FIVE

"General Alatos, sir. This is your new trainee as of today."

A guard stepped into the general's office, dragging a young angel behind her. Alatos nodded in acknowledgment, his eyes remaining on the papers he was reading. The trainee stared at him apprehensively. He hid slightly behind the armor-clad guard as he surveyed his new Dominion leader.

The general appeared battle-hardened. His skin pulled tight over his cheekbones, and his stern, steel-gray eyes were lined with creases. His charcoal hair was cropped close to his temples with a sprinkle of silver. He was adorned in a blood-red toga, and he sported black armbands around his biceps. The young angel stiffened when he noticed a nasty scar on the general's right arm. It looked suspiciously like claw marks.

General Alatos had magnificent wings. The feathers were a pure black with a dusting of silver. At the moment, the general leaned against a large metal desk.

The guard pushed the young angel forward. "It's the one whom you requested, with the multicolored wings? His transfer from the Virtues was completed just hours ago."

Alatos raised an eyebrow but continued reading the file.

The guard cleared her throat and bowed. She placed her fist over her red chest plate. "Will this be all, general?"

The general glanced impatiently from his papers, setting the files on the desk. "Yes, yes. You're dismissed. I will take this one from here."

As the door clicked shut behind the guard, Alatos approached the new trainee.

The young angel shifted nervously. The general grasped the trainee's forearm. He pulled the limb out straight. He inspected the angel's hand...squeezed a bicep. The young angel bit his lip but remained silent.

"You're not what I expected." The general dropped the young angel's arm and circled him. He flicked the braid which fell passed the angel's back. Fastened to the braid, a gold charm in the shape of a music note reflected the hard office light.

The youngling sported hair faded into a Mohawk, the top dark midnight. Toward his neck, the strands became a golden blonde. His eyes were just as mismatched, one a vibrant electric blue, the other a deep-sea green.

Alatos ran a finger along the angel's adolescent chest. The rough calluses of his fingertip left a red mark on the soft, smooth skin. The boy gripped his pants with a fist; the maroon material was the only covering he wore. His wings were still small, following the pattern of his hair and eyes; all beautiful shades of green and blue. The general reached back and stretched out one of the wings, his fingers threading through the soft, midnight feathers nearest the young angel's shoulders. The boy sucked in a breath, surprised by the intimate touch.

The general flapped the youngling's wing manually. The feathers glistened an iridescent gold, and the general nodded curtly, an eyebrow raised.

The inspection was making the young angel queasy. His throat was tight, and he swallowed.

Alatos continued circling the new trainee. The general's small smile was his only sign of approval. The youngling watched him, goose bumps spreading over his flesh. The general's gaze hardened while the inspection continued.

Finally, the general paused in front of the angel and grabbed the youngling's chin.

"What is your name, little angel?"

"Zhanerious."

Zhanerious…Zhanerious…

"Zhanerious?"

Zane groaned in his sleep, waking slowly. Someone was…talking…to him, maybe? His body was heavy, stiff, like death warmed over.

He rolled onto his back and covered his eyes with one arm. Then he adjusted his pillows and snuggled back under his blankets again. He thought he heard a light chuckle. "Are you awake?"

Zane frowned. Somebody *was* talking to him. But wasn't this his bed, his place? It certainly felt like his mattress and smelled like his sheets.

Then, who—?

Warm lips pressed against his. All thought stopped as energy flowed inside Zane's body, a river crashing through where only a trickle had been before. Instinct took over as he awakened. He placed a hand behind the kisser's head, pressing them closer, deepening the kiss. The person tried to pull away, but their protest was muffled between them. His brain was still fuzzy enough the noise didn't quite register, and Zane rolled his would-be lover beneath himself.

The person's chest was hard against his, the material of their shirt riding up. There were more protests even as he unbuckled their jeans, edging the denim down the man's waist, but with the fog of sleep around his mind, Zane could only listen to the power beneath his skin, the rush of lust beginning to build. Zane was delighted to realize he had on only his boxers and he ground his hips into the person beneath him, causing a lovely friction.

Muffled protests turned to soft moans…pushing away turned into pulling Zane closer. It was becoming rapidly clear; his new partner was indeed male. A mischievous smile brightened his face. Zane pulled his newfound lover's legs around his waist, a finger delved beneath their waistband.

Releasing his lips from the kiss, Zane grabbed a fistful of hair. He pulled his partner's head back and started working on his neck. They moaned loudly, bucking into Zane's hips. Hands ran up and down Zane's arms…one reached to grip Zane's arm, fingernails digging into a bicep. The other slid slowly up his spine, over his bare skin. A sharp whip of pain lanced through Zane's body, sucking the air right out of his lungs, stopped him cold.

The events from the night before rushed back. His eyes snapped open. He grabbed the hand on his back and held it down on the mattress. With his mind completely awake now, Zane investigated his partner.

The man before him panted. His green eyes were glazed over. His brown hair was a mess. But he was definitely the person Zane had pulled from the alleyway. Except for one little detail; his injuries from the night before were gone. Zane's eyes were greeted only by the unmarred skin of a lean, healthy body.

Zane pulled himself away. He backed off the bed until he leaned against the closet door.

The man sat up. He studied Zane, and Zane studied him as they caught their breath.

"Okay," Zane finally said. "One question. Who the hell *are* you?"

The stranger moved to the side of the bed. He straightened his clothing and hair. "I am Damaceous. I have been sent to investigate the rise of demonic activity in this area."

Zane stared for a moment, blinking slowly. Then his eyes narrowed, lips thinning as a he squeezed the bridge of his nose, and exhaled a loud, frustrated sigh. "Okay...dude." He held a hand in the air. "You're making absolutely zero sense. Your name is Damaceous...uh...right?"

"Correct."

"Why are you talking about demons?"

Damaceous appeared genuinely confused. "Because they exist."

"Actually, you know what?" Zane said, half to himself. "I think I'd rather just call the police and let them sort out this loony bin." Zane started toward the bed; his phone sat on the night table. But, Damaceous tackled him from behind.

He pinned Zane face down on the floor.

"No police!" Damaceous hissed into his ear.

"Fine, whatever." Zane stopped struggling. "Can you get off of me, at least?"

Damaceous leaned back, shifting his weight but still pinned Zane's arms to the floor.

Zane glanced up. The man's gaze had shifted.

"What happened to you?" Damaceous said. "What are these scars?"

Zane immediately understood what the man was asking about; his back was covered in old scars. Shame welled within the singer. The tissue, he knew, was raised and discolored, an ugly disgusting mess of skin. The worst of the wounds had been in the center of his upper back, where an old tattoo of two wings was disfigured on one side. Years ago, he had tried to cover his arms and back with tribal tattoos. Unfortunately, the scars even then were too sensitive — even for basic human touch. Getting tattoos on his back had been a failure. To protect himself from pain or pity, Zane never went without a shirt. *Ever.*

Damaceous touched the area of the winged tattoo.

Zane gasped. A jolt of pain lanced through his chest and nausea welled up inside his stomach.

"Don't…!"

Damaceous barely heard him. "What *happened* to you…?"

"Nothing…I don't know," Zane grumbled. "Just get off of me."

Damaceous let Zane push him aside. "But, Zhanerious!"

"I don't *know*, okay?" Zane stood and stalked to his closet. "The doctor's think I was abused or something." He put on a white undershirt, immediately comforted. Turning on his heel, Zane left the bedroom, brushing passed the other man. "And, by the way, my name is *Zane*. It is *not* whatever it is you keep saying."

Zane made his way into the kitchen. Damaceous followed close behind.

It wasn't a dream, Zane realized. He slowed, scanning the kitchen table. Bloodstains and Damaceous's cut up shirt still covered the kitchen table. He decided to bypass cleanup and opted for a cup of coffee.

Damaceous sat on one of the stools at the table. He was careful to avoid the mess.

Zane leaned against the counter while the coffee brewed. "You want a cup?"

"A cup…?"

"Of coffee."

"'Coffee?'" Damaceous asked, still confused.

Zane facepalmed. "Ya' know. Coffee. It has lots of caffeine and helps most people, like…I don't know, be able to go to work and *not* hate the world…as much?"

"Hmm. I had not heard of such a device. Is it dangerous?"

Zane chuckled, the tense atmosphere gradually dissipating between them. "Only if you have four or five cups in a couple of hours. But, it's *really* good."

Zane grabbed the trash can and began cleaning the table as they waited for the coffee brewer to finish. By the time he had finished, the smell of coffee hung in the air. Zane poured them both a cup and handed one to Damaceous.

Ah, ecstasy, Zane thought as he sipped from his mug. He leaned forward on the newly cleaned surface. "Now since I've got my coffee, how about you try explaining again?"

Damaceous pondered for a moment. "I'm not authorized to share information with entities outside of Heaven. Especially ones I'm not sure I can trust yet. I would be more willing to explain my circumstances if you told me how you ended up on Earth as a Fallen."

"Why are you calling me a Fallen?" Zane demanded. "And how are you completely healed? You were beaten to a pulp last night. These are basic questions, man. Tell me that much, at the very least?"

"Of course. You are an angel. More correctly, you are Fallen; an angel who has been cast out of Heaven."

Zane was speechless. He waited for the stranger to smile and admit he was joking.

When Damaceous continued staring back blankly, Zane leaned backward with his arms crossed. He studied the other man's face, lips pursing while his gaze traveled over healthy skin, not a scar or bruise in sight. "And the healing? An angel thing?"

"Yes."

"Okay…but why?" Zane asked.

Damaceous blinked. "It's something we've always done. Our energy…our power connects us to each other. We can exchange energy to help speed the healing process within our bodies. For some angels, it can be intimate…a way to share your emotions without using words. I've heard those with a powerful bond can even share memories with each other."

"Oh, you…No, I meant, uh…" Zane frowned. "Wait. That's why you kissed me?"

Damaceous glanced away with a blush. "It can be done through a kiss, like in your case, but the energy exchange doesn't happen without the conscious will to do so by one party. A physical touch becomes more complicated. It takes many centuries of practice to accomplish and even though I've tried…I haven't mastered it yet. Which is why the exchange happened between us like it did. I apologize."

"Okay." Zane sighed. "But, you're here, too. I'm assuming this means you're also 'Fallen,' then?"

Damaceous shook his head. "No. I was sent here. I'm only a visitor. This is part of my duty. Normally, when encountering Fallen, our orders are supposed to be execution."

"Wow. Thanks for not killing me, I guess?" Zane said. "This…is a lot to process." He ran a hand through the blonde hair on his neck.

"So…I'm not just some freak of human nature. I'm a supernatural being. An angel," he muttered. "I'm not sure if I feel better or worse…"

Zane's grip tightened around his coffee cup. "Well, excusing my latest identity crisis…" He caught Damaceous's gaze. "You know me? Or who I was, right? Why would I become Fallen?"

Damaceous's expression fell blank, his lips thinning. "I cannot say more. Not until you explain yourself, too. I'm especially interested in the scarring."

Zane sighed, rubbing his neck. "But, I mean, we just met. Aaaand…this kinda' thing is personal."

"I don't understand." Damaceous's expression was perplexed, genuine confusion on his face.

Zane squeezed the bridge of his nose, frustrated. "Personal, private, *secret*. Something you would only tell to, like, your best friend, maybe. Or only *ever* tell your significant other. 'Personal,' ya' know?"

Damaceous nodded.

Zane rolled his eyes. "And what is with the way you talk, dude? It's so…I don't know. Formal."

"My apologies, my contact with this modern age of humanity has been limited," Damaceous explained.

"Right…" Zane said, resigned to the task. "I must be losing it to go along with this."

He let out a breath.

"I don't have any memories. At least, not passed a certain age. My childhood is…blank. And whatever happened to me, it must have been awful. Parts of me hope I never find out what happened. But, honestly? I would give anything to have a sliver of memory, good or bad. I mean, what about my parents or friends? You're saying I'm an angel, so…maybe I don't *have* parents."

"Correct. Angels do not give birth, they are created. The Virtues raise the younglings until they are old enough to be placed into their dominions. Normally around ten years of age."

Zane pursed his lips, unsure whether to be happy or sad he'd never had a parent of his own. "Honestly," he said, "the first thing I remember is waking up in a hospital. My boss at work, Cyrus, he was standing next to the bed. He told me I had been found, dying, in an alley. The same one I found you in, actually.

"The doctors kept me in physical therapy for months," he continued. "Cyrus was the one who called an ambulance and paid for all my medical bills. Since then, I've been working for him. First, as a busboy and, now, as part of the band. Cyrus even set me up in a place near the club until I could afford this apartment a few years ago. He's been …kinda'…like the father I couldn't remember. Ya' know?"

Damaceous frowned. "This Cyrus is a demon."

"No," Zane protested. "Not true. He's never been anything but nice to me. He sheltered, clothed, and fed me. Cyrus gave me a job."

"A demon does nothing which would not benefit himself in the end."

"He wouldn't…"

"He's using you."

Zane slammed a fist on the table, anger welling painfully in his chest. "He's taken care of me my whole life. And…we can either continue, or you can leave. But talking about Cyrus's role in my life is *done*."

Silence fell between them. A muscle twitched in Damaceous's jaw, but he eventually nodded in acquiescence.

Zane sighed, relaxing against the counter behind him. He rolled his shoulders, the muscles in his back twinging from the tension. Stress always made his old wounds ache.

"As you said, you have no idea why you were in the alley?" Damaceous asked. "No idea how you are Fallen?"

Zane raised an eyebrow. "I just told you. No."

"And, your injuries? Why they never healed?"

"No clue."

Damaceous sighed in frustration. "Even a Fallen normally retains their ability to heal. Albeit drained of energy, the rate of healing would be even slower than for a human. But doesn't explain the scarring. I may have to return and research this some more."

Damaceous moved to stand.

"Yo. Hold up. You promised to tell me about your stuff, too. I just laid out some pretty personal shit. The least you can do is keep your end of the bargain. Like who you are, and why you keep spouting crap about being from Heaven."

"Yes, of course."

Damaceous settled back onto the stool. His fingers tapped the coffee mug. "Since you have trusted me with your...secrets, I shall also endeavor to trust my information will stay between us."

Zane nodded in agreement. He took the seat in front of Damaceous, eager to listen.

"I am an angel." Again, Damaceous sighed. "Specifically, I'm from the Powers Dominion. I act as an investigator, and I help protect humanity against demonic influence. My supervisor sent me to this area. We have been noticing a rise in demonic activity. I am supposed to find the source and try to...remove it, in a sense."

"'Rise'?" Zane asked. He took a swig of his coffee.

"Well, it has become pretty commonplace for human souls to disappear here and there. Demons make deals and humans…are ignorant when it comes to matters concerning the supernatural. They think nothing of disappearances these days. Recently, more and more of the humans are going missing. Azrael's Cherubim had even made a note of it in their regular soul reports."

"The who did what?"

"High Council members noticed the rise and brought it to our attention. It makes this matter of even higher importance."

"Oh." Zane tried his best to follow the explanation. "A question. If you're an angel, does this mean all the religions and their rules…are right?"

Damaceous scoffed.

"Not at all," he said. "Each holy manuscript has been written by man. While parts were guessed at correctly, none have come close to the truth. Demons were never originally evil but, merely beasts, dragonkin. Lucifer corrupted them with dark magic. This is not to say all evil comes from Lucifer or demons. Humans can be just as horrible, if not worse, than any demon."

"So, Lucifer is the only actual bad guy?"

Damaceous chuckled. "Anyone, or anything, can be 'bad,' given the right circumstance. Our history lessons taught us Lucifer fell into an obsession, using his magic for selfish gain. But he *was* created with the power to corrupt. Perhaps, he was always destined to Fall."

Zane's eyebrows scrunched, and he frowned. "It's not an excuse," he said. "He could've found a way to use his magic for good somehow."

"Such is the endless argument of ethics and philosophy. Are we born evil or do we choose evil?" Damaceous asked. "We may never truly know the answer. I'd like to think it's a choice. But, it's why the Virtues Dominion have a sect dedicated to keeping the balance between the world and religion.

"Many humans need hope," Damaceous continued. "They need something bigger than themselves to believe in. They need to think someone protects them. As long as the belief is not taken radically, it's fine. Unfortunately, there are many bad apples, as humans like to say, in every religion, who have gone too far. The Virtues fight a losing battle in this regard."

Zane scratched his head. His brain was overloaded. "Before...you mentioned you know who I am...what happened to me?"

Damaceous knit his brow.

"This is what I don't understand, either. You started off in the Virtues Dominion for a couple of years. You became a musical prodigy, performing more than once for our High Council."

"Whoa, I'm impressive." Zane waggled an eyebrow, pleased with his past self. "How do you even know this?"

Damaceous blushed. "I...I enjoyed your performances. You played beautifully."

Zane smiled and winked.

Damaceous cleared his throat. "After a few months, General Alatos transferred you to the Warriors Dominion, which happens only with those chosen for leadership. I remember because it was odd. You were an artist, not a warrior. You should have stayed for Jophiel, the Commander of the Virtues, to cultivate. A couple of years after you transferred, we were informed you had decided to Sleep. No one ever thought to question the report."

"What does 'Sleep' mean?"

Damaceous tapped his cup impatiently.

"You ask a lot of questions...For a young angel, it's not uncommon during the first few centuries for them to Sleep after expending their energy, sometimes for decades. Therefore, when I saw you at *Infernal Avarice*, I couldn't believe you had Fallen. You are still exceptionally young, even for an angel."

"All right," Zane stated. "Let's say I take this—angels, demons, and all—at face value, okay?"

Damaceous nodded. "Yes."

"You're saying my workplace is filled with demons, right?"

Damaceous nodded again. "Yes."

"I'm supposed to be a Fallen angel, right?"

Again; "Yes."

"Why haven't I ever seen any demons there? I feel like that's something I should have noticed."

"It's rare, but my working theory is you have lost too much power. All angels can see a demon's true eyes. You were already weak before I took your energy the other night."

"I was just exhausted from playing onstage. Of course, I was weak." Zane stood and set their cups in the sink. "And what do you mean 'other' night? This was only a few hours ago."

Damaceous raised a brow. "Zhaner—Zane. You slept for over twenty-four hours after I drained you of energy to heal my human body."

Zane whipped around. "Twenty-four hours? Shit!"

He ran back into his room. Damaceous followed.

Zane grabbed his phone, checking the date. The screen showed several missed calls and texts.

"Son of a bitch!" he swore. "I was supposed to work last night. It's Saturday already!" He paced back and forth. "I am so screwed..." He turned to Damaceous. "This is *your* fault! You drained me...or kissed me...or...whatever...Crap!"

Damaceous's face turned pale. "I am terribly sorry." He held out his hand and seemed about to take a step forward to comfort Zane.

A knock on the door made them both freeze in place.

SIX

Both men turned toward the door. "I sense an evil presence," Damaceous whispered.

Zane scoffed, rolling his eyes. *Dramatic much?*

"Who's there?" he called.

Garrett's familiar voice filtered through the door back at the entryway. "It's us."

Zane's eyes widened. "Shit. Cyrus must've sent them."

"One sec!" he called. "Just—uh…" Zane glanced at Damaceous. "…getting my boxers on!"

A light giggle came from the hall.

"Oh, darling!" Maribel sing-songed. "No worries. Come as you are…!"

Zane started toward the door. Damaceous grabbed his arm.

"Don't answer."

Zane frowned. "And why the hell not?"

"Have you listened to a word I've said? Your friends are demons. Do not invite them inside. I've placed wards around the apartment, and your friends are unaware of my presence...for now. But, if they come in, they might try to kill us both when they realize who I am."

Zane stared at Damaceous, eyebrows scrunched into a perplexed expression. He sighed. "Anyway...wouldn't they already know 'what' I am at this point? I see them at work all the time."

A loud pounding came from the door. "Zane!" Rylan shouted. "Open up already, the boss has a message for you. Put your little winky in a towel and open the fuck up!"

"One second, asshole!" Zane shouted back. He glanced at Damaceous. "Can I open the door or not?"

Damaceous let go of Zane's arm and nodded. "Yes, you can open the door. But, do not let them inside..."

Zane moved forward, but Damaceous grabbed Zane's arm again.

"Be careful. I don't know if your powers have reawakened...*Don't* let them see fear in your eyes."

Zane nodded, his brow furrowed. He was *so* going to get wrinkles like this. He was normally a pretty calm dude, but this was stressing him the hell out.

He shrugged his arm out of Damaceous's grasp and moved into the hall. He glanced back.

Damaceous had disappeared.

Gripping the door handle, he took a deep breath and braced himself. Impatient noises were coming from the hallway outside the apartment. He quickly opened the door, like ripping off a Band-Aid.

Apparently, he had surprised the rest of the band. They had their fists raised, as though they had all decided to knock at once.

Rylan scowled, grabbing Zane by the collar of his shirt. He pulled Zane into the hall.

Maribel giggled. "Now, now. He's here…"

She sidled up to Rylan's side and ran her finger along his neck. Rylan looked at her then glanced back at Zane, who had gone a shade paler.

With another growl, Rylan released his hold on Zane.

"Jeez, you're always so frickin' grumpy," Victor muttered under his breath.

Rylan glared at him.

Zane took a moment to shut the door behind him. "Soooo…what's up, guys?" He plastered a polite smile on his face.

"Wow," Victor responded. "'What's up?' he says." He walked over, slinging one arm around Zane's shoulders. "What's up is you, my man—" he poked Zane's chest "—are about to lose your spotlight to little ol' me and my amazingness."

Zane licked his lips. His mouth was dry. He shoved off Victor's arm then forced out a chuckle, rolling his tightening shoulders. "Heh. As if you could compete." His eyes flicked to each of his bandmates after they remained silent.

A cold chill crept up Zane's spine with each glance. When he tried looking through his peripheral view, their eyes appeared normal. But when he stared directly, their eyes changed. The whites of Maribel's turned a dark pink, not entirely frightening but Garrett's turned pitch black with white pupils. Victor's glowed like blue diamonds, and Rylan's burned a bright yellow.

Zane took a deep, settling breath. "So, is Cyrus angry with me?" He turned to Garrett, staring just above the drummer's head so his demonic eyes wouldn't appear.

Garrett nodded. "Yeah. Last night we lost a lot of customers, they were really upset you weren't there." The drummer rubbed a hand through the scruff on his face. "Mr. V. had to cut off refunds after the first couple of hours. The boss lost a few grand. *Angry* would be putting his reaction lightly, mate."

Zane winced. "Damn."

Rylan took a step forward. "I had better not lose a cent because of this bullshit. And if I do, I'm coming for my cut...from your hide," he seethed, his face inches away from Zane.

Zane was unable to meet his eyes. His pulse rising, he said, "Fuck off, Rylan."

Maribel moved between them. "Yeah, yeah, testosterone this, testosterone that. It's a wonder how we manage to play so well together." She placed a hand on Zane's forearm. Zane reached back and gripped the door handle, his knuckles white. He forced a smile.

"Look, darling," Maribel said. "Mr. V. wants you to come in early after missing last night. Don't make him wait long, he's not exactly happy, baby."

Zane nodded, bobbing his head. "I'll be there."

Maribel cheered, releasing Zane's arm.

"Okay then," Victor said. "We're going to go. We'll let Cyrus know you're coming in. Okay?" He pushed the other band members, steering them toward the elevator.

Zane waved. "Yup. Got it...See you guys later tonight." He waited for the elevator to close before he turned the knob of the door to his apartment. But he suddenly felt weak and collapsed backward into the apartment.

Damaceous heard the *thud!* He poked his head around the corner. Seeing Zane lying on the floor, he gasped and hurried to check on his condition. The investigator pulled Zane inside the apartment and shut the door.

Damaceous squatted before Zane, concern in his eyes.

Zane's hand grasped his wrist. He struggled to keep his eyes open. "Hey."

"What happened?" Damaceous demanded. "Are you all right?"

Zane shook his head.

Damaceous frowned, deep in thought. "Did any of them touch you?"

Zane tried to sit up, but the effort it took was ridiculous. Finally leaning forward, he let out a sigh of relief. "All of them did, except Garrett. We were talking. Rylan was an ass, per usual."

"Why did you faint?"

Zane narrowed his eyes at him in annoyance. "No idea. I got really tired suddenly, and their eyes were...." He shuddered. "Just...yeah."

"I tried to warn you."

"Yeah, you did. But, if I hadn't answered, my boss would've ended up more pissed off. I already have to go in early and..." Zane made a disgusted noise. "I can't even get off the damn floor."

"You realize, now, everything I've said is the truth?"

Zane's stomach dropped. His throat tightened. "Which means...the boss is...Cyrus is..." His voice broke off, unable to speak through the hurt.

"A demon," Damaceous finished. He laid a hand on his shoulder. "Are you okay?"

Zane looked up after a moment. Damaceous froze in place. Everything slowed as Zane cupped his jaw then pulled him forward, capturing his lips with his mouth, the force surprising them both. There was the same rush of energy as earlier when he'd woken in bed.

Damaceous stopped, his expression filled with confusion. "I don't understand." But his voice was breathy. "Are you okay?"

Zane held up a finger, running the tip over Damaceous's lips to shush him. He brought his mouth to the brunette's earlobe and drew him close into his arms. The angel leaned hesitantly against Zane's chest.

"I just need this…a moment to not think," Zane whispered.

Damaceous's eyes were glazed over, and his face was flushed.

A strand of brown hair fell across the angel's face. Zane brushed his hand through the soft, brown mess. Fisting the strands, he pulled the brunette's head back boldly. Zane's tongue flicked out and traced Damaceous's earlobe. Damaceous gripped the waistband of the singer's boxers, his fingertips brushing heated skin.

Damaceous shivered. Zane licked his lips in appreciation and pulled him close, capturing his mouth again in a long, passionate kiss with a chuckle, the sound rumbling deep from his chest. He pushed Damaceous backward onto the floor.

He nudged a knee in between his legs. Then he pressed his weight on top of the younger man. Damaceous moaned, the sound delicious to Zane's ears. The singer slid his fingertips along Damaceous's chest then, through the brown mop of hair.

He lingered over Damaceous's mouth and locked their gazes until his eyes focused. "Are you okay?" He planted gentle kisses on each corner of Damaceous's mouth. "Is this okay?" he said.

"Yes..." Damaceous replied. He closed the distance between their lips then settled back on the floor, eyes crinkling as he smiled. "...This is okay."

It was Zane's turn to smile, kissing one side of Damaceous's neck. He sucked in a breath. Damaceous stared back at him, his brown hair standing up in weird places, his eyelids heavy. A rosy tint covered his cheeks.

Zane chuckled, then sighed in frustration. He rolled off the younger man, stretching out beside him. Damaceous took the opportunity to peck him on the cheek.

"Thank you. You are a very skilled kisser for such a young angel."

Zane snorted. "You're welcome?"

He gazed at the other man, noting the lovely glow in his green eyes. They were beautiful. He could stare into them forever…

Sitting forward, Zane caught his thoughts before they went any further. He'd leave it alone. Because now, there was work and an angry, demonic boss to face.

Keyword; *demonic.*

How was this his life now?

Zane sighed in resignation. "All right, well…"

He turned and kissed Damaceous on the lips. "I've got things to see, bosses to talk down, and, later…" He waggled an eyebrow. "…people to do."

SEVEN

Zane arrived at the side door of Infernal Avarice twenty minutes later. He had dressed in record time, slipping into a tight, charcoal V-neck tee and his best pair of jeans. He'd made sure to style his hair a little extra tonight. Parted to one side, he moussed the majority back, but let a few strands fall naturally. The singer paired his clothes with leather hiking boots and a studded belt.

Zane felt compelled to reaffirm for Cyrus he took his job seriously. Missing a night meant the biggest ass-chewing of his life. But if he could draw in a large crowd tonight, all would be forgiven. The thought of Cyrus's own betrayal stung more than Zane had words, a part of his heart was still in denial.

Zane cracked open the door. He stuck his head through, checking the coast was clear.

When he saw no one was in sight, he let out a breath of relief and stepped over the threshold.

He made his way backstage, his boots clomping loudly across the floor. When Zane was behind the curtain, he set his guitar on the stand. He opened the case, twiddling the strings with a fingertip. Man…he was stalling. He just needed to buck up and go to Cyrus's office. The singer took a deep breath, exhaling sharply. He was a man, he could take a lashing. *Just have to walk over there and —*

"Boo!"

A hand clamped onto his shoulder. Zane jumped, his breath catching in his throat. He spun around. But it was only Victor.

"Jezuz, dude!" Zane shoved the blonde's shoulder.

Victor laughed hysterically, slapping his thigh. "Oh my god! You shoulda' seen your face!" Victor gasped for breath. "You thought I was really gonna' kill ya'!" He leaned against the singer, smacking his chest repeatedly.

Zane's mouth made a thin line. His eyes narrowed. "Yeah, yeah, ya' got jokes." But his lip twitched. Victor's laughing was infectious. Soon he, too, chuckled at himself. He shoved the idiot away again half-heartedly and rolled his shoulders, massaging his neck muscles with one hand.

Victor straightened, calming down with a deep breath. "You all right, man? Back bothering you, again?"

Zane waved him off. "Yeah, fine. I better get up there to see Mr. V."

He headed toward the office. Ascending the stairs, he paused for a moment to look back down to the stage curtains, knowing Victor was still there, and shook his head. For all his idiocy, the guy knew how to lighten the mood. It was one reason they'd become such good friends. Without him and Garrett, there was no way he'd have kept his shit together over the years. With that in mind, Zane continued climbing the stairs.

Uneasiness crept back in as he approached Cyrus's door. He could see the blinds on the office windows were closed.

Not a good sign.

Lightly, he knocked and waited.

Seconds later, the door opened.

Cyrus stood in the threshold, his expression unreadable. Gold flashed across his eyes.

Zane took a step back. His eyes widened, and fear slithered through him. But, no, Cyrus's eyes were brown.

"Hello, Zane. Nice of you to join me this evening," Cyrus greeted, ice in his tone. "How about we talk over a glass?"

Zane audibly swallowed. He nodded in quick agreement.

He sat at the table on the balcony as Cyrus disappeared back into his office. A moment later, Cyrus returned with a decanter of top-shelf whiskey and two tumblers. He deliberately set the glasses on the table, pouring them each half a glass, then set the decanter to the side. He took the remaining chair at the table.

Zane waited. But the man merely crossed his legs and took up his glass, sipping his whiskey.

When Cyrus settled the glass back on the table, Zane finally spoke.

"Cyrus, Mr. V'...I'm sorry for not being here last night. It has been such a weird —"

Cyrus held up a finger, shushing Zane mid-sentence. He collected his glass and polished off the remaining contents. He poured himself a second drink...and just sat there.

Zane had expected yelling. But Cyrus wanted him to squirm.

Zane stared at his boss, straight in the eyes, not flinching as the sclera turned golden yellow, the irises a deep purple. But a piece of his heart broke.

Cyrus quirked a brow. "Have we gathered ourselves?"

Zane straightened in his chair.

"Well, you seem ready enough," Cyrus determined. "You're still an employee here, if you wondered. But, after last night, you owe me for my losses."

"And how do I repay those?"

Cyrus's smile was smug. "With the private performance I asked you to do months ago."

Zane groaned. He lifted his glass and downed the contents in one swig. The whiskey burned from his throat all the way to his stomach, giving him courage. "We've been over this a couple of times. The guy creeps me out. I don't want to sing for some random client."

Cyrus's eyes iced over as if the temperature around them had dropped a few degrees. "He's not random. He's a major backer of this establishment. After your stunt last night, you have no choice. His payment for the performance will make up for what was lost, and then some. Deal with it."

Cyrus stood and walked to the stairway, waving for someone to come up. "He's here now to work out the details. Go practice *after* properly greeting our client."

Zane groaned again. He stood to greet the man who stepped onto the balcony.

The man was older...probably mid-fifties, Zane guessed. His salt-pepper hair was cropped, and his eyes a steel gray, the same as his suit. His tie, which was a deep maroon, stood out against all the monochrome. The man offered a crooked smile, offset by his strong jaw. His posture was ramrod-straight, and there was a coldness in his eyes.

Zane unconsciously straightened his own shoulders, more than a little intimidated.

The man walked over to greet them. He shook Cyrus's hand, and then the singer's too. He squeezed Zane's hand just hard enough to cause him to wince.

"Hello, Zane." The client smiled, but the display of warmth didn't quite reach his eyes. "It's nice to see you've finally come around. I cannot wait to see such a...raw performance."

Zane's grin was strained. "Yeah, no, of course. Nice to see you again, too, Mr. Elvorix." As had occurred the first time he had met the client, sweat broke out along his spine from discomfort. No matter how many times they'd met, Zane's instincts screamed for him to run in the other direction.

"Alexander, please."

Zane nodded.

"Right...Alexander."

He extricated his hand from the man's grip, wiping it on his jeans to remove the sweat. "Well, I've got practice, so...I will see you again, later. At a time, the boss...Cyrus will appoint. Yup...so...bye..."

Zane smiled, but the other man stared with amusement. He retreated down the steps, trying not to run after such an embarrassing stammer. He wouldn't want to offend Alexander, or else Cyrus would be more upset.

When Zane was out of earshot, Alexander turned to Cyrus. His expression changed from warm to calculated. "You sent for me."

The two men retreated into Cyrus's office. When Cyrus was settled behind his desk, and Alexander had situated himself comfortably in the guest chair, Cyrus spoke again.

"There may be a slight blip in my situation."

Alexander's frown deepened. "Such as?"

"We encountered an investigator sniffing around the other night. I had him removed quickly enough, but I'm not sure if he noticed anything."

"This...could be a problem. Powers are like sharks in the water, always sniffing for blood. But all too common for your kind. Is this all you wanted?"

"No. Zane didn't come to work last night."

Alexander's eyebrows rose. "Interesting. Do you think it's related?"

"There's no way to tell. I doubt it, but the timing is suspicious."

"I can try to find out more on my end."

Cyrus sighed, irritated on multiple levels. "We should move up our timeline. With our level of activity, we knew this could catch their attention. I don't believe we can operate for much longer. We are so close to the border, even Pride will become suspicious sooner rather than later. They've already had their ambassador keeping tabs on me."

"Yes, but he's been here for years. If Baelozar were aware, we'd have heard about it," Alexander replied. The older man stood, walking over to the window. Alexander peeked between the blinds, surveying the stage below. "You've been able to run this place with little complaint for decades. What's changed?"

"Well, Zane's popularity has helped attract more customers. But it also had the unintended consequence of bringing too much attention. Record companies are calling for him. A local magazine just published his picture and an article. We were able to work *under* the radar before. If someone starts sniffing around now, all our work could be lost, especially if news of what we're doing got back to the wrong people."

Alexander chuckled. "*People* is too general a term, Cyrus. And you were well aware of exactly how popular he might become from the beginning. But besides this…article, you've hidden him well so far." He let the blinds fall and turned back from the window. "I need more time."

Cyrus tapped his desk in annoyance. "And, Khamael?"

"As loyal as he's always been," Alexander said, his tone irritatingly calm. "Just because Zane decided to skip a night of work once, does not mean the incidents are related. Don't be paranoid."

Cyrus pursed his lips. "My paranoia has kept me alive for eons." His disbelief still hung in the back of his mind. "In the eight years of his employment here, Zane has never missed work. Not even when he was just a busboy—such a disgusting job."

Alexander's lips thinned, eyes narrowing in anger.

Cyrus held up his hands. "Fine. I'll drop it for now. In any case, we should schedule the performance while you're here," Cyrus reminded him.

He sighed to himself. Then Cyrus opened a drawer in his desk and pulled out his large planner.

EIGHT

Applause rose, deafening his ears. The youngling bowed low, the tips of his wings brushing the ground. He smiled, his chest ready to burst with pride. Members of the High Council, all of whom were seated directly in front of him, stood as one, nodding their approval. Straightening, Zhanerious exited the small arena. He stepped quickly down the paved hallway, excited to share the news.

He made his way to the arched doorways as many angels walked up and shook his hand. All he could do was acknowledge their approval and continue. He made his way to Alatos, who stood a little removed from the crowd. The general's expression overflowed with disapproval, an emotion Zhanerious had begun to recognize.

Zhanerious bowed his head, his braid falling forward. "My performance is finished, general."

Alatos grabbed his arm, and they headed back to the Warriors compound. The general kept a strained smile on his face when others came forward to congratulate Zhanerious; the smile disappeared once they had left.

The compound reminded the young angel of the Grecian palaces he had read about while studying human history. The palaces were often built with stone walls, marble columns supporting this and that piece of architecture with hard tiles on the floor, cold and Spartan. The building itself stretched on for miles, having to accommodate the army within its walls.

"You've been onstage quite often these days, youngling," the general stated. Frustration was evident in his voice. His grip tightened, and the younger angel grimaced in pain.

Zhanerious tried to keep his breathing steady. "Sir, you seem upset. But, my audience, the High Council, was pleased. I'm confused."

Alatos glanced back. Instantly, his body froze, and the young angel's mind went on high alert. His brain sent signals to his body, but none of his limbs reacted. Fear set in. He was paralyzed in place. With some effort, he found his eyes could move though, and he swiftly took in his surroundings.

They now stood in his bedchamber.

The walls were white marble, matching the rest of the compound. His bed rested across the room, with the headboard pushed into the corner. The maroon sheets matched the general's banner. Instruments lined his bedroom, and pages of sheet music were piled onto his desk in the corner. This sight normally reassured him. But only horror grew within him, and his physical paralysis sent his mind into a panic.

*Alatos released his grip. "Do you like this little trick? I've been working on it for some time."
He studiously circled his trainee, his gait slow and predatory. "I'm glad to see this power is...effective. This could be used on the battlefield." He raised a hand and stroked the soft feathers along the upper ridge of Zhanerious's smaller wings.*

Zhanerious whimpered, the general's touch making him shiver.

Alatos stood before him again and relocked his gaze. "You will not perform anymore. You need to be here. *Where I can watch over you. Understand?"*

The hold over Zhanerious's limbs released, and the young angel crumpled to the floor. His body visibly trembled.

Alatos bent and seized his chin. "Do you understand me, youngling?"

Zhanerious's eyes widened. He bobbed his head hastily.

The general smiled with satisfaction, straightening. He left the room.

The young angel picked himself off the floor and climbed onto his bed. He sat near the edge, his wings hanging off, and pulled his knees to his chest. He didn't cry, his mind reeling from shock.

He just sat still for a long while, in utter silence.

Light streamed in from the window across the room, falling onto the bed. The brightness of morning glared harshly, smack dab into his closed lids. Zane grumbled in his sleep and tried to reposition himself to a spot where the sun couldn't reach. *Damn.* He really should have invested in those blackout curtains from the mall.

Shielding his eyes with his hand, he opened his lids and smiled. Only a brown mess of hair poked out from the cocoon of blankets and pillows next to him. The bastard had stolen all the covers while they had been sleeping. No wonder he'd been cold last night.

Zane chuckled as he did a full-body stretch, his muscles stiff and crampy. Then, he got out of the bed.

He walked over to the window and pulled the blinds shut, glorious shade darkening the room just enough to be tolerable. Zane then proceeded over to the angel in his bed. He pondered for a moment, wondering how to retrieve his covers.

A little while later, he set a tray of delicious-smelling food near the foot of the bed. Sitting on the edge of the mattress, Zane cupped his hands and waved them toward the cocoon of blankets until he saw the mess of hair twitch.

Slowly, a forehead—and then sleepy eyes—emerged. Damaceous peered over to the tray. He sat forward and pushed out of the covers. Zane watched as he crawled closer, hunger on his face. Zane had prepared a bowl filled with different colored berries — strawberries, raspberries, blueberries — and some cantaloupe on the tray. A large plate had four sunny-side up eggs, and a smaller one was piled with bacon. A glass of milk and a glass of orange juice sat neatly beside two plates with a set of silverware for each of them.

"This smells amazing." The angel situated himself until he sat cross-legged and hunched forward toward the food. Damaceous blushed when he saw Zane trying not to laugh at his eagerness. "Did you cook all of this...?"

Zane frowned, wishing he'd made coffee instead. "Nope, I ordered room service."

"What's room service?"

"Just eat your breakfast."

Zane stabbed his fork into the berries and sighed with resignation. This guy really needed more "How To Act Human" lessons back in Heaven — especially with an emphasis on sarcasm.

Now that he thought about it, Zane didn't know what angels did. Were the streets paved in gold? Did they float around on clouds and play harps all day? Or did little cherub angels shoot love arrows from the skies, like in the legends of Cupid?

He popped another berry in his mouth and watched Damaceous gobble down a piece of bacon.

The look of delight on Damaceous's face while he ate made Zane chuckle; his past offense forgotten.

"Ya' know," Zane said. "For an angel, you sure eat like a human. *And*, you hog the covers like one too."

He reached over, flicking Damaceous on the forehead.

"Ow!" Damaceous rubbed his forehead and reached for another piece of bacon. "What are you talking about?"

"You stole all the covers last night…I was freezing!"

Zane dipped a piece of toast in egg yolk then stuffed it in his mouth and sighed. His eyes rolled back in ecstasy.

Damaceous sucked in a breath. He blushed while Zane moaned around the bread, memories of their make-out session the day before popping into his mind. "Well, we sleep, eat, and bleed like humans. We can even die…eventually. But on Earth, I'm not allowed to access my normal power range unless it's an emergency, or I'm returning to Heaven. This lets the Powers investigate undercover, with little risk of exposing our true intentions."

Zane nodded. "This's why you were so beaten up the other day? Wouldn't it have been considered an emergency? You could've died."

Damaceous grabbed a piece of toast and dipped it in the yolk, following Zane's example. "No. My mission is undercover. Even if I'm suspected, like in such case, I can't reveal myself. My human body was damaged, but I was never in danger of dying. After a few weeks of Sleep, I would have recovered and continued as before. It would take an evolved, intelligent demon twice my age to do any real harm. Even legionnaires are harmless unless they're in packs."

"Just how old are you?" Zane asked. "And, I wondered...could you tell me more about Heaven, too? I know I asked a lot yesterday, but maybe it'll jog my memory or something."

Damaceous picked up the glass of milk and drank half the contents before setting it back on the tray. Then he leaned on his knees with his elbows, chin resting on a fist. "This tasted wonderful!"

"Thanks."

"You're most welcome. But, to answer your question. I'm around nineteen thousand years old, give or take a century."

Zane's jaw fell open, a berry falling back onto the tray.

Damaceous smiled.

"General Remiel and his lieutenant, Ashliel, they're even older than I am. Ashliel just saw her thirty-thousandth birthday a few years ago. Remiel is around four or five hundred thousand years old. He always bumps it up every time I ask."

Zane blinked at Damaceous with shock.

"In heaven, you were still considered a trainee. You're incredibly young by any standard. Normally, you would spend the first one hundred years growing, learning, and being free, being happy. The next thousand is spent studying and training in a dominion. But the Warriors Dominion is different, they start early. I told you before—you were considered a prodigy. Your talent for music even caught the attention of the Seraphim. You gave a performance every month."

His words flowed over a corner of Zane's consciousness, whispers of familiarity in his mind. A flash of wings, the applause of a large crowd, and his fingers twitched, longing to play an instrument he'd never touched.

Zane shook himself, and the sensations vanished. "I still can't believe you're so old, Dam'." He stood with the tray. "Should have guessed with the way you talk."

Damaceous chuckled. "I apologize. I have not had enough interaction with this modern world. It has changed quickly in just the last one hundred years. Keeping up can be difficult."

"True. There's a ton of slang out there now. Especially here, in America. Even people from other countries find American English a pain in the ass to learn."

Zane walked out of the bedroom to clean off the tray of food.

"No," Damaceous continued from the bedroom. "The language isn't an issue. I speak every language — whether ancient, dead, known or unknown to humankind. It's one of the many subjects we study in Heaven; it's key to my dominion's ability to investigate. We have to be able to communicate wherever we are."

"Really?" Zane shouted from the kitchen. "Cool!"

He reentered the room, wiping his hands on his boxers. Zane came around and crawled to the headboard, leaning against a pillow. He tried to relax his muscles, his back twinging in tiny painful spasms. The spasms weren't a common occurrence, but stress was always a trigger. And lately, he had experienced stress from all directions.

Damaceous turned to face Zane. "What do you normally do on a regular Sunday afternoon? Do you work again tonight?"

Zane shook his head. "Nah…I get to chill today and tomorrow. These are my days off. The rest of the week we practice. Weekend days, Thursday through Saturday night, the club is open."

"Ah."

"Yeah, pretty typical when you work the nightlife, though. And, it's a living, ya' know? Doing what I love. Not many people can say that."

"But you aren't human."

Zane's eyes narrowed in thought. "Yeah...I guess I'm not. I'm...Fallen. It's just hard to accept." Zane covered his eyes with his arm. "I've spent my life so fucking *grateful* to Cyrus. I thought he was someone who cared about me. I was just an orphan, no family...except for him. This fucking sucks." Zane snatched the pillow beside him and threw it across the room. "I *hate* that he's lied to me this whole time."

Damaceous pursed his lips. "I'll help you bring him down. It's my job."

The singer scratched the back of his head. "Appreciate it. I mean, these past couple days have been ridiculous. Normally, I'd have called you an idiot and dropped you off at a police station." Reaching over, he pulled Damaceous on top of him. The singer cupped his face between his hands and brought Damaceous's lips to his. "But I can't say I'm not glad to finally know more about my past...and meeting you hasn't been all bad."

Zane slowly released Damaceous. The investigator touched a hand to his lips, his expression troubled.

Zane cocked his head to the side. "What's wrong?"

Damaceous shook his head.

Zane grabbed his arm. His stomach started to knot. He hadn't meant to become attached to Damaceous so fast, much less display his affection. This man—*er,* angel, he reminded himself—had given him a glimpse into his past. He had given him intimacy. Those were things Zane had never known. Who wouldn't start to develop feelings?

Damaceous brushed off Zane's arm and stood from the bed. His expression was pensive. "I'm sorry. I think you've misunderstood the situation between us, Zhanerious." There was that name again. "Maybe I have been too...cavalier with our interactions. It's not right for me to be close to a Fallen. I would be remiss if I did not try to stop this before any more misunderstandings occur."

Zane tensed. His jaw twitched, cocking to the side, and his fists clenched; hurt stung in his chest. "I wasn't trying to imply anything other than I was happy you found me."

Damaceous nodded. "I am also glad. And, I will investigate your situation immediately." His words fell coldly upon Zane's ears. Zane couldn't bring himself to return Damaceous's gaze.

"I thought it didn't matter. I'm still an angel, right?"

"To share energy, your stature as a Fallen does not matter. Your situation is…unique. I should report directly to my general. He'll want to know what I've learned."

"Are you coming back?"

Damaceous hesitated. "I'm not sure."

"Wait…you're just gonna leave me here? To deal with all this on my own?"

"I don't know."

"Fine. Then, leave…just, just get the fuck out. Goddamned asshole." The words lashed out, bitterness tainting Zane's voice.

Damaceous's eyes narrowed, and his lips thinned. A glimmer of something deeper shone in his eyes. He turned to leave the room.

Zane watched, unsure of what he should say or do, guilt constricting his chest further. He regretted his words; Damaceous hadn't deserved his bitterness. He gripped the sheets in his fist before pushing off the bed. "Damaceous, I'm sorry. I didn't mean it. Please, wait!" The apology spilled out. He should never have said something so cruel. Damaceous turned around, his expression unreadable.

"Why the sudden change? Moments ago, everything was fine. Now, you're rushing off and…" Zane's words fumbled over each other as he tried to explain his confusion.

From the other side of the room, Damaceous cracked a small smile, eyes sad. He walked back over to Zane and pressed a light, chaste kiss upon his forehead.

Zane's throat tightened at Damaceous's tenderness. His jaw clenched, confusion still clouding his mind.

"I'll try to return as soon as I can."

Damaceous left the room. A moment later, there was a sudden flash of light outside the bedroom.

Zane rushed to the doorway. He wiped a hand over his face and slumped against the frame.

The hall was empty. Damaceous was gone.

NINE

Damaceous stepped through the portal leading to Heaven. He landed on sands as white as snow. A beach curved in a half circle, forming the gulf of an ocean. The water was crystal blue but slowly turned darker as the ocean deepened. A mile offshore, small islands dotted the sea, lush with trees and flowers.

Even from this distance, he could see winged figures lounging on the beach of one island, picnicking. A small breeze blew overhead. He gazed up to see a group of young, carefree angels heading out to join the others. Zane himself should have been among them, Damaceous realized, laughing and enjoying his first one hundred years, just as Damaceous had done. Sighing with resignation, he closed his eyes and concentrated. His body began to glow. Above him, one of the younglings stopped midflight to watch him transform.

Damaceous's limbs and torso grew and expanded, his hair falling passed his shoulders, curling at the ends. His muscle mass doubled, his jaw sharpened and widened. Large wings sprouted from his back, each feather tipped with silver, the rest a luminescent royal purple. Within moments, Damaceous had transformed into his original angelic body. Black, billowy pants covered his legs.

He stood roughly seven feet tall, lean, carefully cultivated musculature covered every inch of his body.

Damaceous stretched his wings to their full span then stretched out his arms and inhaled deeply, readying for the flight ahead. The large angel rotated his head, his thick, wavy hair falling across his eyes as his bones cracked.

He took a moment to pull the loose mess of hair back into a tie and waved to the youngling whooping above him. The angel waved back then continued toward the island ahead. Seeing another angel transform from a human, or vice versa, wasn't unusual; but only a few select angels from the Powers Dominion needed to use a separate form on Earth.

Damaceous turned his back to the wind. With his wings outstretched, he bent slightly and let the warm breeze carry him forward, up and away from the rich white sands of the gulf. In the sky, the landscape was clearly visible. The rolling hills of green, set among occasional pools of blue, gave him a sense of homecoming.

Even after only a few days away, he felt renewed to be in his homeland again. Only small areas of Earth came even slightly close to the beauty which lay before him. The mainland was covered in small oases teeming with waterfalls and wildlife, continuing farther into the distance than the eye could see.

Beside every waterfall stood columns of white stone. Curtains hung between the columns, creating roofless housings. This allowed angels to engage in unhindered takeoff. Only those structures which required privacy were enclosed. These buildings were found near the capital; the headquarters of the Powers Dominion, and the main hall of the Warrior's compound.

The skies were clear and bright — as they always were. Damaceous could see buildings from miles away. He turned with the breeze and headed toward the capital.

The city, like Heaven, was divided into three territories — one for each dominion. The mountain sat in the center of the dominions, which surrounded it, the capital built at the base. Dwellings dotted the side of the mountain, taking advantage of rocky cliffs and drop-offs.

Facing the mountain, the Powers headquarters lay to the eastern edge of the city. The building stood tall, an opaque glass dome on the roof. To the west, the Warriors compound was a ranch-style structure, the main corridors enclosed. Behind the building, training grounds stretched for miles. Even now, a division of soldiers practiced maneuvers, their Archangel shouting commands.

The Virtues building was sprawling like the Warriors compound, but stood three stories tall, directly along the southern edge of the capital. Used as an education center, the center was filled with historic artifacts of the realms. A small arena had been built behind the compound to entertain all angelkind. The High Council's building was located atop the mountain. As Damaceous flew in from the south, the Council building's golden dome became visible.

The city itself buzzed with angels landing and taking off in all directions. Now and then, as Damaceous drew closer, a passing angel waved to him in acknowledgment. Picking out different dominions was easy; the army wore dark maroon with light armor plating whereas the Powers were adorned in shades of black or grey.

The Virtues Dominion was filled with artists, muses, scientists, and healers who wore whichever shade of color suited their style. The other dominions never minded wearing one color; these angels weren't known for their personal vanity.

Damaceous's lip twitched.

He remembered Zane, primping himself in front of the mirror the night before. His vanity assured his place as a Virtues—there was no doubt in Damaceous's mind. Yet, somehow, the angel had been transferred to the Warriors Dominion.

He frowned as he landed in front of the Powers headquarters. The structures reminded him of government buildings on Earth. Two sets of majestic stairs led to the entrance. Statues of past generals kept the watch, and support columns lined the front wall, to intimidate lawbreakers and inspire the rest.

Gathering his thoughts, Damaceous ascended the stairs, entering the building. The interior had a large, central atrium extending from the ground to the ceiling, allowing for easier travel from floor to floor. He immediately flew to the top level and made a beeline for the general's office. He slowly approached the general's door, where he knocked then waited patiently.

"Come in," a low voice commanded, resonating out in the hall.

Damaceous entered, his head low. He fisted his hand over his sternum and bowed. Straightening, he walked over to the desk where General Remiel sat signing paperwork.

The general scowled and unconsciously scratched his dark goatee with annoyance. He had feathers of a soft, light-beige, belying his striking appearance. His jaw was sharp and narrow, his nose was aristocratic and pointed but crooked in the middle. His eyes had a small, almond-shape, their color a swirl of silver and blue, which shone brightly against his dark-umber tone skin.

His hair was shaven on each side, but in the middle, long braids reached his shoulder blades, secured every few inches by silver circlets. Matching circlets decorated each arm, squeezing tightly around his biceps and wrists. A dark-gray toga angled across his chest, fastened by a silver brooch, which was knotted into the cloth over his left shoulder.

Damaceous waited patiently for the general to finish his work. There was a guest chair across from the general's desk, but he remained on his feet.

Soon, Remiel set his feather pen in its placeholder, a bottle of golden ink sat beside it. He stretched backward, small cracks and pops sounding as his body eased out of the cramped position. The general stood, reaching across the desk to greet Damaceous. The two angels grabbed each other's forearm and smiled — the custom salutation between angels.

"Good to see you."

Remiel returned to his seat and gestured for Damaceous to begin his report.

"General Remiel, sir," Damaceous started. "I just returned from my current assignment. I would've waited to inform Captain Aaryn, but I have information you should know firsthand. I was recently sent to Cincinnati."

Remiel's eyebrow quirked upward, but he made no comment about Damaceous's jump up the ladder of command. During the next few minutes, Damaceous related the events from the last few days; his discovery of Zane, the beating he had received from the low-class demons, and his time spent in Zane's apartment. He left out certain personal bits, of course. Remiel listened, his chin resting on his hands until Damaceous had finished.

"What of the demonic activity?" The general's expression was unreadable. "You were sent to find out what caused it and why humans are disappearing in the area."

"Yes, sir, of course," Damaceous answered. "I believe the rise surrounds a nightclub. I'm hoping to find out more by working with Zane — the Fallen I discovered there. He lives and works among them. With his help, I can discover exactly what is going on."

Damaceous paced while he talked. "In the meantime, I want to find out why he Fell in the first place. Were we not informed this youngling was Sleeping? How is it he's on Earth, and no one is aware of what happened, sir? I find the entire situation disturbing. I want to investigate further by questioning his dominion for answers…possibly check any documents they may have."

Damaceous paused his pacing when Remiel shook his head in disagreement.

"No. Your top priority, like your supervisor, Captain Aaryn, initially ordered, needs to be the disappearance of humans in the area, relating to the rise of demonic activity. As of now, stay away from this…Zhanerious, or Zane, and continue your investigation. You know our rules about Fallen."

"But, Gen—"

"Even if his situation is strange," Remiel continued, extending a finger to silence his subordinate. "He is Fallen. He would have broken the laws which protect the realms. Only then, and after considerable deliberation, would he have been banished to Earth and stripped of his abilities. This process cannot happen without a high-ranking angel—a general or above—overseeing his punishment. Therefore—"

"General!"

"*Therefore*…his status is not your concern. He was banished for a good reason, I'd imagine. Whether you agree or not, my decision…is final."

"But, sir. He has no memories from Heaven. He wasn't even aware of who or *what* he was. Zane is barely into his second decade. How can I just leave him?"

Remiel met his gaze, a tiger looming in the darkness. His eyes flashed dangerously.

Damaceous's mouth went dry. His chest knotted, tightening until he felt like he couldn't breathe. He waited for the hammer to drop.

"Damaceous," the general said. "You are hereby ordered not to engage with this Fallen anymore. Continue your investigation of the demonic activity, without his help. This is a formal order." Remiel's voice reverberated throughout the room. "Do not make me repeat myself."

Damaceous gritted his teeth. A muscle in his jaw twitched, but he bowed in respect...The general was his superior. Orders were orders. Although he wanted to deny his growing affections for the Fallen, they had already begun clouding his judgment.

"I'm sorry, my friend," Remiel murmured. His tone had softened, apologetic. "I know this is a difficult situation. But you must remember how easily we Powers can be corrupted. We are the ones who must immerse ourselves amongst humans the most often. The influence of a Fallen could be detrimental to your mental health. I cannot lose one of my best investigators. You are invaluable."

Damaceous sighed. At this point, everything was out of his hands. The amount of evidence was not enough to prove his theory about Zane—and meant nothing without the general's support. He chewed on his lip, contemplating his options.

After a moment, he nodded.

"Yes, sir, I understand," he said. "It is not my place to question your judgment, General. You have lived far longer than I."

Damaceous offered his hand. Remiel took the offer, clasping his wrist as they shook. Remiel had always treated him like a younger brother. And he knew how the general hated when he was forced to bark orders at him.

Remiel was known for his stubborn attitude, bravery, and wisdom. He regularly attended High Council meetings, one of the few generals who had ever dared to stand his ground when they made rulings about angelkind and Earth. He was respected, one of the best angels to ever lead the Powers Dominion. Damaceous had been a lucky youngling to have been trained and cultivated by him after reaching the end of his first hundred years.

"How fairs Lieutenant Ashliel these days?" Damaceous asked, settling into the guest chair.

Remiel smiled wide. An air of companionship broke the tense atmosphere. "She is well. I believe she's with our youngest trainees today. They were scheduled to learn about the Great War."

Damaceous chuckled, rolling his eyes. "Of course. She decided to teach it; it's one of her favorite topics. She seems to know more about the war than those who were there."

The Great War had been reduced to legend nowadays. Members of the High Council were the only remaining angels who might have first-hand knowledge of the event; the ancients of ancients. Occurring over one hundred and seventy-five millenniums ago, the war caused the greatest devastation man, angel, or demon endured before or since, most records of the Atlantic Empire lost.

It began during the existence of the supercontinent, Pangea, when all the continents of Earth were joined. To modern times, Atlantis was a myth, a legend. Any evidence to support its existence had long turned to dust...except for the few rare artifacts preserved in Heaven. But, before the war, the largest empire man or angel had ever known had thrived, Atlantis as the capital, the heart of civilization.

The war was supposedly caused by Lucifer's jealousy of humanity, but the actual truth behind his actions remained a mystery. Lucifer created a demonic army out of once loyal and peaceful beasts to destroy mankind; he'd nearly succeeded until the angels stepped in. By then, an intervention was too late to prevent bloodshed. The opposing forces virtually destroyed each other over the ensuing one-hundred-year battle, nearly erasing every trace of mankind from Earth's existence.

The two armies eventually retreated to their own corners of the universe, and each species thrived separately. The humans stripped themselves of magic, alchemy, and disavowed the supernatural, unintentionally leaving their race at the mercy of Lucifer and his demons.

The angels decided to bear the mantle of protecting humankind and divided themselves into three dominions. Over time, small wars broke out—but no confrontations as bloody as the original Great War had ever again come to pass. Damaceous hoped to never see devastation like it; the small battles he had been a part of were more than enough to placate his desire for war.

"Yes, I believe I saw Lieutenant Ashliel head to the education center not too long ago."

Damaceous and Remiel turned to see Alatos standing in the doorway.

Remiel's face became expressionless. He offered a brief nod of respect to his fellow general. "Thank you, General Alatos. What brings you to my office?"

Alatos smiled, but his display of warmth didn't quite reach his eyes. "I was standing outside the door while your subordinate delivered his report. I hadn't meant to eavesdrop, of course. But I couldn't help but hear this information about a Fallen. I believe you said his name was Zhanerious, yes?"

Damaceous narrowed his eyes. Alatos ignored him, waiting on Remiel's acknowledgment.

Remiel nodded. "May I ask why you find this a curious matter, general?"

The other general chuckled softly. He sidled closer to the desk. "He was my subordinate. I'd be happy to provide any information regarding his Fall, but it's as you said. This matter concerns only my dominion. He wouldn't have been banished without cause, I assure you."

Damaceous stiffened. "You can't deny it was reported he Slept. His Fall should have been made public. Not kept in secret."

Remiel banged his fist on the desk, a warning.

Alatos furrowed his brow. His amusement with Damaceous's accusation was evident. He sneered. "Why, of course. A mere oversight on someone's part, I'm sure. The paperwork can easily be retrieved if you'd like to review it."

"No, general. It's not necessary." Remiel waved a hand in dismissal. "My *subordinate* and I are more than pleased to take your word for the happenings within your own dominion. I'm sorry if my investigator has overstepped."

"Of course, of course. No need to worry." Alatos's voice was smooth, making the hairs on Damaceous's neck stand on end. "I'll be on my way, then. I only came to remind you of the Council meeting this eve."

Remiel raised an eyebrow. "You are attending?"

"Of course."

When the general did not elaborate, Remiel sighed. "Thank you for the reminder, I will be there. Be well, general."

"Yes, you too."

With that, Alatos left the room.

Remiel crossed his arms over his chest and glared at Damaceous with a deep, disapproving frown.

"My apologies, General. I did not mean to undermine you in any way." Damaceous bowed, but Remiel remained silent. He merely pointed to the door, his movement swift but unmistakable.

With his dismissal, Damaceous ducked his head, blood burning his cheeks as he exited the office.

Remiel retook his seat, his wings resting against the back of the chair, the tips brushing the ground lightly. A bad taste lingered in his mouth—one which only arose around Alatos. The angel had not been as calculating when they were younglings together, five hundred thousand years ago. Then, they had been as close as brothers.

The general had always been arrogant, his ambitions alienating his peers—except for Remiel. But, when they were assigned separate dominions, he developed a charm and charisma—angels flocked to his side—even Remiel lacked. As the two generals rose through the ranks, they eventually became distant...a circumstance Remiel still regretted.

Over time, Alatos had proven to be slick-minded, with a knack for strategy. When offered, he'd accepted the mantle of dominion general. Remiel himself was the only one who could challenge him in one-on-one combat...except for members of the High Council.

Like Remiel, Alatos was a highly respected authority in Heaven; many considered him the army's greatest general. Even so, rumors and whispers of cruelty associated with the general would still find their way to Remiel's ears.

Remiel sighed. There were more pressing matters to worry about, and plenty of paperwork to finish before the meeting.

He picked up his feathered pen and dipped the tip into the golden ink.

TEN

Crack!

Zhanerious sprang into a sitting position. He was instantly awake.

Crack!

The sound echoed, making the angel jump. He tucked his wings tightly against his back, gripping the sheets of his bed. He shivered but, there was no chill in the air.

Zhanerious gulped big breaths of air.

Crack!

He jumped out of bed, knocking over his violin.

Zhanerious crossed to his doorway, walking as quietly as possible, his bare feet on the cold floor.

This was the third time he'd been woken in the middle of the night by strange sounds. They had started the day after new trainees had arrived at the dominion. Zhanerious couldn't help but wonder what kind of training his superiors were performing this late.

With caution, the angel stuck his head through the doorway. His mouth was dry.

There were no guards in the corridor, and Zhanerious stepped out into the hallway. He was nervous...but slightly excited. He had never been allowed to interact with new trainees here before, not since his time within the Virtues.

Zhanerious watched his fellow Warriors from the sky, during the flights he took every afternoon while they ran through drills and lessons.

He had trained with the Virtues for two years before being transferred to the Warriors Dominion at the request of Alatos. Afterward, the young angel had been virtually locked away in his room or, at Lieutenant Khamael's insistence, secluded in a private courtyard to practice basic battle skills.

Zhanerious had become proficient in hand-to-hand combat and swordsmanship, but he was far from being naturally talented, unlike most angels who were drafted into the Warriors Dominion. It made his transfer even more curious.

But his seclusion often confused him the most. The Virtues believed in nurturing; they constantly surrounded each other. After months had passed, he'd begun to accept his new environment. Any time Zhanerious voiced his discontent, Alatos would become unusually cruel.

More than once, he had returned to his room, bruised and bloodied, blaming himself over the defiance. If he was caught now, there was no telling what would happen to him...but his curiosity was overwhelming. Perhaps these trainees would become his new companions, and friends for centuries to come.

How he desperately *wanted friends...*

Crack!

The sound was closer, causing Zhanerious to jump again. He hugged the wall and held his breath. He now stood at the end of the corridor and peered around the corner. There was another hallway, and at the end, a room ordinarily kept locked. But tonight, light shone around the edges of the doorway. His adrenaline raced when he saw another familiar door, Alatos's office.

Crack!

Zhanerious bit his lip. A war raged in his mind. Should he risk the chance to see the new trainees...his possible future companions? Or should he go back to his room and ignore the noise?

Common sense told him he should return to his room. But...if he could just meet them...become friends. Maybe they would help convince the general to let him be a real part of the army. He was tired of being locked away alone.

Always *alone...*

This might be his one chance.

Gathering his courage, Zhanerious took a deep breath and tiptoed forward, keeping his wings tight against his body. When he was almost halfway down the hall, muffled moans drifted from the room. Another voice echoed out, but he continued to move closer, straining to hear the words.

Dread set in. His breath quickened, and a cold sweat broke along his spine. His instincts screamed for him to leave.

Approaching the door, he plastered himself against the wall, trying to peek inside.

"Why have you stopped, youngling?"

Zhanerious froze, sucking in a breath. A dark figure walked passed the door, their features obscured by the light.

"Do you want to be banished? You're only following orders. Don't be afraid. Your fellows must endure if you all want to survive. Pain is a necessary part of war...."

There was a small whimper.

Zhanerious strained his neck, scooting forward, inches at a time.

"But we aren't—!"

The voice cut off. Choking noises floated to his ears. He moved ever closer, his feathers scraping against the wall.

Finally, he could see inside.

A young angel hung by her wrists from the ceiling. Her body faced the wall, knees scraping the ground. Chunks of feathers were missing from her small wings, and gashes bled freely down her back. Metal shackles encased her wrists, red with irritation and blood; evidence of her struggle to break free. The angel's hair had been cut short, matting against her skull. Her whole body was covered in filth, her robes torn to pieces. The thin material barely covered any part of her skin.

Zhanerious put a hand to his mouth, and his nails dug into his cheek. The horror of the angel's condition made him nauseous.

The angel slowly turned her head...just enough to catch his gaze. Her pale green eyes were filled with a vile hatred so deep, so all-consuming, Zhanerious stumbled backward, tripping over his ankles. He stood then hurried back down the hallway. Hearing a noise behind him, he quickly ducked into Alatos's office. He ran behind the large desk, curling underneath it.

His heart thundered, and his mind raced. Every scenario he imagined to make sense of what he'd seen was more horrible than the last.

Footsteps approached the door.

Zhanerious tried to quiet his breathing...Could the angel in the hall hear his heart beating from across the room?

After a moment, the footsteps moved away, and he let out a long breath.

The young angel remained where he was, crouched behind the desk. His limbs shook uncontrollably, and his organs seemed to convulse inside his body. He gripped his arms, holding himself in a tight embrace.

After a while, the trembling subsided. Zhanerious poked his head over the desk...It was quiet.

The angel pulled himself into the general's chair and leaned on the desk, his head in his hands.

Reaching over, Zhanerious clicked on the lamp, the darkened room making him paranoid.

He was unable to focus, his mind fuzzy. The disturbing image of the other angel kept flashing across his eyelids.

Then, a file on the desk caught his eye. He pulled the papers over, his brow furrowing. Words like "trainee" and "Fallen" jumped out at him. He read further and gasped in disbelief.

The file detailed all the trainees who had arrived within the last few days, the female included. Seven in total. Each one had endured unspeakable torture to...

"...ensure their souls be sentenced to Fall."

Zhanerious couldn't believe what he was reading. Pages upon pages detailed experiments, worse than what he had just witnessed...Why would the general experiment on his own? Why would he want angels to Fall? It made no sense. All angelic youths were fervently protected, their very innocence considered a precious commodity to be nurtured over time until the angel matured. Even Zhanerious knew this; the Virtues Dominion had treated him with the utmost care.

The general was endorsing behavior which was treasonous...abhorrent.

His face turned grim. The general's corrupt behavior could not stand.

Zhanerious shut off the lamp. Then he closed the file, tucking it into his robes. He exited the office cautiously and returned to his quarters. There, he stuck the file inside his violin case for safekeeping.

Tomorrow, he would go to the Powers Dominion. He had to stop the madness before it was too late, and innocents were doomed forever.

ELEVEN

Garrett walked down a hallway carved in stone, the heat from underground rivers of molten lava pressing against his skin. The walls of the corridor were lit with torches, the light reflecting off mirrors anchored to the walls every few feet. The chain on his pants clinked, his steps echoing over the stone, his stride slow, practically stalling. He glanced into one of the mirrors as he drew closer to his destination.

Garrett frowned. His glamor remained, showing his human appearance. He gazed into his dark eyes and for a moment wondered what life might be like without another skin. Unlike most demons, he actually...liked the idea of having humanity. Sometimes, with Zane and Victor...Garrett could forget he was a demon.

Perhaps...he should request a replacement.

Garrett sucked in a breath, glancing around. Thankfully no other demon was about to see him sweat. He shook himself, his hands trembling, and took a moment to slow his breathing.

His real name was Sinohne.

Sinohne, the lieutenant to the Demon Lord of Pride.

He repeated the title to himself a couple times, drilling his identity into his skull. If he was going to continue, Sinohne knew he had better cast off his petty doubts before his master strung him up for it.

If another demon found a weakness with him, the lieutenant? Sinohne would be eating his own entrails, imprisoned and tortured for years...decades even. Any chink, any perceived blow, and his lord's vengeance would be legendary. The Demon Lord of Pride was second only to Lucifer, himself, the Dark King. There was no room for weakness or insecurities, no room for ridiculous dreams.

He blinked — and his glamor vanished.

The sclera and iris of his eyes were black, but his whitened pupils were devoid of color, narrowing like a cat. His hair remained the same, but his face had slightly lengthened, his cheeks sharper, his nose a bit wider, his eyes larger but more angled in the corners. His canines had sharpened, his nails had lengthened into claws.

Horns jutted out of his temples and twisted backward, curling toward his ears, the color of polished silver. Sinohne's skin matched his horns, patches of scales covering the vulnerable parts on his body. His tail lifted, wrapping around his waist like a monkey, the end an angry arrowhead. He was dressed in a half-chest plate with leather straps wrapped around his shoulders and back, his legs clothed in black leather.

Sinohne always left his midriff bare, proud to reveal the jagged scar which cut across his belly and slashed down his thigh. The scar was a remnant of a battle long past, one he'd barely survived but had earned the demon his reputation as the "Silver Death." Staring back into the mirror, he straightened his shoulders and lifted his chin.

Satisfied, Sinohne continued along the hallway, his clawed toes clicking on the stone. He approached the chamber doors and knocked loudly.

The double doors opened simultaneously. The servants bowed their heads to him, walking backward into the chamber. Across the room, a lithe figure lounged on a settee, his legs dangling off one side. The lord was draped in robes of luxurious clothes and jewelry, rings for every finger. His hair was long, tumbling down in multiple shades of red and brown. All his braids and curls fell to his hips, his claws polished to a shine.

Baelozar. The Demon Lord of Pride.

His horns grew out of his temples, curling against his skull. The horns were no longer than five inches but gleamed dark mahogany. His face was feminine, all soft edges and long lashes.

Baelozar had round, bright-emerald eyes. His eyes gave off an eerie aura, glowing with power, the sclera a deep violet.

Nearby, a servant held a tray of food. The servant dangled various fruits into Baelozar's mouth every few moments. Baelozar was the living embodiment of Pride; he delighted in showing off his control over others, and the power he wielded.

Striding boldly to the settee, Sinohne waited for an acknowledgment.

Baelozar raised an eyebrow and turned his head toward him. He stuck out a hand, and a servant scrambled to take it, using sandstone to file his claws to fine points.

"Lieutenant Sinohne," Baelozar spoke, his voice sickly sweet. "What brings you into my esteemed presence? You are supposed to be monitoring the filth of greed."

Sinohne bowed his head. "Yes. Your orders were highly accurate and well placed, my lord. But you also ordered me to provide reports of any activity outside the norm. You were correct—and your intelligence, as always, is beyond compare, my lord."

Baelozar smiled and leaned forward. "Something has happened, then?"

He patted the spot beside him. Sinohne knelt at the lord's feet, not daring to sit upon the settee.

Baelozar's smile widened, spreading from ear to ear. He reached to pet Sinohne's hair as if he were a child being soothed by his mother. "You always know how best to please me, my pet. Tell me, what are those foul creatures doing? What does the beast, Culzahr, want on Earth?"

Sinohne frowned.

"I have not ascertained his plan yet, my lord. He keeps it close, even after all these years. But, the Fallen—the one who sings for us? He didn't show for work on Friday. It has never happened before. Not once in the ten years since Culzahr brought him there."

Baelozar stayed quiet for a long while, petting Sinohne's hair.

"Angels do not fall ill, Lieutenant. Tell me what you know!"

He grasped Sinohne's horn and yanked his head back. Out of eyesight, one of the servants gasped.

Sinohne swallowed. The pleasure which had exploded through his body when the lord touched his horn made him nauseous. His groin hardened against his will. He kept the rest of his body perfectly still, refusing to show any reaction, knowing that's what Baelozar wanted. It was a tactic Baelozar often used, trying to humiliate his lieutenant, to control him however he could.

Such was his nature.

Sinohne licked his lips, gathering his will to speak. "I don't believe he was ill, my lord. He didn't give an explanation when we approached him the next morning. There must have been another reason to explain his absence. I'm not yet sure what it could be, my lord."

Baelozar was content with his answer and released him.

Sinohne dared not disrespect Baelozar by rubbing his horn and instead, waited for his next response.

Baelozar resumed petting his hair absent-mindedly, distracted by his own thoughts.

"Culzahr places a lot of importance on this angel. You must find out why, my pet, and soon. Lucifer has become anxious. He looks to me to find out who intends to undermine his rule. We must prove it is Culzahr...Do you understand?"

Sinohne stood and bowed low to Baelozar. Grabbing his hand, the lieutenant placed a chaste kiss upon his ring finger.

"Of course, my lord. You will not regret giving me this responsibility."

"Take your leave, then."

Sinohne quietly exited the room. When he was finally back out in the corridor, and the doors to Baelozar's chamber had closed, he exhaled a long breath. He rubbed at his horn now, trying to rid himself of the lord's touch. His body was still brimming with the effects, his pants tight against his groin. Sinohne quickly cast open a portal, renting the air with his claws and mumbled an incantation. He returned his glamor and stepped through to Earth.

He climbed into his waiting truck, which was parked in bum-fuck-nowhere. A half an hour later, Garrett drove into the parking lot of Infernal Avarice, just in time to see Victor climb off his crotch-rocket motorcycle. He was clad in multicolored, leather gear and his tan, Timberland boots.

Victor pulled off his helmet, his hair sticking up in all directions. Sweat dripped onto his neck. He hadn't yet noticed Garrett. This gave Garrett time to appreciate just how well-fitted those leather pants were. He bit his lip and groaned in frustration. Then he climbed out of his truck, slamming the door shut.

Victor whipped around. "Whoa! When did you get here?"

Garrett shrugged with a nonchalance he didn't feel. "I just arrived. Why are you here?" He walked over to Victor, his movements slow, predatory...his eyes glued to Victor's body.

Victor pulled headphones out of his helmet. He scratched his neck as a blush filled his cheeks. "The place is closed. I like to come on Sundays and practice singing the lead parts of our songs. Taking lead this past Friday wasn't just some gift of mine, ya' know?"

Garrett smirked, but on the inside, he was impressed. He'd been suspicious for quite a while, but perhaps Victor and Maribel were innocent in whatever machinations Culzahr had going. As innocent as a demon could be, anyway. While wards of Greed, they were considered Rylan's personal slaves, given by their demon lords to curry Culzahr's favor.

For Victor to do something like this implied ambition. For what? He couldn't say. Perhaps it was just part of Victor's nature as a demon of Envy. Or perhaps...

No. He couldn't push his own thoughts onto others. Nor his own weaknesses.

"You okay?"

Garrett snapped back to reality to find Victor staring at him in confusion. He must've been silent for some time.

"I'm fine."

Victor appeared skeptical but didn't reply. Instead, he peeked toward Garrett's truck. A smile crept over his face.

"You wanna go somewhere?"

Garrett narrowed his eyes. His insides flipped, excited at the prospect of getting the demon alone.

"Where?"

"Anywhere. For a few hours. Just us."

He had a hopeful glint in his storm-blue eyes, sparkling like a small puppy.

Garrett smiled, glad to accommodate him.

Victor grabbed the other demon, pulling Garrett back to his truck. Garrett held open the passenger door, the metal creaking with rust. Before hopping in, Victor removed his leather jacket and gloves, his muscles bunching.

Garrett sucked in a breath, forcing himself to look away...which lasted damn near two seconds.

Victor placed his stuff in the bed of the truck, along with his helmet. As he reached over the side of the truck-bed, his limbs stretched in such a way, Garrett's mind fuddled and he lost his grip on the door. He tried to hide his reaction, moving to the driver's side and climbing in the truck, sitting behind the wheel.

He pushed open the passenger door to see Victor left in only a white tank top. The shirt was soaked with sweat, and Victor's nipples showed through the material.

Garrett swallowed and turned the ignition, starting the engine.

He had an older truck, the seats one long bench. It was big enough for two people and a small child. Some of the cushion was missing in places, but Garret didn't mind; it gave the truck character. The outside was a faded navy blue, rust creeping around the edges.

Victor swung into the seat, sliding all the way over, leaning against Garrett's side.

Garrett stiffened but continued to drive. He'd need more space to control the urges still roaring through his body; otherwise, he might cause an accident.

He decided to head south.

They drove for a while, neither man striking up a conversation. The silence passed comfortably. Victor moved and leaned against the window of his door, watching the scenery go by. Whenever Garrett glanced toward Victor, there was an expression of longing the lieutenant had never seen on his face before. But he had seen it in his own reflection.

Garrett's eyes focused back on the road. First business.

Trees passed by while he drove further down the highway. Eventually, the silence of the demon next to him started to grate his nerves.

He cleared his throat.

Victor glanced over. "What's up?"

"I can't drive forever. Anywhere, in particular, you wanna go, man?"

Victor turned back to the window without replying. His mood seemed troubled. Blowing out a sharp breath, Garrett pulled off to the side of the highway and shifted into park. He turned to the other man and grabbed his arm, pulling the blonde toward him. Victor didn't protest. Instead, he moved to rest against Garrett, his back to the other's chest.

The contact soothed Garrett's irritation instantly.

"What's on your mind, Vaxihir?" Garrett murmured into his ear from behind. He massaged his left shoulder, thrilled to be touching the other demon. He'd never been able to hold him this close before.

Saying Victor's demonic name out loud had the effect he thought it might; Victor stiffened for a moment before relaxing against him again.

"Don't call me that."

"Then, speak. *You* wanted to go somewhere."

A semi drove passed. Garrett's truck rattled with the backdraft.

"Pick somewhere before we get hit."

"You're the one who pulled over."

"And, we're not leaving until you speak what's on your mind."

He squeezed Victor's stomach with the arm he'd wrapped around the other man's waist.

"You're normally happy-go-lucky. This gloominess isn't like you. Even Zane would notice."

Sighing, Victor dropped his head backward, resting a cheek on Garrett's shoulder.

Garrett sucked in a sharp breath. Victor's scent drifted to his nose. Sweat, Old Spice deodorant, and pine mixed together. An effective tool of temptation.

"I know. I know," Victor said. Garrett's throat bobbed as the other man continued. "It's just been strange the last few days. Last night was so...weird. Zane was there, but it just seemed *off*. Zane having disappeared Friday? When has he ever no-showed? Was he sick or something?"

Victor scoffed. "I thought he couldn't, you know? He's an angel. A Fallen angel...but, still, an angel."

"He was covering for something else."

"No, yeah, I get it...I mean, I don't know." Victor pulled away to face Garrett. "That's not even what's doing for me. I know I'm a demon, but...he and I are friends. We've all played together for years now and hung out outside of the band. You, too. It's hard when I...remember it's all fake. And, one day, you guys won't be around." He bit his lip, his frustration evident.

Garrett had never realized how much Victor relied on their friendships. "What're you trying to say here?"

"Can't you feel it? Zane didn't see *me*. As if we were just meeting. It was wrong. I felt…" Victor sighed, dismissing his last words, unable to explain his emotions.

"Hey, now. Don't think too hard, you might hurt that big boney head of yours!" Garrett teased him, poking him in the temple.

Victor laughed, smacking Garrett's hand away. The moment of levity was brief, as Victor's expression turned grim again. "Rylan acted strange, too."

Garrett raised an eyebrow. If Culzahr's lieutenant was involved in something, he needed to know what. "How so?"

"Well, he wasn't a douche bag last night. When I gave him my extra earnings for singing lead Friday, he was…decent to me. I normally sleep on the ground. He let me sleep with him and Maribel on his horde. And, when we woke up today, he said I had the day to myself. Which never happens! You know how he is."

Garrett's lips thinned…Yes, he did.

The bastard was controlling, absurdly possessive. Victor was never allowed out alone. When he was with Zane and Garrett, Rylan had to know his every move. His behavior made the years working together extremely trying. Zane and Garrett clashed heads with Rylan multiple times over his treatment of Victor or, frankly, his hostile personality.

Ironically, Zane liked to compare Rylan to a demon. It gave the other staff all a good chuckle — to the singer's confusion. But Zane had never requested new members. Perhaps the kid was too grateful to Culzahr to say anything about his choices.

Garrett winked. "Greedy bastard."

Victor smiled. "Yeah." He swiped a hand through his hair and rubbed his palm over his face. His body relaxed, and he moved over to lean against Garrett's shoulder.

"Thanks for listening to me whine." Victor chuckled to himself. "I think this may be the longest conversation we've ever had. Rylan would hate me being alone with just you…"

Garrett's eyes found his gaze, the air becoming heavy, his lust firing on all cylinders. He reached over, cupping Victor's cheek, and pulled his face closer. Leaning in, he pressed their lips together in a long, slow kiss.

Victor moaned, a low guttural sound muffled by their lips. Garrett's lip twitched in amusement, deepening the kiss. He pulled the other man onto his lap, his legs straddling him, his back against the steering wheel. There was no denying their mutual attraction.

Garrett rubbed his fingers over the other man's chest, tweaking his nipples and eliciting another low moan. Releasing Victor's mouth, he latched onto his collarbone, nibbling his skin, salt on his tongue. Victor's hands were in his hair, pulling him closer. His hips were grinding on him, creating sweet friction, and Garrett squeezed his sides, thrust upward as his frustration grew.

Another semi drove passed. The whole vehicle shook, startling both men out of their lust-filled haze. Then they locked eyes for a moment before Victor burst into laughter. His whole body shook with it. Garrett tensed as the other man's hips rubbed against him.

"We shouldn't stay here."

Victor rubbed a tear from his eye, catching his breath. "Yeah, I suppose not. Should we go back?"

"Hell no." Garrett lifted the other man off him and placed him back on the seat.

Victor smiled. The dark-haired demon next to him delighted him to no end. He had always put Victor before himself, backing him when Rylan became too much to bear. No other demon had ever treated him this way, and he often wondered if Garrett really was one sometimes.

His very nature and personality were the opposite of everything he was supposed to be. Garrett had been appointed the royal ambassador between their two factions, the most powerful in Hell. Pride was always at odds with Greed, but Culzahr begrudgingly allowed Garrett's presence to curry favor with Lucifer.

Garrett pulled the truck back onto the highway. They drove for a little while longer before he saw an exit sign boasting hotel names, went to the nicest one of the three and parked. He jumped out, motioning for Victor to stay put. Ten minutes later, give or take, he returned and waved for Victor. They strolled around to the side exit and headed to the elevators.

Garrett pressed the button for the third floor. He turned to Victor and shoved him against the wall of the elevator, immediately claiming his mouth with his own, heart pumping inside his chest. Without releasing Victor's mouth, he picked the demon up and wrapped his legs around his waist, pressing the demon into the wall even harder.

Victor gripped his shoulders, the material of his shirt bunching in his fists. He was by no means a small dude, the display of strength from Garrett really turning him on. He was already ridiculously hard, the leather pants he wore uncomfortable as hell, his cock straining against the cloth.

Garrett's tongue penetrated his mouth, swirling around, dancing with his own. His mind clouded, pleasure and release the only thoughts left to him. The doors pinged, opened. Garrett lifted Victor from the wall and slung him over his shoulder, hand gripping his ass.

"Hey!" Victor pretended to protest, but his efforts were only a half-measure. "I can walk, ya' know!"

"Yeah, yeah. Save it for someone else." Garrett pulled out the key card for the hotel room door.

Victor laughed and shook his head, rolling his eyes. "Okay, Tarzan."

Garrett's comeback was a hard slap to his ass.

Victor yelped in surprise. "Let me down already, Garrett."

He started to struggle against Garrett's hold, and the other man released him just as the door swung open. Victor stumbled backward, tripping over his feet and landed on his butt.

Victor glared daggers. "Thanks, you dick."

Garrett chuckled while he closed the door. "No problem." He crouched then offered his hand, smirking and unapologetic.

Victor took the offer and pulled himself to his feet. He peered around their room. To his left was a wide bathroom with an open shower.

Beyond the bathroom, a private Jacuzzi was nestled into the corner, unlit candles and bath salts placed on the edges. To Victor's right was a king-sized bed, covered in a salmon-colored comforter with flower patterns on it. The window on the wall in front of him was covered floor-to-ceiling with large, ugly green curtains hanging from each side. All in all, it was a pretty average room with a desk, a television center, and a minifridge. He nodded to himself, satisfied.

Garrett walked to the window and drew the curtains closed. The light in the room dimmed to a low glow from the lamps.

Victor proceeded to open the minifridge, curious about what he'd find inside. "Oooh!" he exclaimed. "They got chocolate! Ooh! And, little mini-bottles of vodka and whiskey!"

Garrett rolled his eyes as he sat on the bed. Victor's leather pants stretched tight over his butt. Garrett tilted his head to the side, able to appreciate the angle a little more, and sighed. "So, how does it feel to have a day to yourself?"

Victor jerked, banging his head on the minibar. He rubbed the back of his head then finally turned around to face Garrett. "I'm just enjoying myself. It's been fun so far." He settled on the floor, cross-legged and ripped open a candy bar, chewing noisily. "It's pretty cool knowing I don't have to check my phone every minute in case I miss a text or a call. He really is a pain sometimes. But, he's my master so...I guess it's a moot point when you're just...property." He grew quiet, frowning, and his eyes became distant.

Garrett regretted mentioning it. Victor was young, but as a demon, this was just a fact of life for them. Garrett might not technically be a slave, but he still reported to Baelozar. If Garrett pissed him off, there was no telling how he'd end up. He should not even be caring about this other demon in front of him.

The two demons may have become friends, but Garrett would be required to return to his own faction. They'd be enemies because Greed and Pride hated each other. His ambassadorship had been meant as a brief ruse. He should remember to stick with his own.

Still...Victor's frown bothered him.

Bothered him in a way he couldn't describe. It was a weakness he couldn't break away from, even knowing whatever was between them would end, *had* to end, eventually.

Fuck it.

Garrett slid to the floor, onto his hands and knees, crawling over until he was inches from Victor's face, an arm on either side of the man's hips. The blonde swallowed, anxiously licked his lips.

"I want to kiss you." Garrett gazed into Victor's widening eyes. "Don't be nervous."

Victor took a deep breath through his nose, his heart thumping hard enough he was afraid it might pop out of his chest. Garrett's eyes bored into his, an abyss he could fall into and...never find his way. Not like he'd want to, anyway. "What do you really look like?"

Garrett jerked back as if he had been slapped, dropping his gaze.

Victor could've smacked himself. *Why did he say something so stupid? Frickin' idiot!* He scolded himself and started to move away.

Garrett grabbed his arm. Victor glanced back to see Garrett's expression change rapidly as if he argued with himself. After a moment, the other man's eyes refocused, his facial expression unreadable. "You're a demon."

Victor frowned and tried to move again, but Garrett held firmly to his arm. "Wait. Let me finish. You're a demon. The four of us, you, Maribel, Rylan and I, are all demons. Cyrus is a demon."

"Thank you, Captain Obvious," Victor said with his usual snarkiness. "What's your point?"

Garret glared. "What I'm trying to say is…we all come from different factions and have different ranks in Hell."

"Yeah, that's been established."

"You don't understand, V'."

"Understand what? We've known each other for seven years. And I have yet to see under your glamor. Hell, you've seen *me*. Why is it every time I ask to see the *real* you, you clam up?"

Victor moved toward the curtained window, Garrett's hold loosening. He still had his candy bar and decided to take a giant bite, chewing angrily, his back to the room. Chocolate always soothed his nerves.

"But that's why you don't understand, Victor. You don't even know my real name."

"It's Gadruhm. You're an ambassador to help keep the so-called peace between Pride and Greed. Not like it's made any difference," Victor grumbled between bites.

A tail of bright silver snaked around his waist, pulling him back against a warm, solid chest. His heart skipped a beat, dread a pit in his stomach, the candy bar forgotten as it fell to the floor. Arms the same silver as the tail wrapped around his chest, trapping him, holding him still. Slowly, he was turned around to meet a gaze which squeezed the breath out of his lungs.

It couldn't be. This wasn't a demon named Gadruhm — if that demon had ever existed. No, he was a much, much, much *more* legendary demon. A demon who became an enormous reason Pride was singularly feared as a faction. Baelozar commanded one of the deadliest, scariest fuckers in all of Hell, known for a particular set of silver looks and unique, dark eyes. A creature who had battled angels and demons alike, his kill number in the thousands, easily. He was the only demon to ever survive a battle with a Thrones, the enforcers of the Angelic Council, and he had the scar to prove it.

Sinohne, the lieutenant of Pride.

"Ho — how?" Victor stammered, fear licking his spine.

"I am not an ambassador, Victor." Sinohne's voice was deep and gravelly.

"I...am a spy."

TWELVE

"A spy!"

Sinohne winced, the other man's voice too loud for his sensitive hearing, and his pointed ears twitched.

Victor struggled against Sinohne's hold, his expression filled with anger and hurt. His efforts were wasted, Sinohne's strength overpowered him. Eventually, he gave up. "Let me go."

Sinohne bared his teeth and let out a small growl. Victor visibly shrunk before him, eyes widening, his face a shade paler. Sinohne sighed. He hadn't wanted to scare him, instantly experiencing guilt. "If I release you, will you please let me explain?"

Victor just stared for a few moments.

"If I don't, will you kill me?"

There was an unfamiliar pang in his chest; the fear and betrayal he had heard in the question was difficult to bear. He released Victor's arms but kept a tight hold with his tail. He pulled Victor toward the bed with him.

The blonde did not resist, but his eyes darted around, seeking a means of escape. When they were seated, Sinohne grabbed one of his hands; the fingers trembled beneath his touch. He had never seen Victor act this way with him. He hated that he was the cause.

"Are you going to kill me if I don't stay silent?"

Sinohne shook his head. "*I* would never dream of hurting you...But, I can't guarantee your life is safe if this news comes to light. More than likely, Lieutenant Rhaisur himself would kill you."

Victor's shoulders slumped, dejected. Sinohne grabbed his chin, being careful with his claws. "I don't want to lose you, V'."

Victor's brows narrowed. "But you've been lying to us this whole time...lying to me."

"Demon?"

Victor chuckled. "Really? This's the best reason you could come up with? 'Hey, I'm a demon, what'd you expect?'" Victor laid a hand on Sinohne's tail, his smile faltering. "It would be easier to say you had orders. Maybe you hate it. Or, you're protecting something."

"Someone?"

Victor stared at the demon, the pad of his thumb rubbing against his tail, the silver skin surprisingly soft. By most standards, Sinohne's eyes might be considered eerie. His sclera was black, but the pupils themselves were a hollow white.

It was a trait unique to the demon, unlike the rest of the Pride faction who had purple sclera. To Victor, Sinohne's eyes appeared beautiful, ethereal. Far less terrifying than he had ever imagined of the legendary demon. The tips of his pointed canines poked out, lips parted just ever so slightly.

Despite the betrayal, Victor was genuinely tempted to kiss Sinohne.

Sinohne sighed. "You're right. I was ordered. To be a spy. To feed my lord information about Culzahr—and his plans. But, for what it's worth, you were never supposed to be a part of the equation…" He fell silent.

"Why then? If you were just supposed to be here to get information and to sabotage or something. Why become involved with me, become my friend? Is it all a lie? Are you using me, too?"

"You're enchanting," Sinohne blurted out, surprising them both.

Victor blinked. "I am?"

"Yes," the silver demon said. His eyelids lowered, heat entering the smoky depths. He reached forward, trailing a claw over Victor's earlobe. "You have life. You have such a…a way about you, I could not…cannot resist. But, after all this time, you and I are completely alone. And if I don't taste you, taste what you have…I will go *mad*."

Sinohne jerked Victor forward with his tail, captured his mouth in a deep kiss. The silver demon wrapped his arms around the blonde's waist and released his tail. Victor's hands dove into his hair but winced when his lip caught on Sinohne's canine.

Sinohne noticed and hesitated, pulling away.

"No, it's okay," Victor assured him.

Sinohne frowned and, in a blink of an eye, morphed back into his glamor.

Victor sighed. "You really didn't have to…"

Sinohne shook his head. "No. Without my glamor, I'd only have hurt you again, worse than a bloody lip."

"I don't believe that."

Sinohne captured Victor's mouth, silencing his protests. He pushed him onto the mattress, delving his tongue inside and swirling it around his mouth. Victor moaned, hands roaming Sinohne's back and sliding under his shirt. There was no resistance as he started pulling the shirt until Sinohne had no choice but to remove it. Victor undid Sinohne's zipper, working his hands inside, then palmed his length.

Pleasure spiked through Sinohne's body. His cock grew hard. Victor stroked him, up and down. Sinohne grunted, his control starting to shred. He pulled Victor's lips to his then left kisses on his neck, and on his shoulder. His tongue danced over his ears, playing with his piercings. Little goose bumps spread where he touched Victor with his lips, the demon shivering beneath him.

Sinohne leaned to the side. He used his free hand to work the other man's shirt loose…left the material hanging on Victor's shoulder. Victor's nipples had hardened, the nubs ripe for the taste. He didn't waste another second, sucking one nipple between his lips.

"Mmmm…" A moan worked its way out of Victor's throat, heightening Sinohne's excitement. Soon, both men panted. Sinohne worked to remove Victor's leather pants and had made progress until he realized they both still wore their shoes.

"Shit…" Sinohne muttered in frustration. He pulled away from Victor's grip to bend and remove their boots.

Victor chuckled. His pants were bunched around his ankles, his shirt hanging off his shoulders. His lover was untying his shoes for him, and his erection jutted out, a nice draft in the room.

Good times.

Sinohne glanced back with a grin. "It's never easy, is it?"

"Nope, never. That's why it's worth it."

Victor pulled at the other man. He kicked off his loosened boots and pants, shrugged off his shirt. He was naked...and not one bit ashamed. Victor knew he had a damn good body, toes and all...Hell, he chose it, right?

Sinohne licked his lips. The sight of all his skin made the demon's mouth water. He quickly wiggled out of his own pants and boots then climbed onto the bed—and on top of Victor. He moved in between the other man's legs, grinding their groins together.

Victor's head fell back. He moaned, gripping the comforter beneath them. "Oh damn, that feels good." He nibbled Sinohne's chest and stuck out his tongue, twirling the muscle around one nipple.

Slowly, Sinohne thrust with his hips, working himself and Victor into a frenzy until the blonde left scratches on his arms. This only heightened his pleasure, and he groaned. Victor's eyes were glazed over, and his hips were thrusting, the tip of his cock leaking pre-cum.

"Damn, V', you're just the sexiest thing..." Sinohne whispered.

Lifting himself up, he flipped the other man over and pulled him to his knees. He took two digits, plunging them into Victor's mouth, who sucked on them greedily. With his other hand, he reached between Victor's legs and stroked his cock. Victor arched his back, moving into his grip, moaning around his fingers. Sinohne pulled his hand away from his mouth and slowly inserted a wet digit into Victor.

"Ah!" Victor moaned. "More...hurry!"

Happy to oblige, Sinohne inserted the second digit, spreading his fingers to widen the hole. Soon, he was able to insert three fingers, the muscles around the tight entrance loosening. He twirled his fingers around until he hit that tight bundle of nerves.

Sinohne groaned. "Are you ready?"

Victor nodded to him, his eyes glazed over with pleasure.

Sinohne positioned himself behind Victor. In one hard thrust, he seated himself all the way to the base. Victor gasped, gripping the comforter. Sinohne chuckled. If Victor had had his claws out, the blanket would have been shredded. Victor's insides squeezed the hard length, pulsing around him like a branding iron.

Victor moaned, his voice muffled into the bed. "You have...to move...I can take it. Move!"

Sweat dripped down Sinohne's forehead as he clutched Victor's hips, trying to maintain self-control. It was difficult enough, not reverting to his demonic form. He moved his hands over the blonde's butt cheeks, gripping them tight. He liked seeing his cock inside Victor. He liked being able to enjoy it. He pulled out and plunged back in, keeping a slow, deliberate pace for quite a while.

Victor's arms eventually gave out, unable to hold himself up any longer, his face smushed into the pillow.

Sinohne smirked and hooked his arms underneath Victor's legs. He lifted them, continually thrusting inside. He picked up the pace, thrusting harder and harder. Victor's head and arms thrashed around, delirious with pleasure, his moans getting louder and louder until he was yelling and cursing Sinohne's name. When Sinohne knew they were both close, he dropped Victor's legs. He then flipped the other man onto his back and reached to kiss him, thrusting back inside in one smooth motion.

Victor came a moment later, hot fluid hitting his chest.

This was the last straw. Sinohne let loose, cumming hard.

They both collapsed.

After a few minutes, Victor grimaced. He was super-sticky, and Sinohne was heavy. He tried to push the other demon off, but his arms didn't want to work. "Hey...we can't stay like this..."

Sinohne grunted, turning his head to meet Victor's eyes. He smiled softly. "Yeah...I know. Give me a sec..." After a moment, Sinohne moved off and leaned forward. Victor groaned, his hips and back stiff.

Sinohne pecked him on the lips. "Be right back." He stood and walked into the bathroom.

Victor heard the shower turning on, and then Sinohne walked back out into the room. When he was closer, he scooped Victor into his arms.

Victor blushed. "Why do you always feel the need to carry me around like a girl?"

Sinohne scoffed, kissing him with a mischievous smile. "When are you going to feel the need to try to stop me?"

Victor just blushed harder. He crossed his arms.

Sinohne walked them into the bathroom, straight into the spray.

THIRTEEN

Sweat poured down his spine, his muscles bunching, contracting, a sweet, slow burn working its way up his biceps. Zane took a deep inhale of oxygen and exhaled, his breathing heavy but controlled. He stared at his arms in the mirror then raised the weights one more time before setting them back on the floor to rest. The grunts and groans of the gym surrounding him were like white noise to his hearing, but they did little to drown out his racing thoughts.

Damaceous had returned to his world the day before. Zane was aggravated to no end about it, deciding to de-stress. So, here he was getting his grunt on, along with the other gym regulars. He liked this place. It was bright, always crowded. Some might have preferred the opposite, but Zane was a social creature by nature. He was…less alone this way. Other than work, the gym was his only home-away-from-home; his place to let loose and grind away at his anxiety.

Zane sighed, sitting forward on the workout bench to take a break. He pulled at his shirt to let his skin breathe a little. His whole back and chest were covered in sweat.

He had been blind-sided yesterday, the sudden disappearance had come from nowhere. He'd assumed Damaceous meant to stay, to investigate. One minute they were laughing, joking, and having a good time. Then, Damaceous was gone. Especially after he dropped the "your whole life is a lie" bomb.

Who does that and just *disappears*?

Zane dropped his head into his hands, pulling at his hair in frustration. He was going crazy. His emotions were all over the place, anxiety through the roof. He really wanted to talk to his friends, Victor and Garrett. But, shit…they were demons!

Demons.

From Hell.

Of all the freakin' things….

He was supposed to be an angel. Given, they might believe him when he started talking but—what if they attacked him? What if the whole reason he didn't know who, or what, he was, was the point of whatever was going on? What happens if he admits he's aware of it?

Fuck.

Zane sighed. His anxiety was taking over his mind. His shoulders were tight, and his back twinged painfully every few moments. Whenever he was stressed, the past injuries bothered him, especially between his shoulder blades. Usually, he could breathe deep, relax...and the spasms would subside after a while. This time, the pain only seemed to worsen. He grimaced, rubbing his neck.

Zane looked at his image in the mirror, noting the stress lines on his face, dark bags from a restless night of sleep under his eyes. Standing with another long sigh of resignation, he shook out his legs, the basketball shorts sticking to his skin. He grabbed the weights off the floor and returned them to the rack against the mirrored wall.

"Are you using this?"

A guy in a green shirt busted out leg lunges near a barbell Zane wanted. The man waved him off, giving Zane the go-ahead. He took the bar back to his bench, putting it on the stand.

He added weights on both sides of the bar, proceeding to settle himself underneath it for a set of bench presses. He gripped the metal and paused, the steel cold against his palms. Normally, Victor would be there as a spotter, egging him on. Being alone was weird. Zane's throat tightened, but he forced himself to breathe deeply. This was his new reality, being alone. He lifted the bar and began to knock out his reps.

"Are you a moron, or are you actually having health issues?"

Zane jumped, the bar fumbling from his grip. A hand reached out, catching it before his face was damaged. Zane twisted his neck to see storm-blue eyes filled with confusion. "Victor? What're you doing here?"

Victor set the bar on the stand, leaning forward.

Zane twisted to face the man. "How'd you know I'd be here?"

"Dude, really? Whenever you're stressed, you're here...after Friday, I figured you were probably stressed. Plus, we always come here around noon." Victor shrugged. "I'm your best friend. I *know* you, okay?"

"You checked Facebook."

Victor leaned against the mirrored wall, crossing his arms. "I mean, really? I'm your friend. And...yeah, okay, I checked Facebook. *You* checked in."

Zane snorted. "Well, I have to keep my fans in the know. I am a 'rising star' and all, remember?"

"Oh, God. Just 'cuz you got *one* article, doesn't mean you're famous, okay?" Victor said. Zane laughed, and Victor's grin widened. "So, you gonna' tell me what's really going on?"

Zane's lips thinned, his chest tightening at the reminder. A steady hand gripped his shoulder. He glanced back to see Garrett. "You're both stalkers, you know that?"

Garrett laughed. The brunette sat beside him on the bench and waited for Zane to answer Victor's question. "It was nothing, you guys. Just a fluke, I promise."

Victor looked less than convinced but shrugged. "It's whatever, man. Just know, you can talk to us. There's nothing you could tell us that would be too weird."

"What do you say we help finish the next set?" Garrett suggested.

Zane's mouth went dry, remembering why he had attempted to avoid them in the first place. "I, uh, actually need to run to the bathroom. I'll be back. Watch the bench."

The two men glanced at each other with skepticism.

Zane twisted around, tripping over a free weight left on the floor. He fell, smacking his head onto a nearby machine. Stars burst behind his eyes, pain flashing through his skull. He grabbed his head and cursed.

"Holy shit, dude! You okay?" Victor helped him off the floor. "Uh...you should probably go wash that off."

Zane felt the injury on his head, his fingers coming back spotted with blood. A towel was placed over his head, Victor holding pressure to the wound.

"Yo. Go on. Take a shower or something." Victor scanned the room. He seemed…nervous. But, why? Zane glanced at Garrett. His eyes darted around but with more discretion.

"Yeah…I was headed there, anyway. I'll see ya' guys later."

He took over the hold on the towel and grimaced. The cloth smelled like old gym socks, the one Victor always used but never washed.

When he made it into the locker room, the man with the green shirt was there, gathering his stuff out of a locker. Zane gave him a passing nod as he went to the shower stalls.

"Whoa. What happened, man?"

Zane shrugged. He held out the towel in his direction, showing off the bloodstain. "Just hit my head. No big deal. Gonna' shower and head out."

Zane opened a curtain, finding an empty stall. He turned the knob and let the water flow, checking the temperature until it was warm enough to enter. While he waited, Zane began slipping out of his clothes in the small area in front of the shower.

The curtain to his stall was pulled open, Green Shirt standing at the entrance. The man sniffed the air, picking up the nearby towel and held it to his face.

Zane turned to face him. "Uh…Can I help you? Trying to shower, dude." The man was a total weirdo, sniffing the towel like you would a Thanksgiving dinner.

Green Shirt moved closer, dropping the towel on the floor.

Zane stepped backward, holding up a hand for him to stop. "No, really. You need to leave."

"It's okay, man. I can help. Those are some nice tattoos…" Green Shirt's eyes were focused on Zane's head. Zane had only just removed his shirt, but the comment was disconcerting. He felt exposed as if he was already naked. The man's eyes looked hungry.

"Thanks. But, I'm good. Can you go now?" Zane replied.

Green Shirt was unexpectedly against him. He shoved Zane into the wall, a hand around his throat, cutting off his air. As his anxiety mounted, the whites of Green Shirt's eyes changed to a deep red with charcoal irises, and his rounded pupils narrowed to cat-like slits. Fangs slipped out over the demon's bottom lip when a forked tongue flicked out and tasted the wound on Zane's head.

Zane shoved him, but his strength did little against the creature. The hand around his neck squeezed tighter, and white spots began to appear in Zane's vision as he struggled.

"Be still, little angel." Green Shirt knocked the singer's head into the wall to make his point clearer. The creature leaned forward, sniffing the wound.

Zane felt its tongue lick at the blood dripping onto his temple, a warm slippery sensation. "Let me go!" He clawed at the creature's wrist. It was no use. He wasn't strong enough to get away. Zane was getting dizzy, the lack of oxygen starting to take effect.

The creature laughed.

Zane made one last effort to get away and headbutted Green Shirt. It was a stupid thing to do, making his own vision blur even more.

The demon growled, but his hold didn't break. In fact, he only appeared amused. "You can struggle all you want. No one will help you once I take you out of here."

"How?" Zane asked. The sound was so quiet, Green Shirt was forced to bend closer to hear him. Zane bit his earlobe as hard as he could.

Green Shirt shrieked. His grip finally loosened when the creature grabbed for his ear.

Zane kicked him away, falling backward into the spray of the shower. The creature became tangled in the plastic curtain, pulling it off the rings, and then fell to the floor. The singer struggled to his feet. He had to choke back nausea caused by his dizziness. Zane managed to grab his shirt and moved to leave the stall, stepping around the tangled demon.

A hand caught his ankle, toppling Zane to the ground. He flipped onto his back but was too late to stop Green Shirt from jumping on top of him. A hand swiped out. Zane barely missed losing his pretty face by holding up an arm in defense. The skin on his forearm split open, blood gushing out of the wound.

"Hey!" Someone shouted behind them. "What's going on here?"

Green Shirt snarled, fangs bared, but was gone in an instant, running out of the locker room. Zane groaned, curling onto his side and clutched his arm into his chest.

A portly man in a grey shirt and sweats bent down to help Zane stand on shaky legs. "Oh, my goodness. What *was* that? You okay, man? You're cut up pretty badly," his rescuer asked.

"I'll be okay. Thanks."

The other man scratched his head. "Did that guy have pointed teeth and weird eyes or was it just me?"

"Uh...I didn't see anything..." Zane muttered, grabbing his stuff out of the shower stall and pulled on his shirt. He moved to the towel dispenser, wrapping his arm in a bunch of brown paper towels. As he shuffled out of the locker room, Zane spotted his friends but left the gym before they could ask him about his arm.

Outside the building, Zane leaned against the brick. His heart thumped a mile a minute. His breath came in short gasps as anxiety took over. The singer's eyes darted around, watching for his attacker. Lucky for him, his apartment building was only a couple of blocks down the road. There was also a store with a pharmacy along the way. Zane made his way down the block, walking fast.

He trembled with adrenaline, his breathing still erratic. As Zane walked, the people he passed stared at him with puzzled looks. Blood from his arm dripped onto the sidewalk; he was bleeding through the towels. He had finally stepped through the doors of the nearby store when someone grabbed his shoulder. He twisted around, swinging his arm out in defense.

"Whoa! It's me!" Garrett dodged his fist. Zane froze, his face paling. Garrett reached for his injured arm. "Are you okay?"

Zane jerked away. "I'm—I'm fine. What do you want?"

Garrett held out Zane's forgotten gym bag. Zane blinked. He hadn't even noticed he had left it behind. His wallet and keys were in it.

He let out a breath. "Oh. Sorry. Thanks. Is that all?"

"Yeah. That's it. What happened to your arm? I heard someone was attacked in the locker room. Was it you?"

"No," Zane lied. He glared at Garrett, daring him to contradict what he'd said.

The other man crossed his arms after dropping the bag. "Well, first aid is aisle six. Since you weren't attacked and all."

Zane glanced toward the aisle. "Where's Victor?"

"He had to get back."

"Oh."

Silence extended between them, his lie hanging in the air like an elephant.

Garrett sighed. "Look. Just get yourself fixed up. First, you no-showed on Friday. Then, you tripped and banged your head. It's still bleeding by the way. And, now, your arm looks like Freddy Krueger had a field day." The brunette squeezed his nose and heaved another big sigh. "I don't know what's going on. Just…take care of yourself. We can't have our lead member out over dumb accidents. Cyrus is already difficult to manage. For all our sakes, get it together."

"I'm sorry."

"Don't worry about it. It's just not making my job any easier." His friend stepped close before Zane could react, whispering out of other customer's earshot; "And, stop bleeding everywhere. You smell like candy and sunshine. It's making you a target for ones like the thing earlier."

Zane's eyes widened as Garrett left him to exit the store. Shaking himself, Zane picked up his gym bag and hurried to the sixth aisle, grabbing bandages and a first aid kit. After paying, the singer rushed home to care for his wounds, trying not to think about the implications of Garrett's words.

FOURTEEN

He blinked and stared into the mirror, leaning on his hands. He was so tired. His arm throbbed, still healing from where he'd been wounded three weeks ago. Damaceous still hadn't returned from Heaven, but the truth of his words rung like a gong through his life.

Zane saw the truth every day, and Cyrus's betrayal left a bitter taste in his mouth. He had no choice, feigning ignorance was the only option, but his willpower faded. The sheer emotional strain, knowing he was surrounded by demons who might hurt him, or worse, left him exhausted. But he had no way out.

So, he played ignorant. Cyrus had questioned his injury, and he had laughed him off, saying something about a stupid mishap with a bike messenger. The excuse could easily have explained his arm. The wound had nearly killed him, almost bleeding out on the sidewalk.

Zane stared into the mirror of his bathroom and gathered his strength. Strange. His mismatched eyes used to bother him. But such a self-conscious thought seemed petty compared to what he was dealing with now. For the first time, he didn't insert his colored contact. His life hung in the balance, maintained only by subterfuge and lies.

He could control this lie, however, and chose to cast it away....

But what bothered Zane more? His inability to remember his life before arriving on Earth. The memories of his past might be enough to justify the horror he suffered knowing he had to go back on the stage. He felt forced to perform like a marionette when once the stage had been his sanctuary. Whoever said "ignorance is bliss" really knew what they were talking about. Now that Zane knew about angels and demons? He wanted to know everything.

Otherwise, when — not if — he slipped and revealed himself, he was going to die.

Zane wanted to know who he was but mostly...*why*. Why was he chosen to be manipulated rather than some other Fallen angel? But life wasn't fair, and Zane imagined he would probably die while he was still entirely in the dark.

He straightened and smoothed out his shirt. He was all dolled up for the evening, per the client's request. Usually, Zane enjoyed the process of spiffing out his look. Tonight had taken significant effort. Every movement was like walking through wet cement, his body protesting against him. He wore his straight-cut, dark jeans with a leather belt. His shirt was a charcoal button-down with three-quarter sleeves, paired with a steel-gray vest.

To top off the outfit, he wore a bright silver chain around his neck. Zane had even smoothed back his hair with a comb, letting the strands part to the side naturally. Over his socks, he wore polished leather wingtips.

He smiled into the mirror, admiring his choices.

Damn… I make this look good.

He nodded to himself and did a Michael Jackson spin on his toes.

Yup, very, very good.

Satisfied, Zane grabbed his acoustic guitar and essentials then left the apartment. When the elevator arrived at the garage level, he stepped out, lost in thought, and nearly knocked over a red-haired woman waiting to get on. "Omigosh! I'm so sorry!"

She waved him off as she entered the elevator.

Zane smiled apologetically.

The woman blinked, blushing. "It's no problem, really." The woman stared at the magazine in her hand and glanced at him, then used her arm to stop the elevator doors from closing. "Aren't you him? The singer? Your eyes look different, though."

It was Zane's turn to blush, and he rubbed his neck sheepishly. He cleared his throat. "Yeah. It's me. Colored contact. Is that the article from the—"

Her eyes lit up, and she gasped. "Oh wow! I'll have to tell Remus I finally met you."

"You know Remus?"

"Yeah, he's a…friend."

The woman tugged at her blue sundress, the color matching her eyes while the material hung loosely around her petite frame. Her hair was an orange-red, with natural golden highlights woven throughout the strands. A delicate gold chain graced her neck, falling underneath her dress into the crook of her modest cleavage. Safe to say, the woman was beautiful.

And, even better, she was a fan.

For the life of him, Zane was stumped. He'd have asked her out any other time but didn't feel the need. Instead, he reached into the pocket of his guitar case. He pulled out one of his extra picks, a swirly blue one. "Here, would you like this?"

The woman smiled, genuinely happy. She plucked the pick out of his fingers, careful not to brush against them. "Thank you."

"Just tell Remus, the next time I'm over, I want an introduction to his lady friend," Zane said with a wink.

"Of course. I will." She let go of the elevator door then glanced back at him. A swirl of sorrow behind those blue depths. "And...I'm so sorry." Before Zane could reply, the elevator closed.

Zane cocked his head to the side. Then brushed it off with a shake of his head as a more immediate concern demanded his attention. He unbuttoned his sleeve, his arm throbbing from the earlier impact. There was no bleeding, thankfully, and his wound remained wrapped. After three weeks, he shouldn't have to worry, but his body refused to heal.

If he was human, Zane imagined a wound continuously bleeding like this would have killed him already. He had made it so far, but he'd been plagued by dizzy spells and forced to reapply bandages multiple times every day. Most work nights, Victor had played lead guitar because his arm throbbed horribly after a single song.

Zane rubbed a hand over his face. How did he go from never having a paper cut to needing to buy a first aid kit fit for an ambulance? He sighed and headed to his car.

Minutes later, he parked in his usual spot near the back of the lot. Guitar hanging on his shoulder, he entered the building. A round table was set in the middle of the dance floor, a black tablecloth draped over it.

He frowned. The silence of the space bothered him.

Typically, on a weeknight, the band practiced. They'd figure out what songs to cover and line up sets for the coming weekend. The bartender and the bouncers would be busy unloading new shipments of alcohol. A janitor would sweep, push tables into their correct positions. It was the ritual...the same for years. For it to be interrupted...however much it bothered him, it was his own fault. Had he not missed work, this particular client wouldn't have had any leverage to force Cyrus's hand. Yes, he'd learned he was an angel.

Probably a fucking Christmas angel with cherubic little wings to boot.

Or...was it Damaceous's fault? His life had been perfectly fine, and then he'd shown up and kissed him and—

"Zane?"

A voice broke his musings. Zane started. He had apparently been staring the furniture down like the table owed him money.

Across the floor, Cyrus waited, an eyebrow raised.

"Sorry, boss. Should I go ahead and set up?"

Cyrus nodded, eyeing him with suspicion. "Yes. Mr. Elvorix will be here momentarily." Cyrus looked him over, pausing on his mismatched eyes. "A personal touch for the client, I see. I'll allow it, for now." He waited a beat then headed upstairs to his office.

Zane breathed a sigh of relief and hopped onto the stage.

The blood rushed to his head, he swayed on his feet. He gripped the nearby microphone stand to steady himself, shaking off the dizziness. He didn't have a lot of time, but he still needed to do a sound check and a warm-up tuning. Hopefully, he could get it done before the client arrived. There was no choice but to push on and make it through the night...as quickly as possible.

Zane was just about finished tuning the last string when Alexander Elvorix walked in, the front door squeaking loudly on its hinges. Zane met his gaze as he entered then returned to his task.

The client was dressed in a long, unbuttoned leather trench coat; the three-piece suit underneath a blood red. He removed his jacket and handed it to the bar manager, who took it to the check room behind the bar. Underneath his blazer, Alexander wore a steel-grey shirt and tie. He carried a case large enough for an instrument.

Alexander dripped power, his arrogance sensed all the way to the stage where Zane was seated. The man knew he was in charge. Any orders he gave, he expected those around him to obey. Some might get excited when a man with vibes like his walked into a room.

Zane just felt unease, the hairs on his neck standing up, his stomach in knots. Why he reacted this way around the man always confused him, but Zane didn't let it bother him tonight. He took a deep breath to settle himself. His instincts had been way off lately; trusting them now wouldn't be his first choice.

"How are you doing tonight, sir?" he spoke into the microphone.

Alexander smiled, his mouth curving slightly at the edges. He made his way down the stairs and took a seat at the table in the middle of the floor. He settled his case underneath and leaned back in his chair, his arms crossed. "I'm doing well…Zane. What kind of show have you planned for me tonight?"

"Well, I've prepared a few songs, but honestly, I thought maybe you might have a request. There's a list I put on the table for you. I can play any song off it. So, if I already know it, I can play it."

Zane winced inside. He was babbling, his nervousness getting the better of him.

Alexander chuckled. "Why don't you choose, you're the artist. If I like the song, I'll listen." He pointed at Zane's guitar. "Are you going to be singing or just playing guitar?"

"I can do both. If you want. I can sing a cappella…or just guitar, or both. Whichever."

Alexander gestured for him to begin.

Zane took a deep breath. "This song was released recently…and it's catchy. The artist plays with his acoustic. I thought, since this is a private show, an electric guitar might be hard on your hearing."

As Zane began to play, the world around him faded out, and a peace settled over him. Music had always been his happy place. The notes were soothing, the melody slow but powerful.

When the song ended, Alexander clapped a few times. "Brilliant. Another."

"Do you like country?"

"I enjoy a variety of music, especially classical."

Zane frowned, his eyebrows furrowing. "I don't play classical music."

Alexander scoffed, reaching for the case underneath the table, and walked to the stage. He set the case down beside Zane's feet.

The outside of the case was hardened leather. Alexander unlatched both sides then opened the lid. The liner was made of suede, and the client ran his fingers over the smooth texture. Then he pulled a flap of suede back to reveal a violin of dark mahogany nestled inside. The instrument was beautiful, elegant.

But, confusing as hell.

"I definitely don't play the violin, sir. Look, Mr. Elvorix," he continued. "I can play whatever you want, except classical. I'm a contemporary musician but, I only know how to play the guitar in my hands."

Alexander gazed at him with amusement. "Are you sure? Have you ever tried?"

"Even if I did try, I'd need more than two minutes to learn something which takes years to master."

Frustrated, Zane turned to the microphone. "Cyrus! Can you come down here for a minute?" he called. This client was severely warped in the head.

When Cyrus walked out onto his balcony, Zane beckoned him closer.

"Something the matter?" Cyrus asked after coming down to the dance floor.

"He wants me to play the violin."

Cyrus cocked his head, looking to Alexander for confirmation. "Is this true?"

"Yes."

"Then, Zane, I suggest you play the violin."

Zane's mouth fell open. "But I don't know how," he protested, his tone filled with polite frustration. "What am I supposed to do? Screech at him for another hour?"

Cyrus's face remained undisturbed. "If it's what he wants, then, yes. Screech until his little heart is content."

With that, Cyrus went back to his office, leaving Zane dumbfounded.

"Okay, then," he grumbled. The singer set his guitar on the stand beside him.

Cautiously, he picked up the violin, afraid the delicate instrument might break.

Alexander smiled in triumph, returning to his seat.

Zane tried to recall memories of Maribel when she performed. He imitated her stance, placing the butt of the instrument on his shoulder, underneath his chin, holding the bow in his right hand. Immediately, his arm throbbed from the violin's weight, pain lancing up his elbow and into his shoulder.

Zane threw one last glance at Alexander and shook his head. They were both freakin' nuts. He was about to make a fool of himself because this ass-hat just *had* to make him play the violin.

Zane poised the bow over the strings. He had no idea where to place his fingers, guessing from what he knew about the guitar. He cringed—then he pulled the bow across the strings, figuring he'd need hearing aids after this mishap.

The note was low and smooth, ringing out true, clear as day.

Zane paused to look at Alexander then back at the violin.

He licked his lips, mouth suddenly dry. *What. The Shit. Was That!*

He tried again.

Another clear note hummed, high and crisp, blowing his mind out of the water.

This time, Zane continued playing…his fingers knew where to go, a wave of familiarity assaulting his senses. Soon, a low, haunting melody filled the room, and Zane closed his eyes. The melody swelled and ebbed, flowing around him. Like the room, the pain melted away. He had no idea what he played, the song wrenched from his subconscious, out of his control.

When the song finally ended, Zane opened his eyes. His hands trembled, his chest heaved. He stepped back, his arms falling to his sides, hands gripping the violin and bow in white-knuckled fists. He inhaled—short, shaky breaths—and gasped for air. The room suddenly grew small.

"Zane."

He met Alexander's gaze.

Alexander smiled back. "You should look at the inscription. It's on the back."

Zane raised the violin and turned it over. His heart thudded in his chest, beating wildly.

In small silver calligraphy, the inscription read; *Property of Zhanerious.*

He read the words over and over, the implication not quite sinking in.

Abruptly, Zane chucked the violin. Just threw the whole damn instrument across the room. Alexander stood, dodging the violin as it crashed into the wall behind him. Wooden splinters scattered on the floor.

Zane glared. "What the fuck is going on?"

He threw the stool next, walking backstage to distance himself from whatever the *fuck* was happening here. "Seriously, what the fuck is happening?"

Zane was officially *over* this crazy mess. All the demons and the angels could go fuck themselves. He was *done*.

Zane leaned against a wall, hand over his mouth, mind racing. "I want my life back…"

Alexander came around the curtain and headed toward him.

Zane held up a hand in warning. "Stay away from me, man. I don't know you, and I don't know what's going on but stay the *fuck* away from me."

Alexander's eyes narrowed into slits. He slammed a hand against the wall, right next to Zane's head. He leaned in close, and Zane glared daggers, ready to throw a punch any minute.

Alexander chuckled, the sound low. Cold chills crept up Zane's spine. Alexander raised a hand and grabbed his chin, forcing Zane to face him.

Zane bared his teeth. "Get your hand off me, asshole."

"Mm…so cold, youngling," Alexander said. "But you have grown, haven't you? Not nearly enough. Such a nasty little mouth." He sniffed Zane's neck, hot breath tickling the singer's ear. "Even now, I have…an unhealthy fixation. But this has all been for you…"

Revulsion pulsed through Zane allowing him to muster enough strength to push out of the man's grasp. He took a few steps away. "Look, Alexander. You need to leave. I don't care who the fuck you are. You need to leave. Now."

Alexander's grin faded, catching his gaze. When the man moved closer, Zane shifted to take another step back but found he couldn't.

He was stuck.

Zane swallowed. Panic descended over him like an avalanche. Alexander ran a hand over his chest.

Panic turned to anger. His mind screamed for him to run, and he wanted to punch, kick, yell…but he couldn't. His paralysis disturbed him.

"I wanted to make you stronger. But I had to keep you hidden away." Alexander put an arm around his waist, one hand stroking Zane's cheek. He pushed open his shirt, and a fingertip traced the singer's collar bone.

Then, Zane's world unlocked and broke apart. Memories from another lifetime flooded his brain, pouring through his mind like a movie reel he couldn't put on pause…

FIFTEEN

The next morning, Zhanerious woke bright and early. He grabbed his violin case, then waited for Khamael to come to his room.

Waited and waited....

Finally, there was a firm knock.

"Are you ready, trainee?"

Zhanerious opened the door and greeted the older angel. "Good morning, Lieutenant. Sir, I'd like permission to fly over the capital now, rather than this afternoon since I'm supposed to have another performance this evening."

Lieutenant Khamael's expression showed signs of disbelief, but he shrugged. "Well, I do have other trainees to attend. Stay out of trouble. You can fly over but be back within the hour. The general will have my head if he finds out you aren't with me, understand?"

Zhanerious nodded. Khamael was an angel with a tanned complexion, dark, wavy hair, a goatee, and upturned, angular dark eyes. He was built for speed, and he was one of the best-trained combatants in Heaven, rivaling the two dominion generals; the reason he had been chosen to train Zhanerious in the first place.

But, for all his toughness, the lieutenant had always treated Zhanerious kindly when they were alone. Every opportunity he had, he indulged Zhanerious, knowing how alone the young angel had become.

With Khamael's permission, Zhanerious smiled and headed away.

Standing on the grounds outside the compound, he expanded his wings to their full length then pulled them in tightly against his body. He repeated these stretches, expanding and contracting his wings until his muscles were sufficiently warm. Holding his violin case securely, he jumped into the air, his wings immediately lifting him toward the clouds.

Zhanerious soared for a while, enjoying the warm breezes and the sights of the teeming city below. He waved to a few other angels passing by and then remembered his mission.

Swooping low, the youngling headed toward the Powers headquarters, opting to fly toward the back entrance. He landed in a small courtyard, lush with flowering bushes, perching birds, and a small stream, then walked passed the well-maintained greenery and jogged up a few stone steps. He raised his hand to open a large wooden door, but just as his fingers settled on the handle, the door unexpectedly swung open.

He stumbled backward, landing on his butt.

Zhanerious gazed up to see an angel with bright green eyes, his brown hair swept into a ponytail, offering a hand to him. The angel had large wings; dark plum with silver tips.

"Oh!" the angel said. "I must apologize, I didn't see you there."

Zhanerious took the angel's hand and stood. "It's not a problem. Thank you." He grabbed the fallen violin case and headed inside. Here, angels of all sorts buzzed around, wearing different shades of gray and black clothing, an easy indicator of the Powers Dominion. With his maroon pants and sandals, it only made him stand out even more.

After searching for the Powers general with no luck, he decided to ask for help.

"Excuse me?" Zhanerious tapped the shoulder of an angel passing by, papers in hand.

She turned to him and smiled, her braided hair swaying at her side. "May I help you, youngling?"

"I'm looking for your general. Is he here?"

She frowned. "I'm sorry, General Remiel is in a meeting with the High Council. Is it important? I can tell him. I'm Ashliel, the lieutenant."

Zhanerious raised his eyebrows in surprise. "Oh!" He held up the violin case and tugged Lieutenant Ashliel closer to whisper in her ear. "You should take this, sir. There's information about something bad happening in my dominion. I think my general's behind it!"

She took the case, her face grim. "Those are dangerous accusations. What do you think is happening?"

Zhanerious peeked around nervously. "I think...I might have seen it, last night. There was an angel, a girl. She was chained, all torn up. They were torturing her."

Ashliel stared at Zhanerious. "Come with me," she said. "We must inform General Remiel at once."

Zhanerious followed Ashliel around a corner and up three flights of stairs. Finally, she led him inside an empty room.

The lieutenant set the violin case beside him. "Wait here, I'll be back soon."

Zhanerious caught her arm. "I can't! If I don't return to my dominion soon, the general will find out. I can't stay here."

She smiled gently, removing his hand. "It's okay. No one can hurt you here. I must go find my general—Remiel. He needs to look at the evidence himself. I won't be gone long, promise."

In moments, he was alone again.

Zhanerious sat in the only chair and waited, fiddling his fingers. The room was white, with no other furniture than the chair he had already taken and a long, metal table. He suspected the room was used for interrogations of some sort, but not often; a fine layer of dust covered the surface. He ran his fingers through the dust, drawing shapes and making patterns.

The door clicked open, and Zhanerious turned.

His face fell. General Alatos stood in the doorway. Anger lit his eyes, flushed his face.

Zhanerious didn't dare move.

"Get your things."

Quickly, Zhanerious grabbed his violin case and stood. Alatos moved out of the way while Zhanerious stepped through the door.

In the hall outside, Ashliel leaned against the wall and smiled. It was a cold smile...the kind of smile which leaves a lasting imprint, like when a death sentence has just been handed out. Her light-blue eyes seemed to mock him, and she waved, twiddling her fingers.

Alatos pushed him forward. "Thank you, lieutenant, for alerting me to this...situation. We'll be taking our leave now."

Not long after they'd left the Powers headquarters, they landed back in the Warriors compound. Alatos dragged Zhanerious by one wing to his office, feathers falling like a trail of breadcrumbs while the general continued to pull him. Zhanerious winced but held his voice; it would be much worse to express any kind of complaint...

Alatos wrenched the violin case from his hands, dumping it on the floor. The violin fell out, the papers spilled onto the tiles. Alatos gathered the file, setting it on on his desk.

"Now, you know."

He said it matter-of-factly, so...blasé. As if the idea he was behind the torture of young angels was no big deal, no worse than your average hangnail. Zhanerious stared at him, afraid to speak. The general slammed his fists on the desk. The youngling jumped, more feathers falling out.

Alatos turned and grabbed him by the throat. "You know nothing! What did you see? Nothing, do you hear me? How could you possibly comprehend even a little of what I'm trying to accomplish?" He pulled Zhanerious closer and squeezed.

The angel clawed desperately at the general's hand and gasped for breath. The general watched him struggle, then smiled callously. "Well, you're going to understand. You're going to have firsthand knowledge."

His vision blurred, dancing spots in his eyes then, blackness as he passed out.

When Zhanerious woke, he screamed. Searing pain traveled from his right wing, caused him to almost pass out again. He was chained by his wrists to the wall he faced, sitting with his knees under him. Blood trickled down his feathers as pain assaulted his senses.

He craned his neck and moved his wing closer, so he could inspect it, but even those short movements caused him to scream more. When Zhanerious could manage it, he tried again, not moving his wing this time

"Oh...god, no..."

His entire wing had huge chunks of feathers missing like a plucked chicken. The wing itself was bent outward awkwardly, broken in multiple places. Pieces had been ripped off, chunks of meat and muscle just...gone.

He convulsed, vomiting on the floor in front of him. What had they done?

The angel's whole body quaked, the chains on his wrists clanking loudly. He might never fly again... He wept openly at this realization and sobbed for hours.

Finally, he quieted, no more tears left.

Or so he thought.

The door opened moments later.

"Crying already?"

His heart sank. Khamael came closer, alongside Zhanerious, a whip in his hand. He crouched, staring the youngling in the eye and cocked his head. Then, he giggled. The sound had a deep, eerie quality, coming from him. But, his expression chilled Zhanerious to the bone. He saw no hint of the kind teacher he had always known.

"Awake for round two? How delightful. I thought for sure you'd miss this one."

Khamael snapped the whip against his open palm. He rose and moved to a spot where Zhanerious couldn't see him. For a moment there was silence. Then—

—Crack!

Blinding pain followed. Zhanerious gasped. He grabbed his own chains for support.

Another lash. And another.

The punishment went on until he passed out, the pain too much to bear.

The next time he woke, the lashings started again.

The time after, Khamael bashed his head into the wall.

Then, the lieutenant broke his fingers and toes.

The torture continued for days...maybe weeks. He had no idea. It seemed to go on forever.

The last time Zhanerious woke, he was alone. He opened his eyes, barely able to see or lift his head. Blood blocked most of his vision. He wasn't chained to the wall anymore. Perhaps Khamael had removed the chains when he realized his prisoner couldn't move. Beyond the ringing in his ears, Zhanerious could just make out voices arguing some distance away, probably in the courtyard.

Footsteps drew near.

Zhanerious stiffened, tried to push himself against the wall and appear small.

Alatos burst inside the room. He closed the door quickly and locked it. His head swiveled around, looking for another way out. His expression seemed harried. When his eyes fell on Zhanerious, the general snarled. Zhanerious flinched backward, cowering away as much as possible.

Alatos's head whipped around. Voices in the hallway outside grew louder, heading in their direction. Swiftly, the general moved toward Zhanerious. The general pursed his lips tightly, and he snatched the angel by the hair. Zhanerious whimpered, his fear mounting.

Alatos reached out with his other hand. He hauled the angel into a standing position, balancing him against his body. Zhanerious struggled, trying to extricate himself from the general's hold. The general shook him, and his mind fogged over with dizziness.

When he was conscious again a moment later, Alatos was drawing a symbol in the air. A crackling circle emerged...a golden portal opening behind Zhanerious.

"No!" Zhanerious cried, renewing his struggle.

The voices in the hall were closer now. General Alatos looked back, his patience fading.

"Now," he said. "Since you couldn't keep our secrets to yourself, enjoy your days on Earth until I can figure out what to do with you."

He gripped Zhanerious by the hair again, wrenching him backward.

Zhanerious reached out, clutching at the general's robes, fear consuming him. "No! Please!"

Pounding started on the door. "Open this door, at once! I'm here to inspect all rooms, by order of General Remiel."

Alatos covered Zhanerious's mouth, nails digging roughly into his cheeks. Zhanerious grabbed the general's arm, straining to hold on but, his weakened strength quickly waned.

"One moment!" the general responded. His polite tone was sickening. He bent Zhanerious's fingers backward, forcing the younger angel to release his grip. Then, the general shoved the youngling and kicked him in the chest with full force. "Have fun, little buzzard..."

Zhanerious tumbled through the portal.

The ground came fast; wind whipped passed his face. His wings refused to work. Mangled and damaged, the one broken wing plunged him into a tailspin, spiraling the angel through the air. He couldn't control the free fall. He spiraled between two buildings, bouncing violently off a dumpster then onto cold, hard concrete.

Zhanerious landed in a heap of feathers and broken limbs, his head bleeding profusely.

Through his blurry vision, a white pair of dress shoes stepped into view.

"Well, what's an angel like you doing on a planet like Earth?"

Zhanerious raised his head. He saw a man with long, white hair staring down at him. He gagged, blood and puke spattering the ground.

"Disgusting. Get ahold of yourself. You're the late one…"

The man knelt, hitching his white pants higher. "Your wings are going to raise a lot of questions, you know."

"Please…" Zhanerious begged. "I need help…"

The man reached over and turned the broken angel onto his stomach.

Zhanerious cried out, his body in agony.

"Quiet!" Zhanerious met the man's gaze, only to shrink way in fear. Yellow eyes with bright purple irises crinkled with mirth. "What's your name, angel?"

"Zhaner…ious."

"Too long. And, you're not quite what I'd pictured."

"Please…have mercy."

The demon snorted.

"Why should I care about some whiny buzzard who ne-ne-needs my help?" the demon mocked.

Zhanerious tried to think of anything he could offer.

"Music. I'm...a Virtues." It wasn't a complete lie, but he didn't care. Demons didn't have scruples.

He gasped for air, his breathing shallow, his insides burning in pain.

A calculation entered the demon's eye, an aura of evil surrounding him.

"Really? You might be useful after all. This is going to sting but, by the looks of you, I doubt you'll notice. We can't let the pesky humans know about us, can we, my little angel?"

The demon pressed a palm to the angel's upper back. Zhanerious tried to move away, but the demon easily held him still. To his horror, Zhanerious's wings disappeared while a searing pain sprouted from his back.

As his memory burned away, Zhanerious passed out for the last time, clutching a black feather in his hand.

Zane gasped, pain shooting up his left arm, which Alexander squeezed within his steel grip. His back burned, then he felt a strange cracking sensation with a loud, sizzling—*Pop!* His paralysis broke then real wings emerged, ripping through his clothes.

"You!" Zane shoved himself away from Alexander. One of his wings dangled to the side, crippled and lame. Zane raised his fists. "You did this! You and Lieutenant Khamael."

Alexander smiled. "Just now figuring it out? It only took ten years."

Alexander lunged at Zane. The singer ducked, but he was too slow, the weight of his wings hindering him. Alexander grabbed him by his good wing causing Zane to fall to the ground.

Alexander laughed. "You're not getting away."

"Leave him alone!"

A flash of purple feathers blurred across Zane's vision, accompanied by a loud grunt. A huge male angel knelt on one knee before him, facing off with the enemy. His wings were outstretched, shielding Zane from further attack. The stranger's chest heaved, a hand clasped around the hilt of a blade sheathed at the angel's back.

Knocked across the room by the blow, Alexander struggled back onto his feet. The man glared but made no move against them. His rescuer swept Zane into his arms, cradling the singer against his chest.

Zane stared at him in a daze. "Who are you?"

The angel shook his head. "Never mind, let's go."

Cyrus stood on the balcony, stonefaced as he watched the angels exit through the side entrance. He went down to the dance floor again then made his way backstage, where Alexander was brushing off his suit.

"What happened?"

"He regained his memory."

Cyrus nodded. "Ah. My seal must've broken. He's stronger than I imagined."

He picked up a stray feather from the floor. "Without my seal, his memory and the rest of his abilities will return. We both know he's not truly Fallen. He could ruin you."

Alexander's head whipped around. "I know! Why didn't you keep him hidden from the public in the first place? Then, we wouldn't have had to worry about this at all."

Cyrus scoffed. "No. You sent him to me, to Earth. You knew working together would be dangerous. But...he made himself useful enough. The power in his voice attracted thousands more humans for this itty-bitty gem here."

He held a dark-blue sapphire as big as his palm. It glowed, warm to the touch.

"And, with their souls imprisoned inside, I have more than enough power to overthrow the Dark King."

SIXTEEN

The sun had set over the city, dousing the sky in a veil of darkness. They rose into the air, chest to chest, Zane's arms around Damaceous's neck and his head resting against him, their faces pressed together lightly, cheek to cheek. After everything he had just lived through, it was…quiet. Peaceful, even.

They kept rising, the silence only broken by the subtle flap of the larger angel's wings.

Damaceous held Zane's wings close to his body, unsure if the singer's muscles were strong enough to handle the strain after their reemergence.

Zane sighed against him. His mind was totally blank, and he was emotionally exhausted. Had he more energy, he might have cared about being treated like a child, but, for now, it was nice to be held…to be able to lean on another being—one he assumed was there for his protection.

They flew for a while, across the river and just below the clouds, until they arrived above his apartment building.

Zane leaned back to glance at the angel. "How do you know where I live?"

Damaceous frowned, pursing his lips. "Zane. We've met before." His green eyes gazed into Zane's own.

"Yeah, I remember you. I was going into the Powers Dominion, and we ran into each other in the courtyard. You helped me after I tripped."

Damaceous chuckled. "I don't remember. What I meant is, I'm Damaceous."

Zane's eyes widened, his mouth falling open. He sputtered for a few minutes, examining the other angel's features more closely. "How is this even possible?" He ran a hand through Damaceous's hair and pulled out the hair tie. He squished the angel's face between his palms, poked his cheeks.

The larger angel smiled. "I told you. In Heaven, I have another form. My true form."

"You also said you couldn't reveal it on Earth."

"Except for emergencies. And in your situation, I believe this qualifies. A young angel assaulted by a high-ranking general. One, I might add, who used some sort of paralysis on you. Something I am most certainly bringing up to General Remiel when I return."

Zane's face fell. "You have to go back?"

Damaceous frowned. "Yes. But you can come, too."

Zane jerked backward in horror, and Damaceous lurched, almost losing his grip.

"Whoa! Easy!" he exclaimed and readjusted his hold. "You could be seriously injured if you fell from this height."

Zane scoffed. "I've already done it once, what's one more time?" Sarcasm dripped from every word, the memories still fresh. He winced, pulling the angel close again. "Take me home, please. There's a balcony outside my place."

Damaceous nodded and flew over the side of the building, counting the floors. After a few minutes, he located the apartment. He landed on the balcony, and Zane entered his home.

He walked to the middle of his living room. He glanced around. Everything was wrong...as if nothing belonged to him, but to a stranger had who never truly existed. The singer stood, looking lost for a while.

Damaceous just observed from the balcony. He was unsure what to do or how he was needed. He honestly had no idea what memories the other male might be recalling.

Finally, he stepped inside the apartment, careful to close the sliding door and the blinds.

Humans may not have seen their flight but, if some had, leaving an open show to the world and displaying the existence of angels was not a good idea.

When Zane hadn't moved for more than ten minutes, Damaceous slid closer and lightly placed a hand on his shoulder. "Would you like to go to bed? I can help."

Zane nodded.

The other angel took Zane's hand and led him to his bedroom. Zane's face was pale, as though the life had been drained out of him. He seemed hopeless and afraid...listless. Damaceous sat him on the bed and began undoing his shirt. He started to rip it away when he saw how badly it was shredded in the back, and there was no saving it.

Zane straightened, looking insulted. "Yo. That's my shirt, dude," he griped. "It's a nice one, be careful."

Damaceous rolled his eyes. Such a small thing to bring him to life again. "It's a lost cause. Your wings demolished both the vest and button-up."

Zane reached behind him to feel the damage and cursed. "Fine...just cut it off then. No point in trying to make it all nice and neat," Zane grumbled. "Dammit. I loved this outfit."

Damaceous smirked.

"Hey, don't judge me. I need to wear nice things onstage. This wasn't cheap. And, I liked this one."

Damaceous shook his head. He pulled out his blade from behind, the sheath strapped horizontally on his waist. Seconds later, Zane's shirt and vest were removed.

Both angels exhaled a sigh of relief.

Zane glanced at the contents of his ruined shirt and vest. He frowned as he kicked off his shoes then glanced at his companion, who kneeled in front of him, his wingspan so wide the two wings touched opposing walls. His feathers…the color was mesmerizing, the dark purple fading to silver tips. It reminded him of the galaxy crafts people made online.

And, Damaceous was *huge*. Compared to his counterpart, he was at least a foot taller. His brown hair fell to his shoulders, the ends curling. Not to mention his muscles, which were on display in all their shirtless gloriousness. If that was a word…Zane assumed it was. Otherwise, he had no way to describe his sudden urge to drool.

Damaceous's body was impressive, to say the least. But his eyes had remained the same, bright green with long lashes, warm and inviting, sharp and perceptive. Zane was glad *something* stayed consistent in a time when everything else in his life was topsy-turvy.

"What should I call you? You have a second name I should know about?"

The brunette glanced up at the question. "Damaceous, of course."

Zane nodded. "So…where've you been? It's been almost three weeks."

Damaceous shook his head. "We can talk about this once you've had some rest."

Zane's jaw clenched, and he narrowed his eyes. "Oh? And how am I supposed to rest? People out there are trying to kill me. If I go to sleep, they might come in here and finish me off…What? Am I just supposed to trust you? Fuck that! Fuck you, angels. Fuck. You."

He stood, pacing. Damaceous stood with him and grabbed him around the waist.

Zane shoved out of his hold. "I don't want you to comfort me like some traumatized child. I'm a grown man. I've been through hell and back these days. If I could fly, I'd be halfway across this country, getting as far away from this nightmare as I could."

"I know." Damaceous sat back down on the edge of the bed. "You're agitated, rightly so. But you are not yet strong enough to hold up your wings, especially the injured one. Sit with me. We'll talk. I'll answer all your questions until you're comfortable enough to rest. But you must sit down. Before you fall down."

Zane stared at him for a moment before exhaling a deep breath. Then he sat on the bed.

They both had to turn toward each other to make room for their wings.

"Where've you been?"

With arms crossed, Zane glared at Damaceous with distrust. The older angel tried not to smile. The other male reminded him of a petulant child who refused to go to sleep without a bedtime story. But Damaceous knew better.

The way Zane's eyes darted toward the doorway. The way he chewed his lip. Even his eyes were filled with a deep fear. He had a right to be afraid. Wards kept only demons away. But an angel could, in theory, open a portal straight into his bedroom. He'd keep the information to himself.

"I've been in Heaven some," Damaceous explained. "But, mostly, I've been around here. Keeping an eye on you, observing the club, watching the demons. My general, he ordered me to stay away from you. He says there's no rational argument to support this case, and my…interaction with you has been more dangerous than helpful. You were Fallen, or at least it appeared that way. Now, I know. It was the seal."

Zane cocked an eyebrow.

Damaceous nodded. "Yes. The tattoo on your back? Of the two wings? It was a seal. Only powerful demons or angels can create them. It masked your entire being…masked your powers, memories, everything. I should have recognized it when I first saw you, but...I've never seen one in person and..."

"You just assumed," Zane finished for him. "But...how did I break it?"

"It's likely Culzahr is the one who created your seal. A demonic seal's effect lessens over time whereas a seal made by one of the High Council would be all but permanent. You'd had an infusion of power from me. It may have been just enough...but to break a seal from a Demon Lord?" Damaceous shook his head in disbelief. "I honestly don't have any idea how it's possible."

"Do all Fallen have these seals?"

Damaceous looked away. "Yes."

Zane searched his memory and came up dry. "So, all those innocents General Alatos tortured...all of them...they had their lives stripped away...just like me?" The weight of the tragedy he had witnessed all those years ago settled in his mind.

Damaceous gripped Zane's forearm. "What are you talking about? What has he done?"

Over the next hour, Zane told him what he remembered. He fudged a few details, leaving out his days under Khamael's hand, attributing his injuries to his fall through the portal. When Zane was finished, Damaceous's pallor was ghostly. They sat in silence for a while as the older angel processed the information.

"Hold on," Damaceous said. "You said…you said you came to my dominion, looking for help and Ashliel, my lieutenant…betrayed you to General Alatos?"

Zane nodded.

Damaceous's hands squeezed into fists so tight, blood seeped out between his fingernails. "What…the fuck!"

Zane burst out laughing.

Damaceous frowned at him. "What?"

Zane laughed harder, holding his stomach. "I've never heard you cuss before!" He fell back against the bed and continued to laugh, stress lifting from his shoulders.

Damaceous's emotions still ran high, but the sight of Zane smiling took the edge off.

When his laughter subsided, Zane looked at him through sleepy eyes and yawned. "I mean, I know the topic isn't funny, but you? Just hilarious."

"Come on. You need to rest," Damaceous suggested, annoyed. He moved to the head of the bed, propping against the pillows and spreading out his wings comfortably.

Damaceous pulled out a pillow. "Lay on your stomach."

Zane took the pillow and laid down beside him. He was propped up, his head on top, his arms underneath, his face toward

Damaceous. His wings settled, the left spreading out over the other angel's chest, but the right remained close to his body. Damaceous turned on his side and spread his wing over Zane's, creating more room on the bed.

Zane chuckled. "I think I need a larger bed. You look cramped."

Damaceous shook his head. He didn't mention how his feet hung off the end. "I'm fine, just rest. I'll keep watch for you."

Zane smiled, his eyes closing as he sighed. Within minutes, light snoring filled the room.

Damaceous tentatively reached out and traced a finger over the feathers closest to him.

He had never seen wings with so many vibrant colors. One side was blue, like the water off the coast of his home world, the other side was a deep green, like pine trees deep in the forests of the Appalachian Mountains. Along the upper ridge, the feathers were dark as obsidian...but each one reflected a luminescent gold under the light.

Their magnificence rivaled those on the High Council, and angels with such were cultivated to take over positions of high rank. Probably one of the reasons he'd been transferred to Alatos's care. Damaceous wondered how he was going to protect such a beautiful creature...How could a lowly investigator defend him against the most dangerous general the Warriors Dominion had ever seen?

He looked over at Zane's other wing, finally inspecting the damage. From what Damaceous could tell, while dormant, the wing had mostly healed, but parts were bent at odd angles, never having been set properly. Feathers lost had regrown. But chunks were still only thin membrane skin and tendon between the bones. There was no way Zane would ever be able to open the limb properly. Thankfully, most of the painful scarring had disappeared, the skin on his back smooth now. But he needed to be taken to the healers in the Virtues Dominion.

The way he'd healed, Zane would never fly without their help.

Anger welled inside the investigator's chest, thick and painful. Damaceous hated that he couldn't have somehow prevented this outcome. He wanted to take a shot at Ashliel...her betrayal hit a personal note. He scowled and blew out a deep sigh. How had no one noticed what was happening? His fingers traced the tattoo circling Zane's bicep, his musings keeping him awake long into the night.

SEVENTEEN

Hours later, light seeped into the room, and Zane opened his eyes. His companion was sitting against the bedpost, his head dropped forward, eyes closed. Damaceous had fallen asleep trying to keep watch. Zane found it cute, planting a kiss on his cheek. The movement woke him, green eyes meeting his gaze.

Damaceous's cheeks turned red, whether in embarrassment from the kiss, or being caught sleeping, Zane wasn't quite sure. Either way, it was delightfully cute.

Zane smiled at Damaceous. The brunette gulped audibly.

"Good morning, sexy."

Zane straddled his legs, linking his arms around the other angel's neck.

Damaceous's brow furrowed. "Morning. Uh…How're you doing? Are you feeling better?"

Zane leaned forward and pressed against him, running a hand through his brown hair. The silky strands slid deliciously between his fingers. He cupped Damaceous's face and drew him forward, capturing his mouth with his lips.

His tongue plunged inside, taking possession, leaving no room for hesitancy from the other, dancing and stroking. He rubbed an earlobe, and Damaceous responded beneath him. When his grip became demanding, Zane broke the kiss and continued, leaving a wet trail of warm moisture down his neck. Hands squeezed his hips as Zane trailed lower until he was out of reach, the investigator clutching his hair instead.

Zane was face to face, or face to head, with Damaceous's groin, the thin fabric of his pants doing little to hide his excitement. He pulled the material down, and the angel's cock sprang free. Zane licked his lips and took the hard member into his mouth, engulfing the entire head, his hand squeezing the base. A loud moan escaped Damaceous. Zane worked him into a frenzy, bobbing his head, sucking and swirling until the angel's toes curled.

Without warning, Damaceous pulled him back onto his hips. Zane smiled before he was captured in another kiss. He was still dressed in his jeans from last night. They were uncomfortable, his cock straining against the zipper. He worked off his belt while Damaceous tried to kiss him to death, ravaging his mouth. Damaceous's dancing tongue made it incredibly difficult for him to think. Hands ran along his spine, pressing him closer. Hips ground into his, a moan escaping Zane's lips.

"My pants, I need them off," Zane groaned.

Damaceous nodded. He lifted Zane off him and stood, leaving Zane on the bed. Then he removed the singer's jeans and briefs.

Damaceous untied his own pants, letting the material fall to the floor, both their clothes now a pile around him. Zane's eyes studied him, and Damaceous blushed under the scrutiny. Taking a deep breath, he straightened to his full height and expanded his wings as fully possible. It was Zane's turn to blush, intimidated by the larger angel before him, but he couldn't help his excitement. He wanted this creature…he wanted to know his touch.

Damaceous bent forward, cupped the base of his neck. He pulled Zane toward him until they were both skin to skin, groins rubbing against each other.

Zane struggled to remain calm, his breathing shallow, his heart racing. They gazed into each other's eyes while Damaceous enveloped the singer with his wings. He lifted Zane, wrapping the other's legs around his waist. Zane kissed Damaceous again, his hair falling forward, covering their faces.

He wanted to stay like this forever, wrapped around his beloved for ages to come. The thought startled Damaceous, but he found he was okay with it. There was no law against falling in love with another being.

His time spent watching over Zane had been filled with amusement and admiration. He squeezed Zane with his wings, trying to bring him closer. Damaceous wanted to feel every inch of him, wanted to know the other angel was safe and protected within his arms.

Zane grunted and released his mouth, sucking in a breath. "You're gonna' crush me!"

Damaceous chuckled but loosened his grip. With Zane's legs still around his waist, he walked over with him to the bed and sat. He reached across and wrapped a hand around the base of Zane's neck, his thumb rubbing his larynx lightly. He pulled Zane's head to the side, worshipfully kissing his neck.

Zane took their cocks in his hand, stroking them against each other. Soon, they were both rocking their hips together, and Zane bit his lip to stifle his moans.

Damaceous frowned. "I want to hear your voice, let it out." He stroked a fingertip along the inside of Zane's wing where small, delicate feathers and back muscle connected.

A shiver of pleasure made Zane cry out unexpectedly, and he glared at him. "Not fair, you can't use your carnal angel knowledge against me!"

Damaceous snorted and stroked there again—angels considered it an intimate erogenous zone. Only lovers were allowed. He loved knowing it was his to play with.

"Dam'?"

Zane's voice was unsure. He looked away, his cheeks red.

Damaceous quirked an eyebrow. "Yes? What's wrong?"

Zane refused to meet his gaze, and he became concerned.

"What is it? Are you hurt? Is it your back, or your arm...?" He moved to try to check Zane's injury, but the singer stopped him.

"No...I..." Zane bit his lip. "Actually, my back doesn't hurt at all. It's just I've never...done this before."

"Had sex?"

Zane's hand bopped him on top of his head. "No, idiot! I've never been a bottom. Jeez!"

Damaceous scratched his head until realization set in. "Oh."

"Yeah, *oh*. And...well, you're big, like...ya' know, all around," Zane stammered, busy examining the ceiling above. "It's kinda' intimidating."

Damaceous blushed. "You're my first," he confessed, and Zane's eyes widened.

"Whoa. That's...really?"

Damaceous smiled. "I've never been interested before you."

"How's it even possible?"

"There's been plenty of...opportunity but I've always been more focused on my work as an investigator. But with you, your very presence creates an interest I can't explain or seem to shake." This time Damaceous avoided Zane's gaze. "I'm sorry. I hope you're not disappointed with me..."

Zane grabbed the angel's face, giving him a big smooch. "Never, ever. You really are so cute, no matter your size."

Damaceous's cheeks burned hot. His stare darkened, becoming heated. He traced one fingertip along the head of Zane's penis. The singer bit his lip at the touch. His hips thrust upward, craving more. He wrapped his arms around Damaceous's shoulders, rubbing himself against his groin. The investigator licked his lips and leaned forward, nibbling Zane's shoulder.

Zane reached over to his nightstand and pulled open a small drawer, taking out a bottle of lube. "We'll do this together then."

Zane took the bottle, squeezed a glob onto his palm. He grabbed their cocks with one hand, stroking them both, the lube making things slippery. Within moments, both angels were panting.

"Now…you have to…prepare me. Like this." He guided Damaceous's hand to his tight entrance.

Slowly, Damaceous inserted a digit. Zane moaned, clutching his shoulders.

"You must relax." Damaceous kissed him and continued to stroke his member. Zane sighed into Damaceous's neck, his back arching backward.

The investigator inserted a second finger, twisting and stretching, searching for the right spot. Zane jerked, and a hot jet of fluid hit Damaceous's chest. The singer relaxed, his body and muscles going fluid, his mind fuzzy.

"I'm going to enter you now. Okay?"

Zane nodded, his head moving lazily on top of the other angel's shoulder. "Mm'kay…"

Something hot and as hard as steel pushed inside Zane's body. He cried out, in pain and in pleasure. Zane sank his teeth into his lover's neck, muffling his moans and whimpers. Soon, Damaceous was seated to the hilt, the heat of his cock pulsing inside him.

"Oh, god…ah…deep," Zane said between breaths. "It hurts…"

"Are you okay?" Damaceous kissed his neck, licked his earlobe, caressed the inside of his wings. The combined sensations overloaded him, and Zane hardened again in seconds.

"I'll be fine."

"You're...tight. I need...to move. I can't...this is too much," Damaceous whispered in his ear, hot breath sending chills down his body. He stood from the edge of the bed, and pressed Zane against his closet door, hooking the singer's legs over his arms. He lifted Zane off his cock just enough...and then thrusted, slamming into him repeatedly. Zane dug his nails into his skin, the pleasure-pain overwhelming him every time Damaceous hit that special place inside.

Zane convulsed. His back arched as he held onto Damaceous's shoulders, stars exploded in his eyes, his mind shattering. He came, and wave after wave of pleasure assaulted him. Damaceous thrust a few times more inside him and joined him with a loud shout.

Zane's stomach flipped as they suddenly dropped to the floor. "Whoa!"

"I...uh...sorry. My knee gave out," Damaceous said.

After Damaceous had regathered his strength, he pulled out and carried Zane to the bed, settling the angel into the crook of his arm, Zane's head on his chest. A few minutes later, soft snoring filled the room, and Damaceous lifted his head to see Zane had fallen fast asleep.

He brushed a strand of hair out of the singer's face, smiling gently.

Damaceous leaned forward just enough to place a kiss on top of Zane's head and then laid back. "I'm truly honored, love."

They spent the rest of the day—and into the evening—making love. Eventually, worn out, the angels opted to take a breather. Zane made popcorn, and the two birds settled in the living room to watch classic movies from the '90s involving dinosaurs and alien invasions. Another movie had started when someone knocked on the door.

"I'll get it." Zane headed into the hallway. He stopped halfway, realizing he was still naked. "Who is it?"

Muffled grumbling could be heard. "It's us, man. Open up!" Victor called.

"Oh, shit!" Zane scrambled for his boxers. "One sec!"

He ran into his room, scraping his wings against the doorway—and froze. *Shit.* He remembered he had wings. *Shit, shit, shit!* He pulled on his boxers—no way he was getting a shirt on at this point. It would turn into a fiasco of massive proportions.

Damaceous grabbed his wrist. "What are you doing?"

"I gotta' answer the door. Victor and Garrett are out there."

Damaceous shook his head. "They're demons."

"Yeah, I know. Isn't everybody? I just...I don't care anymore." Zane jerked away, heading back toward the entrance.

Damaceous disappeared into the bedroom. He reappeared moments later, pants on, his mouth drawn into a thin line.

Zane peered through the peephole. "Hey, guys. What are you doin' here? Can you come back later?"

"No, we cannot! We told you we were coming over after your private...uh, thingy. We want to hear how it went. Remember?"

"Um...well, I've got company?"

Victor scoffed loudly enough to annoy him. "Too damn bad. Tell her I said she can come back later, dude. It's bro' time." He banged on the door. "Let us in, already."

Forgetting himself, Zane opened the door, prepared to give an annoyed retort. But he paused when Victor gasped. The blonde's blue eyes were wide with shock.

"Bro'...dude...you have...but, how?"

Zane crossed his arms. "Well, I'm an angel, right? As I'm sure a couple of demons are *well* aware of."

Garrett stared without apology, but Victor winced. "We...might have known, ya' know, on some level."

Zane shook his head, rolling his eyes. "Uh-huh. Sure. Anything else you wanna' tell me?"

"Nope. That, uh, about covers it."

Zane's eyed the two of them, considering his options. Eventually, he sighed. "Can I trust you?" he said. "If I let you in here, will you hurt my friend or me?"

Victor scoffed. "Look. Yes, we knew you were kind of an angel. A Fallen angel, but not a full-blown one with wings and all. And, if we wanted to hurt you, we'd have done it. We're good. Right?" Victor elbowed Garrett. "Tell him."

Garrett raised an eyebrow but shrugged.

"Fine. Come in."

Zane ushered the two inside, Garrett closing the door behind them. Damaceous glared when a small *pop!* sounded.

"Wards?" Garrett remarked.

Zane frowned. "What?"

"He placed wards to keep demons out. But their only effective without an invitation."

Damaceous's lip curled. Garrett's arms dropped to his sides, fingers twitching.

Zane glanced between them and then at Victor with a sigh. "Okay, guys, let's not fight. We're all friends here."

"Never!"

"No, we're not!"

Garrett and Damaceous spoke at the same time, continuing to glare at each other. The tension was as taut as a guitar string, neither sure what to make of the other. Garrett mumbled a foreign sentence and growled, pointing at Damaceous. Damaceous took a step forward, unsheathing his blade.

"Whoa!" Zane put a hand on his chest, stopping him. He stood back to back with Victor, who blocked an advancing Garrett. "Can you relax a little?"

Victor turned his head and stared in wonder at the wings against his back, reaching around to touch the feathers.

"Stop!" Garrett caught his wrist, jerking Victor's hand away.

Victor tried to pull out his grasp. "What's the big deal?"

Zane shrugged. "I don't know. I don't mind."

Garrett returned his gaze. "As an angel, your wings are the most vulnerable part on your body. We're the enemy, Zane. Never forget."

Victor and Zane exchanged a look, both annoyed with the other two.

"Whatever…This is Garrett and Victor— my *friends*," he said, gesturing to each being in the hallway. "Let me introduce, Damaceous. He is my…um. He's important to me. Okay? So, everyone needs to get along." He blushed, rubbing his neck. Damaceous came over and placed a hand on his waist, pulling the singer against his side.

Victor's eyes widened as understanding dawned. "Yeah, it's fine with me. You've always played for both teams." He snickered. "Well, any team, really…" The demon turned to Garrett. "Sinohne?"

Damaceous sucked in a breath. *"Sinohne?"* Tension shot back into the room and Damaceous's grip tightened on Zane's waist.

Garrett crossed his arms, his jaw cocked, chin raised.

"Who's Sinohne?" Zane tried to squirm out of the angel's hold, to no avail. He gave up, more annoyed by the minute. "You two are driving me nuts! What's going on?"

Damaceous gripped his blade tightly. "Sinohne is your friend, Garrett's real name. He's famous—rather, infamous—in Heaven for the mutilation and murder of thousands of our kind. We call him…the 'Silver Death.'" He turned and addressed the demon directly. "Are you here to kill us?"

Garrett's black eyes glittered but neither his body language nor his face gave away any secrets.

Victor groaned, exasperated. "He's undercover, man." He pointed at Garrett with his thumb. "This big dumb bastard is playing

Lord Culzahr, and everyone else, for a fool. He's spying on Greed for information for his own faction. Pride thinks Greed is up to something — but no one knows what."

"Victor!" Garrett grabbed his arm again.

"What?" Victor snapped. "It's not like they give two flying shits about what's going on in Hell. And besides, I'd rather this other big dumb bastard didn't try to gut you."

Damaceous's jaw dropped. Zane laughed, slipping out of the stunned angel's hold. He slapped a hand on Victor's shoulder. "I'll have to use that one." He wiped at his eyes, shoulders shaking.

Garrett peered at Zane, studying the angel, his expression less than amused. "Who did this damage to your wing?"

Zane stilled, his smile dying. "I'm not sure what you mean. It's from when I fell out of Heaven."

"Fell? I thought you weren't Fallen." Victor said.

Zane leaned into his ear. "No, I literally fell. I'll explain later."

Garrett pursed his lips. "Don't bullshit me. I'm ten times as old as your generals and twice as deadly. There's a reason your wings are vulnerable. Large arteries and nerves run through them."

"Your point?"

Garrett's black eyes narrowed. A chill ran down Zane's spine. Garrett always saw too much. "Only someone with advanced knowledge of your anatomy could cause this kind of damage. Angels may live long lives, but they aren't immortal. I should know, I've killed my fair share."

Damaceous stepped closer. "Is this true? Did someone torture you?"

Zane avoided his touch. "Even if it is, I don't want to have this conversation. Especially not right now."

Damaceous's eyes brightened like a neon sign as he slammed a fist into a nearby wall, breaking a hole in the drywall. "I want a name."

Zane swallowed, mouth dry. He glanced at his friends.

Victor held up a finger, stepping forward. "Um, Mr. Angel...sir?"

Damaceous's head whipped around. "What!"

Victor became annoyed. "Excuse you? Don't cop an attitude with me." He walked right up to the investigator, fearlessly poking Damaceous in the chest, his face inches away. "I deal with enough bullshit from Rylan. Maybe, intimidating someone who was the *victim* of said 'torture' isn't the best way to get information. Obviously, Zane, here, is freaked out. And talking about being tortured probably isn't on the 'Topic of the Day' list."

Damaceous studied Zane. Guilt bubbled in his chest, his anger deflating. Zane trembled, but the movement was faint. His fists were clenched, his intact wing tight against his body.

"I'm...sorry," Damaceous said. "I didn't mean to antagonize you." He reached out and took a fist into his hand, rubbing Zane's wrist with his thumb. "The thought of someone...mistreating you."

Victor crossed his arms. "People say demons are horrible creatures and say we're evil. But it's easy to forget one important fact."

"Oh?" Damaceous quirked an eyebrow.

"The Devil has wings, bro'!"

Damaceous's eyebrows drew up, surprised. He paused to consider his answer. After a moment, he bowed his head. "You make a valid point, demon."

"Just Victor...please."

"It's fine, V'. Thanks," Zane said, interlacing his fingers with Damaceous's. He led him into the living room. The angel sat on the couch, and Zane curled into his side. Garrett and Victor followed, taking the recliner. The younger demon settled onto Garrett's lap, his legs hanging off the side of the armchair. Zane raised an eyebrow, exchanging a knowing look with Victor.

"By the way, were your eyes always like that?" Victor asked.

Zane blinked. He'd forgotten. "Yeah. I decided to stop hiding it."

Victor gave him thumbs up. "Good, it looks cool. You never should've hidden it in the first place."

Zane blushed, a happy warmth blooming in his chest. "Thanks. Appreciate it, man."

"No problem…Whatcha' watching?" Victor asked, his attention officially diverted to the flat screen television.

"Just the one with our favorite '90s rapper fighting off an alien invasion."

"Hells yeah!" Victor fist-pumped the air. "Have we missed the big speech? Can we watch?"

Garrett frowned. He pinched Victor at his suggestion. "We came here for information, not a Netflix-and-Chill sesh'."

Victor stuck out his tongue at the demon. He rubbed his arm but settled back down. "So, obviously…" Victor gestured to Zane's wings. "Something happened yesterday. Wanna' fill us in? Who was the client, anyway?"

Zane locked eyes with Damaceous before he spoke. "He's not a client. Alexander is actually Alatos, the general in charge of the Warriors Dominion."

"No way! Dude was an angel, too?"

Garrett leaned forward, his interest piqued. "Why is a general on Earth—making appointments and meeting with demonic lords?"

Zane squeezed Damaceous's hand before he answered. "I don't know how much I can say to you guys. I'm not sure why he was there. But he wanted me for something, whatever the reason. I used to be in his dominion. I originally was a Virtues, but they transferred me by his request. Why he has dealings with Cyrus and a demon lord? No idea."

"Wait, wait. Zane...you realize Cyrus *is* the demon lord," Victor said.

"Really?"

"Yeah. His real name is Culzahr. He's lord of the Greed. There's more, too. Rylan? Ya' know, our favorite person? He's his lieutenant, Rhaisur. For now, Maribel and I, we're Rhaisur's slaves. And Maribel...she's actually Mirul from Lust."

"Fuck. For real? Holy shit." Zane leaned forward, curious. "What's your real name?"

Victor's face fell. He'd grown rather attached to his human identity. "I was named Vaxihir. But please. Only call me Victor."

Zane shot Garrett a questioning look, but Garrett signaled not to push the issue further. Zane threw a pillow off the couch in Victor's direction. "Of course, bud. We're bro's, right?" Victor caught the pillow before he was hit in the face and smiled.

"What about you? Garrett or Sinohne? Have a preference?" Zane asked the drummer.

Garrett sighed. "Since there's no more pretense, I'll stick with my actual name. I like the reaction from your kind." He winked at Damaceous.

Damaceous's eyes narrowed, lips thinning.

Sinohne leaned back, his chin resting on his hand. He contemplated the possibilities in his mind. What could a general and a demon lord have in common?

Sinohne glanced at Damaceous, who still eyed him with suspicion. "You know, none of it adds up quite right. Culzahr has no reason to waste valuable time managing a nightclub. He could make millions by having a human sign over a corporation. Why a nightclub in the middle of a Podunk city like Cincinnati? And why use a Fallen? None of these moves make much sense."

"Unless it's not about the money," Victor said. "Greed isn't just about money. Greed equals the want, the need to have more...of everything."

Damaceous agreed. "True. Ambition, money, power."

"Power." The gears in Sinohne's mind turned. He fell silent.

The others exchanged confused glances.

Victor shrugged. "He might be this way for a while. He gets moody." Victor used the remote to start the movie. Every few minutes, he glanced at his phone as it buzzed in his pocket for the millionth time. There were three missed texts and one missed phone call from Rylan.

Where are you?

Don't worry. Be back soon. Watching a movie. Victor texted. His phone buzzed mere seconds after he hit Send.

Come back now.

Victor sighed. There was never an end to the aggravation from the demon.

Movie is almost over. I'll be there soon. He hit Send and shut off his phone.

Victor pushed Rylan's order to the back of his mind and tried to enjoy the movie. But his moment of peace was interrupted when Sinohne sprang out of the chair, causing Victor to fall onto the floor.

The blonde glared, rubbing his sore ass. "What the hell? A little warning, please?"

Sinohne paused his thoughts for a moment to apologize. He helped Victor back into the chair and paced the room. "We may have a larger problem on our hands than we originally believed."

Damaceous frowned. He had whipped his dagger out reflexively, every instinct on high alert, but now placed it back in its sheath. He resumed his seat on the couch, gesturing for the demon to continue.

As Sinohne explained his assumptions, the group stared on in amazement.

This time, Damaceous stood. "If your theory is true, I need to report to my general as soon as possible. We need to act quickly."

Damaceous gestured to the apartment's hall.

Sinohne obliged him, striding forward. When they were alone, Sinohne turned. "Yes?"

Damaceous sighed, resigned to his task. "I don't trust you. But Zane does. You could have easily killed him over the years, and I believe him when he says you've become friends."

"Okay." Sinohne hadn't expected this conversation. "What's your point?"

"I need to return to Heaven. But I refuse to leave Zane without a defense. Between us, you...are the best option. I would like to ask a favor. Stay by his side until I can return."

Sinohne scoffed. "You trust me to protect him? Even lower yourself enough to beg a favor? How gracious of you." He turned to walk away.

Damaceous caught his arm as he brushed passed him. "You are not just any demon, Lieutenant Sinohne. You went dark these last few years, but I'm aware of *exactly* who you are, Your Highness."

"Fine. I'll stay." Sinohne ran a hand through his hair, his eyes narrowed. "For the record, I would have stayed either way. I'm fond of Zane, he's important to me, too. But you still owe me the favor." He pulled out of the angel's grip, returning to the living room.

"Thank you." Damaceous sighed with relief and went back to the couch, placing his blade on the cushion next to Zane. Tip to hilt, the dagger was as long as his forearm, curving dangerously. Runic symbols were engraved along the sharp edge, the hilt adorned in swirling gold. An onyx stone was set into the end of the hilt, polished to a glossy shine.

Zane ran a fingertip over the runes, tracing each symbol.

"This is an angel's blade. Do you remember them?" Damaceous said. "They are powerful weapons, etched with runes of protection and violence. Be careful. Only use it if necessary to protect yourself." Damaceous leaned forward, kissing the top of Zane's head. "I'm leaving now. Sinohne's your protection until I return."

"Okay. But, be quick about it. I don't want to worry about you." Zane offered a smile. He pulled Damaceous closer and captured the angel's lips in a long, upside-down kiss before Zane settled back onto the couch. Sitting in Sinohne's lap again, Victor whooped. Sinohne smacked him on the head.

"I'll be back soon." Damaceous turned and created a portal. A large golden circle grew, becoming as tall and as wide as Damaceous. The other three stared in amazement as he stepped through with a wave. Then, the portal dissipated.

"Whoa...cool," Victor said. "Can all angels just say, 'open sesame!'...and suddenly, new dimension?"

Zane laughed. "Yeah, from what I can remember. How do you guys go back and forth from Hell?"

"We use entry points like mirrors for transport and communication. Some of us use cell phones, but the older generations despise technology." Victor pointed at Sinohne over his shoulder with a thumb.

Sinohne rolled his eyes at his antics. "You're like a child."

Zane glanced at Sinohne. "Ya' know, I appreciate your offer, but you don't need to stay. I'll be fine on my own. He's being overprotective."

"No, he's not. Without wards, you're a sitting duck. You're injured and unskilled, not to mention probably the top mark in both Heaven and Hell now. Even with Victor here, you're better off putting my skills to use."

"Hey, I've got my own set of skills. Not completely helpless," Zane argued. "I spent

most of my time in Heaven being trained by…"
His throat caught on Khamael's name.

Sinohne's expression turned grim.

Victor climbed out of Sinohne's lap and joined Zane on the couch. "I know you've been through a lot. Are you okay?"

Zane shrugged. "It's fine. Let's just watch the rest of the movie."

EIGHTEEN

Damaceous stalked up the steps of the Powers Dominion headquarters. His expression must've been frightening because other angels scrambled out of his path. He headed directly for General Remiel's office. No one would stop him from bringing down the traitors in their midst.

Rounding the corner, he took a moment to gather himself as he stood before Remiel's door. He needed to be calm; otherwise, his information might not be taken seriously.

Raising a fist, he knocked.

"Enter."

Damaceous opened the door to see Remiel leaning over his desk, mulling over the paperwork, per usual. The only time he wasn't dealing with endless paperwork seemed to be when he attended the High Council meeting every week.

Remiel rubbed his forehead, surprised to see Damaceous. "Well, hello." He gestured to the chair in front of his desk. "Please, sit."

"With all due respect, sir, I'd like to make this report while standing." Damaceous bowed.

The general frowned. "You've been on Earth for quite some time. I had hoped we could take a moment and catch up."

"I apologize. But what I have learned cannot wait for pleasantries."

Remiel leaned back in his chair, arms crossed. "Begin."

"The devil has wings." Damaceous smiled, thinking about the feisty blonde who'd gotten in his face. "Someone recently reminded me...One of our own may be responsible for a conspiracy to declare hundreds of angels Fallen over the last few hundred years."

"That's an extreme accusation. Do you have proof?"

Damaceous nodded. "I have an eyewitness account of the crimes. I'd like to receive support for access to the Warriors headquarters and search for further evidence."

"You don't have written proof? Nothing concrete to show me? Witness statements can be refuted and dismissed by the Council. You know this." Remiel leaned forward onto his elbows, the papers on his desk crinkling underneath his weight. "Who are we talking about?"

"General Alatos. Lieutenant Khamael may also be involved."

Damaceous quietly scanned the hallway. Then he shut the door to the office.

"I believe they even have someone in our dominion covering it up."

Remiel's eyebrows scrunched together, his lips drawn into a tight frown. His eyes closed for a brief moment. The general exhaled a deep sigh and straightened in his chair. "General Alatos. The general to Heaven's army, the Warriors Dominion. One of the most powerful angels in Heaven, a highly trained combatant, with thousands more under his command...and all you have are witness statements? Without concrete proof, I can't even *try* to bring it to the High Council for a trial. His reputation alone outweighs anything your witness could say against him."

Damaceous glowered, his ire rising. "At least listen to the rest, sir! See Zhanerious and let him show you the damage to his body. Let him tell you his story. But you must know one thing now. General Alatos is working with the Demon Lord of Greed, Culzahr. We aren't sure how, but we think they've been gathering human souls to overthrow Lucifer himself."

"I thought I instructed you to stay away from that Fallen," General Remiel spoke.

"You did, and I was. But that's just it, general; Zhanerious is not Fallen. He never was!

It's why he was never registered. Someone must have placed a seal on his back which wiped his memory, concealed his powers. But he's broken the seal and regained both. He can testify against them all!"

Remiel held up a hand, cutting him off. "Enough. Everything you've reported is circumstantial, and theories carry no weight with me nor, especially, the High Council. Regardless of what this Zhanerious has seen, we can do nothing without evidence."

Damaceous was shocked. His hands balled into fists, fingernails digging into his palms. "Then give me the support to go find the damned evidence," he requested through clenched teeth.

"Denied."

Damaceous decided to try one last card. "I didn't want to tell you yet but...Lieutenant Ashliel is the one covering everything up for them."

Remiel stared into his eyes, his will an immovable wall. Damaceous seethed, losing his temper. "Why aren't you even considering what I have to say? Is it so inconceivable General Alatos could commit these terrible acts? Or are you involved, too?"

Remiel's expression became unreadable, but his eyes glittered with authority. "Tread. Lightly."

Damaceous sucked in a breath. He had pushed too far. He walked over to the general's desk and slapped down his hand. "At least do me a favor. Check the records when you meet with the High Council. Councilman Azrael keeps track of human souls, right? He knows where all the souls go? Compare the numbers to the Fallen versus the trainees. Compare it to the count of missing human souls over the last few centuries. The numbers will be off, I guarantee it."

He turned in a huff, storming out of the office. "Good day, *General*."

A multicolored feather sat quietly on the desk where the other angel's hand had landed. Remiel picked up the feather, glancing at the door as it slammed behind the investigator. Tension drained out of his body, making the general feel his age for the first time in a while. He leaned backward in his chair and squeezed the bridge of his nose.

A few minutes later, Ashliel entered the office, carrying a new stack of forms for Remiel to read over. The lieutenant's golden red hair was braided to one side, reaching her elbow, and a few strands had fallen across her forehead. Her wings were a soft powder-blue, matching her eyes. Remiel often compared their softness to the clouds in the sky.

Today, the lieutenant wore a sheer gray skirt made of satin. The bottom hem angled across her legs, and her blouse was cut short, showing off her navel. Lieutenant Ashliel was only thirty thousand years old, the youngest angel to achieve a high-ranking position.

Remiel held the multicolored feather out for her to see. She looked at him in confusion, her long braid swaying. But she set the stack of papers on the desk and took the feather between her fingertips. She came around the desk, settled onto his lap, curling into his side. Her flowy skirt rode up her thigh, and Remiel laid a palm across it, kissing her cheek.

"Hello, my love," Ashliel greeted. When the general didn't respond, she frowned in concern. "Is everything all right?"

The general sighed. "We need to convene the Council."

"Without their consent? They'll never approve."

"I know…but it's time. We need to tell them. Damaceous was just in here. He knows, Ashliel. He knows."

"Everything?"

The general nodded, staring into her eyes. "Enough to be dangerous."

Nighttime had fallen across Heaven, and Damaceous soared over the capital.

Remiel wanted proof...Damaceous was determined to get it. He was not going to let Alatos get away with his crimes because of a simple technicality. Zhanerious deserved better. The tortured young angels deserved better. *Heaven* deserved better.

He was about to do something stupid. Damaceous was prepared for the consequences — but it was a stupid move. All his instincts screamed at him, but he dived downward, straight for the headquarters of Heaven's army. He hovered above the building as a guard finished his rounds, strolling out of sight. Damaceous had flown above their headquarters all day, timing their rounds, memorizing their schedule. For the Warriors, security was less vigilant than he'd imagined.

Landing silently, Damaceous slipped into his human form. He didn't want his wings to get in his way, and a smaller form made it easier to move around unnoticed.

Damaceous made his way down the corridor, hugging tightly to the wall. He remembered the layout from the description Zane had recounted about his time here.

Damaceous quickly found his lover's old room and tried the handle. It was locked. He had expected as much and continued, rounding the corner. He frowned, his brown hair falling over his eyes; it was too short to fasten with a tie. He brushed it back and checked the handle to Alatos's office. He ducked inside when it turned.

Damaceous glanced around, walking to the filing cabinets, searching through them. He came up empty. Damaceous headed to the general's desk, pulling open drawers, flipping through the files. *Nothing.* He checked every shelf…anywhere the general might have hidden the file Zane had found before. Alatos could have burned it by now. But Damaceous doubted it.

The general was arrogant. He would want to read about his deeds…to glory in them. The only other place he might keep the file was his personal bedchamber. But Damaceous wasn't sure where it was located. Zane hadn't mentioned it, and Damaceous didn't have long to search.

Damaceous sighed in defeat. He needed to find more information about the building and its layout. Then he would have a better shot at finding the proof they needed to bring down Alatos.

Damaceous slipped determinedly back into his angel form and left the office. Out in the dark courtyard, he started his launch for his takeoff. But as soon as he was in the air, a leather cord wrapped around his ankle, yanking him back to the ground. He landed in a heap on his back. Immediately, he was on his feet, wings tight.

Khamael smiled, his head cocked to one side. "Well, what is a Powers doing in our compound, hmm?" He was already re-coiling the whip in his hand.

Dread settled in Damaceous's stomach. The look in the other angel's eyes chilled him to the bone. He moved into a defensive stance but realized he had no weapon of his own. "I was just leaving, sir." He spoke carefully, determined not to show his anger. "I came to receive an audience from your general, but it's awfully late. I'll just return tomorrow instead."

Khamael scoffed. "Right. You think someone wouldn't see you during the day, watching our detail? What do you take us for? We are the militia of Heaven, your defense against the Legion. Did you really think you could just slip in and out without notice?" he spat. His expression turned from amusement to pure malice.

Damaceous held up his hands, hoping to placate him. "I meant no harm or insult to your dominion, lieutenant," he responded. "But you need to let me leave. I've done nothing to warrant your aggression."

Khamael sneered. Damaceous was about to tell the lieutenant he had no right to detain the investigator when he suddenly heard sharp footsteps behind him. He turned to see Alatos and Ashliel leading several guards, heading directly his way. He scowled at Ashliel's presence.

"You entered my office without my consent, officially breaking and entering," Alatos accused once he stood before Damaceous. "Attempted to find proof, correct? Is this what you were looking for?"

The general laughed. He held up the file in his hand.

Damaceous's eyes widened. Khamael snickered beside him. This was not a good situation. The general handed the file to Ashliel, her bemusement clear.

She walked over to stand in front of Damaceous, then mocked him by waving the file in his face. His lip curled in disgust.

"I'm sorry, Damaceous," Ashliel told him. "But this is one battle you are not prepared to win. You should have listened when General Remiel said to stay away."

"You're a disgrace."

She raised her brows, frowning. She moved closer, her expression cold. "I'm your lieutenant. You will address me as such."

Damaceous's eyes narrowed to slits. He scoffed and spat on the ground at her feet.

She slapped him hard, his head whipping to the side.

He wiped his mouth, his lip bloodied.

The lieutenant stood a hair's breadth away and caught his gaze. A barely audible whisper floated to his ears; "Trust me." There was a moment of fear in her eyes, but then she stepped away. Damaceous questioned his senses as her mocking and haughty expression returned.

"Lieutenant Ashliel, don't worry," Alatos reassured her, laying a hand on her shoulder. "We will take him and teach him manners, hmm?"

She nodded and tucked the file into her robes. "I'll doctor the file to account for any questions then make sure the rest is destroyed. I must return, but do with him as you will," she said. Her eyes held Damaceous's gaze. "We have no use for him anymore." His breath hitched, fear seeping into his skin at her words. She took off, flying into the night.

"Lieutenant Khamael, I leave him to you."

Alatos waved, disappearing around a corner on the opposite side of the courtyard. Damaceous stepped away to create distance while the guards formed a circle. He cursed under his breath. Khamael continued to watch him, his head cocked to the side and his creepy smile back in place.

Damaceous glanced around. He was outnumbered. The lieutenant's skill far surpassed his, but Damaceous refused to be taken without a fight. He whipped around then charged the nearest guard, tackling him to the ground. Shouts rang out as Damaceous disarmed the guard, already brandishing the sword which had hung on their waist.

Khamael chuckled but made no move. He simply flicked a wrist, and the rest of the guards rushed at Damaceous.

The investigator was not unskilled with a sword, easily dispatching with the first two guards. Another attacked him from behind, slashed at his wings, blood spraying the ground. Pain scorched through him. His knee buckled, and he slammed into the ground.

The next attack came. Damaceous barely rolled out of the way, swinging his sword around as he tumbled. He sprang quickly back to his feet and grabbed one guard by his face, smashing it into the head of a second. He kicked his leg out, landing a blow to another's gut then he jumped into the air, wings spread, and swung his sword downward, taking off the heads of two more.

Damaceous turned and extended his wings, finally about to fly unhindered, when—

— *Crack!* —

Khamael's whip wrapped around his neck. Damaceous was jerked to the ground, grasping at the cord.

The lieutenant stepped toward him and pulled on his whip. Damaceous was yanked forward, off his feet, face-first into the grass. Pain lanced through his head, black spots dancing in his eyes. The remaining guards raced over to him and pinned him to the ground. His arms were dragged behind his back, and his wings shoved painfully against his body, effectively overpowered.

"Take him," Khamael ordered. Strutting closer, he knelt onto the ground and grabbed Damaceous's hair, lifting the captive angel's head. "We're going to have so much fun. And I hear the general might come to see you."

Damaceous glared. "Fuck you."

The lieutenant's eyes widened in surprise. He laughed, then flicked his gaze to the guard behind Damaceous.

"See you later," the lieutenant said. He stood and walked away while Damaceous was knocked unconscious.

Ashliel flew away from the compound. Her muscles burned, straining with the effort needed to maintain her blinding speed. She gripped the file in her hand tightly, keeping it close to her body but her braid whipped against the wind, snapping around her head. She didn't slow her pace until her personal quarters came into view on the western side of the mountain. Then the lieutenant touched down onto the small balcony outside and she entered the dwelling.

Her home was nestled in a natural opening behind a ledge, the back wall the side of a rocky cliff. The quarters were circular but rather large; four pillars braced the opening. She had moved her bed against the cliffside, but her desk and a small armoire were closer to the balcony.

Once inside, the lieutenant pulled the curtains on either side of the dwelling closed and sighed.

Approaching her desk, Ashliel laid down the file. Her vaiglás, a clear crystal inside of a golden oval compact rested a few inches away, next to a swirly, blue guitar pick. Ashliel touched the compact with her fingertip. She whispered a name, causing the crystal to glow with a soft, white light. An image of Remiel appeared. She forced a weak smile, her throat loosening at the sight of his face.

"Ashliel?" Remiel asked, concern in his voice.

Ashliel waved him off. "I'm fine," she assured him. "I...uh, I finally have the file."

"Good," Remiel said. "What happened at the compound?"

She looked away, twisting her fingers into her braid. "He has Damaceous," she finally answered.

Remiel's expression hardened. "The fool. Damaceous was determined to find the proof he needed. But his impatience brought us the opportunity to finally gain Alatos's trust and get it. You know this. Don't fret," he reminded her.

Her eyebrows drew together. "He's going to hate me," she whispered.

The crystal's image went blank.

She drew in a short breath through her nose then exhaled, trying to hold back her emotions.

Her hand still stung from his cheek. Ashliel hated herself for it, she'd been suspicious of Alatos, his demeanor changing just subtly enough to ping her curiosity. But she couldn't regret it now.

This was her job. The Powers Dominion not only investigated demonic activity...it was supposed to prevent corruption within Heaven itself. Everything she had worked toward was meant to take down General Alatos and Lieutenant Khamael. If Ashliel hadn't found the discrepancies in their reports, those two snakes might have slithered away with everything.

Or...

Someone else might have noticed.

Eventually.

She was startled out of her thoughts by a touch on her arm. Ashliel drew her blade.

Remiel chuckled from where he stood beside her, one eyebrow—and his hands—raised. "I apologize, my love," he said. "I didn't think I'd scare you. My landing wasn't silent."

Ashliel relaxed, sheathing her dagger. Remiel pulled her to his chest, and they wrapped their arms around each other. He rested his head on top of hers.

Ashliel felt safe in his arms, the only place nowadays.

"He will not hate you," Remiel soothed her. "I won't let him. I know you don't like leaving him there, but we must wait. The High Council cannot reconvene for two more days, even without gathering the information I requested. Damaceous is strong, stronger than even Alatos realizes." The general smiled softly, lips curving. "You should've seen the way he railed against me to try and help Zhanerious. He'll be fine."

Ashliel nodded, sighing against his chest. He rubbed her back in circles, the motion a perfect antidote for calming her nerves.

Remiel had not always been a solace for her. Their relationship had started out tumultuous. Centuries passed until, after a heated debate, Ashliel had found herself on the floor of his office as Remiel claimed her for his own.

She smiled at the memory and squeezed him even more tightly. "What can we do for him?"

Remiel shook his head. "Nothing. He must endure. If we can catch General Alatos in the act, his condemnation is assured. Which is why Damaceous won't hate you. He will hate *me*...for using him. You know we cannot storm into their dominion without cause."

Despite appearances, tensions between each dominion hung on the scales of a delicate balance. General Alatos commanded the loyalty of thousands of Warriors. The Archangels, the battalion leaders, would not take kindly to the Powers leveling accusations against their general without the support of the High Council.

"He'll understand why I made this choice when it's finally over. It will take time, but he will." Remiel brushed a strand of stray hair behind Ashliel's ear and chuckled.

Ashliel shoved herself away in annoyance, smacking her hands against his chest. "This is no laughing matter. One of our own was taken. Protocol be damned. I can't sit here while Damaceous suffers."

Remiel pulled her close again. He leaned in and captured her mouth, her lips pliant against his.

Ashliel's insides went to mush. It was impossible for her to stay mad at Remiel when he held her. She sighed into his neck as Remiel broke the kiss.

"More have already been lost. His part will help prevent future losses," Remiel stated. "We also don't know where in the compound Damaceous is. If we move too early, they might get spooked. He could vanish before anything can be done to rescue him. We need the High Council to review this new information, so we can officially take Alatos and Khamael into custody. Then, we'll have the ability to search the compound."

Remiel kissed her forehead, his lips warm on her skin. "Otherwise, they can chalk Damaceous up as an angel who simply appears to be missing—and our accusations would fall flat. Along with what's in the file, his testimony paired with Zhanerious's statement will be all the evidence we need to tie them to their crimes. I...loathe this decision just as much as you...but as general, I stand by it. All we can do now is wait."

NINETEEN

Sinohne settled back into the armchair in Zane's apartment. The recliner was comfortable, covered in a soft, dark-blue cloth, but he had a crick in his back from sleeping on the chair for the last couple of days. With nothing else to do but wait, they watched random television shows as a distraction, neither one paying much attention.

Zane hadn't slept much. He left the room only to eat a meal or take a shower. Victor had departed soon after Damaceous and hadn't returned, putting Sinohne on edge. He rolled his stiff shoulders to ease the tension in his muscles.

Zane sat in front of the couch, legs underneath the glass coffee table, controller in hand. He was busy searching for the latest hellspawn on his game console while he chewed on the remains of a pizza crust hanging out of his mouth. Sinohne couldn't see the appeal, but if it helped keep his mind off the clock, he would indulge him.

Zane killed a group of creatures with his avatar, blood splattering across the screen then pressed pause, setting his controller aside. "So...?"

Sinohne glanced over, his eyebrow raised. "Yes?"

"Am I the only one who thinks it's odd no one has called about work? I missed *one* day last time, and Cy—Culzahr pitched a fit."

Sinohne nodded in agreement. He'd been bothered by it, too.

Zane let out a deep breath. "Do you really think Culzahr is going to overthrow Lucifer?"

"He can try."

"How come no one has tried before?"

"Who said they haven't? Lucifer makes himself hard to track down. For this exact reason. He's incredibly powerful, but not impervious. He must have a weapon I haven't considered."

Zane retreated into his thoughts. He leaned forward onto the table, his arms crossed and his chin on his forearm. He fiddled with the bandage on his arm, a habit he had started to prevent scratching the wound.

Sinohne sighed and stood, his back muscles protesting. He stretched his arms. "My master, Baelozar, should be apprised of this situation. I wanted to wait for Damaceous to return so I could convey as much information as possible. But I'll figure something out."

"Yeah, sure, whatever you need to do." Zane waved him on. "Go for it."

"I need to request a favor, first."

Zane straightened when Sinohne disappeared into the kitchen. He returned seconds later, a small bowl in his hand, and kneeled at his side, pushing the coffee table out of the way. Sinohne dropped his glamor.

Zane's adrenaline spiked, his Adam's apple bobbing in his throat. "Uh...Wha—what, uh, what is it?" He inched away, trapped between the couch and the table, his good wing within the demon's reach.

Sinohne grabbed his forearm, and he yelped in surprise. "Relax, Zane," Sinohne whispered. "I just need a small favor."

"Well, you're seriously freaking me out. What is it?" Zane tried not to panic but was failing miserably. "This is a bad joke."

Sinohne sniffed the air. Fear and sweat radiated off the angel. He regretted being the cause, but there was no helping it. "Just stay still." Sinohne sliced a claw through the bandage.

"What are you doing?"

Zane jerked away, holding his arm against his chest. He folded his wing in front of himself—a flimsy shield between his arm and the demon.

"I need to contact my faction." Sinohne set the bowl aside and leaned back on his heels. "I'm your only protection now...I can't wound myself without making us both vulnerable. And, I can't leave to find an animal or a human to take their blood. You're already bleeding because of your wound, which *still* hasn't healed. I just need a small amount of blood...for the symbols I'll draw on the mirror."

The explanation didn't help. Zane's pallor started turning green.

"Either way, your wound needs to be tended to correctly. You've done a decent job, but you're not an expert. Injuries from a demon's claw or bite are difficult to mend because we secrete small traces of venom. Without the healing agents in my saliva, these wounds may never heal properly."

He waited, balancing on the balls of his feet, but his tail swished back and forth, unable to disguise his impatience.

Sinohne set the bowl on the table and held out his hand. "I want you to trust me, Zane. I consider you a friend. I would never do anything to put you in danger. I apologize for this aggressive approach."

His words seemed to do the trick. Zane settled his wing behind his back and held out his arm. But his hesitation was evident in the way he chewed on his lip.

"Thank you. It'll be fine."

Sinohne used one claw to cut away the bandages around Zane's arm. The wound bled heavily, just as he suspected. There would still be a scar, but there was no reason for Zane to keep bleeding unnecessarily. He used the bowl to catch most of the blood flow. Finished, he pulled Zane's arm close, bringing the wound to his mouth. He licked the area with his tongue, catching the sweet liquid.

Zane watched in sick wonder as sliced muscle and skin healed before his eyes.

"How—?"

"Wounds like this can only be repaired by either specialized healers in Heaven or the saliva of a powerful demon." Sinohne wiped his mouth. "And you've rewrapped this injury several times in the course of a few hours. As if I wouldn't smell the blood on you after being attacked at the gym. I seem to remember offering my help and being denied."

Zane examined the healed skin in fascination. "I guess I should have let you, huh? My bad. I was really freaked out back then."

"It's understandable. Now...I'm going to contact Baelozar and speak with him." Sinohne stood with the bowl, now half-filled with blood.

"Couldn't you have just called him on a cell phone?" Zane asked.

Sinohne shook his head. "Oh, yeah. And what service do you know that makes interdimensional calls? Let me just ping a local cell tower." Sarcasm dripped through his every word.

"Just saying. It'd be easier. Victor and Rylan text each other all the time."

"But they're on Earth the majority of the time."

"Oh yeah. True."

Sinohne rolled his eyes then headed for the bathroom. He dipped two fingers into the bowl he had placed on the counter. The demon drew a large square on the bathroom mirror, spatters of the liquid dripping onto the sink and the countertop. He placed three symbols in each corner, one on the inside and two on the outside.

The symbols were a mixture of dots and lines, reminiscent of the patterns found in Arabic writings. After each group was drawn, he empowered the marks with a simple incantation; "*Potest Etiam*." The symbols crackled, the edges sparking like paper on fire. A few minutes later, he finished off the last symbol in the center and rinsed his fingers.

Then the demon recited the summoning spell for Baelozar.

"*Excieo*." The last word fell from his lips, and he dropped his hand, waiting. When nothing appeared in the mirror, he frowned. Sinohne's tail twitched anxiously. He placed his hand on the mirror and recited the spell, again.

Nothing happened.

Eyes narrowing, he wiped away one symbol, replacing it with another. This time he tried to contact other demons from Pride. Sinohne made several attempts over the next half hour.

Each one failed.

Zane jumped at the echo of glass shattering. Sinohne reentered the living room, looking shaken. His eyes were unfocused, trapped in his own thoughts, muttering to himself.

Zane led the demon to the couch. "Gar — er, Sinohne? Is everything okay?"

Curious, he left Sinohne on the couch and walked into the bathroom.

His mouth dropped open. "What the ever living…fuck?" His bathroom was like a murder scene. He grimaced, stepping toward the mirror. He tiptoed over the shattered bowl, blood pooling across the tiled floor.

"Ugh."

He tried to make sense of the symbols on his mirror. Flashes of memory were like static, the education the angels had taught him unable to break through the fuzziness. He had regained most of his memory, but it was still more like flipping through an old scrapbook. The memories were there but from another life.

Zane gave up and left the room, closing the door behind him.

"You have a serious mess to clean up in there, buddy," he complained. "I better not lose my deposit over this."

Sinohne's expression was grim. "We need to go to Pride. Immediately."

"What?"

"I tried to contact over twenty members of my faction. No one replied. It's impossible."

"Maybe they're busy?" Zane suggested.

"No. They would never be busy enough to ignore a summons from the faction's lieutenant."

"Captured?" Zane said.

Sinohne growled in frustration, and his eyes flashed.

Zane held up his hands. "Hey, don't get testy with me. I'm trying to help."

Sinohne sighed. "I need to find out what's happening. Baelozar wouldn't willingly ignore my summons, especially when he's been eager for news. I think the only way we're going to get answers is by going there directly."

Zane frowned, sitting on the table, the glass edge biting into his thighs. "You seem worried."

"I am. Lucifer's lines of defense are the ruling faction — Pride — and his heir, Baelozar. If Culzahr wanted to overthrow Lucifer, he'd first have to cripple our faction. Otherwise, the Pride demons inherit the throne."

"Wait." Zane's mind went into overdrive. "Aren't you the lieutenant?"

Sinohne nodded.

"So, doesn't this make you…?"

"The third in line, an heir to inherit the throne."

"Holy shit!" Zane's mouth gaped open for the second time that evening. He ran a hand through his hair.

Sinohne looked away, the skin on his cheeks darkening as he blushed. "Fortunately, Lucifer is ancient and formidable. To defeat him, Culzahr will need powerful allies. Which is why he probably aligned himself with a general from Heaven. Without Lucifer, I doubt Baelozar could hold the throne for long. He doesn't command the respect of the other factions. Except for Belphegor, the Demon Lord of Sloth, who always tries to remain a neutral party."

"What about you? You say they don't like Baelozar. Maybe they would follow you."

Sinohne shook his head. "I'm as powerful as any lord but ruling over Hell would be out of the question."

"Why?"

"Because I don't want to."

"Why?"

Sinohne bared his fangs. "Stop asking so many questions."

"Fine." Zane narrowed his eyes. "But, one more. How are we getting to Baelozar? I can't just go outside and start walking around like this." He gestured to his wings.

Sinohne frowned. "Victor took my truck and hasn't returned." He leaned forward on his elbows and stared at the feathers in front of him, an idea rolling around in his mind. "I want to propose something. But, it's risky. And, foolish."

Zane's curiosity was piqued. "What's your plan?"

"To travel the surface of Hell."

TWENTY

"The surface of Hell?"

"Yes."

"An angel, just waltzing around Hell like no biggie?"

"In a sense."

Zane stood and paced the room. "You're outta' your freakin' mind."

"I can offer you a contract, a deal of sorts," Sinohne said. "You'd be under my protection. We only need to travel along the surface for a short time. Lesser demons would not attack you."

"Even if they smell my blood? Sunshine and candy, remember?"

Sinohne shrugged. "Nothing is ever certain. But you stand a better chance with my protection."

Zane crossed his arms, mulling it over. "A demon making a deal with an angel.

Sounds…strange," he muttered. "Sure…what can go wrong?" He laughed half-heartedly at his own joke. Then he flopped onto the couch beside the demon, prepared for anything at this point.

Sinohne held up his right hand. "Put your right palm to mine," he instructed.

Zane complied, and they interlocked their fingers. "Have you done this before?"

Sinohne shook his head. "No. First time. But we'll be fine. It's just a protection contract."

Their palms glowed, a warm light shining between their fingers. A translucent image of a scrolled parchment appeared before Zane's eyes, floating between them.

"Whoa." It was the coolest thing Zane had seen so far. He stuck his free hand through the image, and it flickered like a hologram. "Now what?"

"Repeat after me," Sinohne said. "Le m'anam, tha mi bòid a dhìon fear mi a' cumail. Beatha air beatha, pailme a-pailme. Ach, briste bond bithidh cheangal an t-sreang. Mhà e." *With my soul, I vow to protect the one I hold. Life to life, palm to palm. However, the broken bond shall link the string. May it be.*

Zane repeated the words as best as he could, stumbling over the pronunciation. When he finally finished, the image vanished, and his palm burned.

"Ow!" He jerked away then, inspected his hand. Nothing was there. He glared at Sinohne. "What the hell did I just say?"

"It's an old spell I learned, courtesy of a druid thousands of years ago."

"Right...That's it?"

"Yup. We are now officially allies, and you're my ward when we travel through Hell."

"Thanks. But, does it end? No small print I should know about?"

Sinohne's expression became unreadable. "The contract can end whenever you want our connection to end. But I've never done this before. There may be unintended consequences. My Gaelic is rusty. Be...careful, okay?"

Zane shrugged. "Whatever. It's fine. Too late to back out now. Next up?"

"Clothes. You can't walk around in just your boxers."

Zane glanced down, having forgotten his boxers, the blocky blue and red stripes making him laugh. "I could run around singing, '*America, the Beautiful.*' And, I'd get a top hat. All the little creatures will line up to march behind me."

Sinohne rolled his eyes. "You really are an idiot. Just as bad as Victor, I swear. Like two peas in a fucking pod."

The comment just caused Zane to grin wider.

"The problem, besides your lack of clothing, is your damaged wing. You can't drag it behind you, or you'll slow us down considerably." Sinohne flicked Zane in the forehead.

"Ouch! Jeez!" Zane rubbed his head. "Well, help me get into a shirt first, and we'll figure out the rest afterward."

He walked into his bedroom, grabbing the nearest black shirt. Sinohne took the shirt from him, slicing open the back. "Step into it. It'll be easier than pulling the material around your wings."

Zane nodded, shimmying the material over his hips. "Neat. It actually worked."

"Alright…and now, I need permission to for this part," Sinohne told him, holding the unused bandage wraps he'd found in the bathroom.

Zane quirked his eyebrow but shrugged. "Sure. Of course."

Sinohne moved behind him. With a delicate touch, the demon maneuvered the injured wing, pressing the limb against Zane's body. Sinohne held the wing firmly, and Zane helped him wrap the bandage like a rope. Finished, Sinohne sighed. The angel felt a hand brush across his feathers, but he remained still. His instincts knew the demon posed him no danger.

"Your feathers are stunning, you know," Sinohne whispered from behind him.

Zane blushed. "Thanks." He cleared his throat, breaking the tension and opened his closet to pull on a clean pair of jeans and boots. As he laced up the boots, Zane's curiosity nagged at him. "So...?"

Sinohne raised an eyebrow. "Yes?"

Zane stuffed his arms into a large, black trench coat he saved for cold nights. It was snug but still fit, if barely. "I was wondering something. Damaceous told me before, about when Lucifer corrupted the demons...how they weren't originally bad. Is that why you and Victor don't seem like the rest?"

Sinohne stepped in front of the angel, the temperature around them dropping a few degrees. "Angels are no friends of mine. Do you really believe Lucifer is singularly to blame? As if there were nothing else wrong, as if humans and angels are all so goddamned perfect."

Zane's breath hitched in his throat as Sinohne's claws extended. Sinohne scraped a sharp tip against his cheek and moved closer. Zane was forced backward, his knees buckling when he hit the mattress.

Sinohne towered above him. "Back then, Dragons roamed, the largest carnivore on the planet, feared by humans and angels, alike. Eventually, as humans so often do, they figured out a way to domesticate my ancestors. Over time, we evolved into dragonkin, their loyal *pets*." He spat the last word. "After a thousand years, we were closer to dogs than dragons. But…we were loved, used as guardians."

Zane shrugged. "Doesn't sound bad."

Sinohne scowled. "Some were cruel. They abused their 'property.' When Lucifer was cast out, he promised the abused dragonkin their revenge. No one realized it meant a new form of slavery; we're shackled to his will, his desires. Not only are we vilified as evil, but most are happy enough to live up to the image. Some, like myself and Victor, don't care for the label. Angels and humans have been nothing but a detriment to us, using us like pawns in a game we can't even control ourselves. Now, we want out. Whatever plans Culzahr has concocted, the end game is Lucifer's death." Sinohne bent closer until his eerie gaze was level with Zane's mismatched eyes.

"Due to my affections for you and Victor, you understand a side of me rarely seen. Do not expect the rest to treat you like we have," Sinohne warned. "Many would kill for a taste of the power running through your veins. Just like the demon from the gym. I won't hurt you due to our pact, and our friendship. But before all this mess? I would've skinned you alive for a simple stare. If you think what those angels did to you was terrible, I've done worse. Far, far worse."

Sinohne straightened and left the room.

Zane's fingers twisted into the covers. He'd almost forgotten about the long history of hate between their kind. He didn't care for the reminder. What was happening now was just another ripple from a war no one remembered.

Zane took a moment to retrieve the blade Damaceous had given him, then shoved it into one of the pockets of the trench coat. He met Sinohne in the hallway as the demon returned his glamor. "I'm sorry."

"No. Don't worry about it. You were simply asking a question out of curiosity," Sinohne said. The tension between them dissipated. "I don't hate angels...or humans. I hate what I became because of them."

Zane exhaled a deep sigh. "Hey, don't worry." A mischievous grin spread across his lips. "I'll keep your secret." He poked the demon's shoulder.

Sinohne sent him a flat stare. "About?"

"I won't tell anyone how cuddly-wuddly you are over Victor. I saw you two, all handsy in the chair, ya' know."

"Asshole." Sinohne chuckled, shoving Zane down the hall as they left the apartment. When the elevator reached ground level, they stepped out into a silent parking garage. Only the sound of traffic reached their ears.

Sinohne turned to Zane, held out a hand. "Don't let go of me when we're in Hell. I can cast my glamor onto you, but it will only work while in constant contact."

Zane nodded, his heart beat picking up pace again. "What about the other demons?"

"If you see one, remain as calm as possible, unless I tell you otherwise. We mostly live underground because the surface is inhospitable. Only the Legion live there. They're more animalistic, living by instinct alone. Wrath can command them but, when unleashed, those demons become unpredictable."

"Weren't you in the Legion?"

"Yes, I went later. The time Damaceous spoke of…I earned my rank as Baelozar's second."

"Ah."

"Are you ready, angel? Tell me if you don't want to go."

Zane lifted his chin. "No. I want to see Hell. I may never get another chance, and we need to find out what's going on. This is the fastest way."

Sinohne dropped his glamor.

A woman walking toward them with groceries screamed and dropped her bags, running in the opposite direction.

"Whoops." Sinohne grinned, his fangs showing. Zane pitied the poor woman but could understand her reaction. Smiling like that, Sinohne was as terrifying as the boogeyman.

The demon clawed at the air, a portal opening before them. The black circle grew, widening enough for them to step through.

"I thought you needed a mirror?" Zane asked, surprised.

Sinohne's toothy grin widened. "We, Pride, are royalty. We all have our secrets to keep."

He grabbed Zane's arm, pulling him through the portal. Once on the other side, it closed behind them.

Zane gazed around. Sinohne gave him a moment to take in his new surroundings.

The air was acrid. Zane squeezed his nose, gagging as the smell of rotten eggs burned his sinuses. A hot, steaming wind whipped against them, drowning out all sound but for the howling in his ears. There wasn't much to see as they walked, the ground a barren wasteland. Crumbling structures of ancient ruins surrounded them, corroded metal sticking out of cement here and there. Hell was almost like a mirror image of Earth but decayed and dying.

Zane stepped over the cracked ground, his boots crunching on the bones of creatures he had never seen before. The worst was the heat.

A river of lava flowed a couple of miles away — where the Ohio River should have been. It made the atmosphere unbearable, like a thick coat hanging in the air, pressing down on them. His actual coat stuck to his skin, overheating his body. The humidity made the air virtually unbreathable. Zane struggled, taking short breaths while he clutched Sinohne's hand.

Sinohne was not fazed, used to the environment. "We must head south, opposite from the bridge!"

He pointed to the broken structure over the river of lava, and they began their trek through Hell. Ten minutes turned into twenty…thirty. Their hike went on forever for the angel, his limbs growing heavier with every step he took. The two companions climbed over stone and rock, harsh sand and dirt whipping at their bodies.

To Zane's relief, Sinohne finally stopped and gestured to a massive rift in the ground before them. He pointed, and Zane squinted, unable to make out what the demon wanted him to see.

"We're here," Sinohne shouted over the wind.

He wrapped an arm around Zane's waist. Before the angel could question him, his stomach dropped as Sinohne jumped them into the rift.

Did Zane scream like a little girl?

Why, yes. Yes, he did.

He clutched onto Sinohne's shoulders, his eyes squeezed tight, yelling for dear life.

"I don't wanna' die!"

Sinohne landed smoothly enough he had to shake the angel to get him to notice. Zane opened one eye, whipping his head around.

They stood on a ledge facing the wall of a sheer cliff, not falling to their deaths. He let out a *whoosh* of breath and punched Sinohne in the shoulder.

"What the fuck, dude? A little warning, please!" Zane hugged the cliff side.

"My bad."

Sinohne proceeded forward, stepping through the cliff wall as if it didn't exist.

Zane hesitated before following, stepping through with extreme caution. On the other side, he let out another large exhale. "I'm getting really sick of all these new surprises."

Sinohne rolled his eyes. "Welcome, little angel, to Hell's royal faction; Pride," he announced. "Do not leave my side and do not make eye contact...with anyone. If we see others, you are my slave. My property, nothing more. Only address me by my title; Lieutenant Sinohne, Master, or Sir. Take your pick. Understand?"

Zane frowned, then he nodded. "What do you think we'll find here? Won't your lord want me dead?"

"Best-case scenario, Baelozar will try. I'll convince him otherwise. You're valuable. He'd be foolish to dispose of you."

The angel paled. "What's the worst-case scenario?"

Sinohne, ignoring the question, turned away, starting down the corridor ahead.

Zane hurried after him. "Hey, wait up!"

Mirrors with dark, ornate, wooden frames hung every few feet on either side of the corridor. Every so often they passed heavy, wooden doors, all open, the rooms filled with treasures and luxurious furnishings. Sinohne stepped inside each chamber. His shoulders became stiffer with every empty room they passed. Zane kept quiet, but his stomach knotted with anxiety. When they approached a pair of large, wooden double doors, Sinohne told him to wait. The demon moved closer to the doors, listening.

"What room is this?" Zane whispered.

"The main greeting chamber, where Baelozar sees his minions."

Sinohne pushed lightly and the heavy, solid wood swung open. Immediately, Zane's nostrils were assaulted, the air reeking of burned flesh. He gagged, covering his mouth.

Before them, a giant puddle of black fluid covered the floor, body parts strewn everywhere; clawed feet, hands, torsos, tails...there was a pair of legs, cut off at the knees, still standing as if a laser had vaporized the rest of the body. Near the other end of the room, charred furniture legs and scraps of cloth laid in front of a large burn mark on the wall.

Zane leaned into the door, his knees weak. "My god...what happened here?"

Sinohne turned on his heel, roughly pulling Zane out of the room. "We're going to work," he said, his voice thick. He stalked back down the hall, wildly ripping mirrors off the walls.

Zane barely avoided the glass shards which flew around like shrapnel. "Why?"

Sinohne growled. "Because Lord Baelozar is missing and my faction smells like death. The only damned demon ballsy enough to try, is that bastard, Culzahr. I'm going to find the greedy beast and tear his skin from his bones!"

Zane followed Sinohne down the corridor, through the cliff wall, and Sinohne jumped them to the top of the rift. On the surface, the two headed back toward the river of lava.

Sinohne clutched the angel's hand, lost in thought, trying to control his rising bloodlust. The rest of their journey together remained silent, solemn. Sinohne was glad of it, he didn't want to hear words of comfort. All he wanted to do was pluck out Culzahr's eyeballs, carve open his chest then lick his claws clean. He'd savor the moment when the demon breathed his last.

Zane's hand was suddenly wrenched from his grasp.

Sinohne whipped around to see Zane sprawled across the ground. He scanned the area. "Are you all right?"

Zane grimaced. He took Sinohne's hand to stand — then froze.

On top of a crumbling wall, a creature stared at them, cocking its head left...right...uncertain of what to make of the pair. The creature had three long claws on each paw and spindly arms and legs like a sloth. Its muzzle jutted out, razor teeth lining every inch, saliva dripping off the tips. It had bat-like ears, little beady eyes, a round body covered in scales, and two horns jutting straight out of its forehead.

"Wings-s-s-s...I smell the blood...the wings-s-s," a loud, haunting noise called.

When the ground beneath them shook, Zane blanched. Sinohne stepped in front of the angel and hissed. The creature bristled, its back arching, but it scampered away.

Sinohne yanked Zane to his feet. "Run!" he bellowed into Zane's ear, gripping his hand tight. They took off, the ruins around them shaking. A second tremor rent the ground, and Zane was thrown forward against a wall, small pieces of cement falling on top of him. Dazed, Zane found Sinohne beside him, brushing off debris.

"Win-n-n-g-g-g-s-s-s!"

Another loud noise thundered in the air, closer this time. Warm liquid trickled onto Zane's forehead, and he wiped his face, blood staining his palm. "Shit."

A shadow fell across the ground like a storm cloud. Zane twisted around, horror chilling his veins. A creature as tall as a skyscraper towered over them. The demon had a massive torso and legs like an elephant. A large mouth encompassed the entire bottom half of its body, a circular hole of unending teeth.

"Oh, Fuck! Run!" Zane shouted.

And they ran, flying across the sand, tugging each other along as the ground shook with each step of the massive creature.

"This was a very bad idea!" Zane yelled.

Sinohne laughed, but the wind carried the sound away. He looked ahead, running toward the bridge. The massive creature following them wasn't alone anymore. Creatures from little children's worst nightmares had come out of the woodwork. Some of them gathered on the bridge while others surrounded Sinohne and Zane.

Sinohne jumped into the air, his claws extending as he roared. He was a flash of silver, decapitating any creature who came too close to his charge. Zane refused to be the rescued princess. He withdrew the blade in his pocket, shrugging off his trench coat. Sinohne's actions caused a frenzy, some of the demons backing fearfully away as the two closed in on the bridge.

Zane ran, choking on the heat and the smell, his lungs burning from the effort. He was covered in sweat, his clothes soaked, his hair falling into his eyes. He tripped, falling to the ground when a demon swiped at his ankle. Zane rolled away and quickly regained his feet. When the creature's hand shot forward a second time, Zane slashed out with the blade.

The demon screamed in agony and blood sprayed the ground. Zane didn't wait around to finish the job, instead, running across the bridge. More demons grabbed at him. He dodged out of the way, their claws slicing through skin and feathers.

Sinohne returned to his side, his beautiful silver skin now covered in splashes of black fluid. The demon quickly charged forward and rent the air with his claws, a portal opening before them.

Zane had almost reached it when a slimy pink cord wrapped around his waist and jerked him into the air, the blade slipping out of his hand. Sinohne bellowed angrily from the ground.

Zane strained his neck to see his captor. Terror gripped him; the cord was a tongue. He was being pulled toward the massive creature's mouth, its rows of teeth spinning.

Sinohne grabbed the blade off the ground and leapt into the air. "Zane!"

The angel turned as Sinohne tossed him the dagger. Zane fumbled to catch it properly, and the blade sliced through his palm like butter. He yanked out the dagger, forgoing the pain so he could get *the fuck* out of the giant's tongue.

The creature screamed as he hacked at the slimy limb, blood making the hilt slippery.

With one last cut, Zane dropped toward the ground with alarming speed. Sinohne dove, catching him before Zane smashed his pretty face on the bridge. The silver demon slashed open another portal and jumped through, it vanishing quickly behind them.

They skidded across the ground, landing in the parking lot outside Infernal Avarice. Zane inhaled large gulps of normal air, sprawled atop the demon's lap. Sinohne panted, leaning his head against the wall. He glanced down and caught Zane's gaze.

They both burst into laughter.

Zane slapped Sinohne's shoulder in mocking reprimand. "That was a very bad idea. Holy cow! Did you see the size of him? I would've been like a damned Hot Pocket! What in the hell *was* that?"

"It's one of the ancient creatures from the Hell dimension. And they just love snacking on angels. You're all like little chicken wings to them." Sinohne snorted and started laughing again. "I haven't seen the Legion so crazed since the wars. It was nuts!"

Zane agreed and, wired on adrenaline, giggled like a fool. He surveyed the parking lot, his car still where he'd left it the other day. The thought sobered him, and he leaned forward. "We should go inside."

He stood, his palm aching with the effort.

Sinohne got to his feet, shaking out his right hand.

"Hey, what'd you do?" Zane asked.

"It just burns a little."

Zane caught his arm. He turned up Sinohne's palm. A circle with a star and strange symbols had appeared, the skin blackened. "This is the same palm we used to form the contract."

Sinohne pulled out of his grip. "It's nothing. Don't worry about it. How's your hand? You look a little banged up yourself."

Zane raised his hand, but the injury had almost healed. "Yeah...I should probably not try to catch sharp pointy things anymore." Zane shook his head. "Don't change the subject. We need to talk about this mark on your palm."

Sinohne walked toward the side entrance. "Later. There are more important things to deal with." He paused, glancing back. "You fought bravely…for an angel."

TWENTY-ONE

Zane opened the door, peeking his head inside. On tiptoe, he eased over the threshold.

The door slammed.

Zane whipped around.

The fuck? he mouthed to the demon.

Sinohne shrugged, unconcerned, and continued forward.

They stood in the middle of the dance floor, Zane glanced about. The building was unusually silent. Lights were on, but he could see a chain locking the doors to the front entrance.

"I don't think anyone's here..." Zane whispered.

Sinohne frowned. "Why are you whispering?" His voice echoed in the empty building.

Zane held a finger to his mouth. "Shhhh!"

"What? If we're alone, no one will hear us anyway."

Sinohne hopped onto the stage, sitting on the edge. His tail twitched anxiously. Zane followed him, leaning into the platform, unease pricking at his neck.

They waited for a while until Sinohne lost patience. The demon pulled his cell from his back pocket. Zane raised an eyebrow, honestly wondering how the phone had fit within the tight leathers. His lips twitched at the thought, and he turned away, stifling another laughing fit.

Sinohne selected a number from his contacts then held the cell to his ear. After a few rings, the call was answered. Sinohne narrowed his eyebrows, his expression darkening. "Ah…hello, Rylan."

Zane strained his ears, trying to hear the voice on the other end, but to no avail.

"I was hoping to speak with Victor. He has my truck. Do you know when he'll be returning…Oh? Indisposed?"

Sinohne glanced at Zane, his lips drawing into a thin line. "We've been waiting here at work. Strange. The doors are all chained…Yes. Zane is here, too." He paused. "No, we'll wait."

Sinohne ended the call, setting the phone on the stage.

"What's going on?"

Sinohne turned to him, crossing his arms over his chest. "Bringing them to us. I prefer a setting on my terms." His glamor reappeared. "Prepare yourself. He sounded too pleasant for my liking."

Zane raised an eyebrow. "When is Rylan ever pleasant?"

"Precisely."

"What if Cyrus...er, Culzahr—fuck, whatever—is with him? Can we stop him?" Zane chewed the inside of his lip.

Sinohne exhaled a deep breath. "If Culzahr shows, I have a chance against them. Either way, this will not be peaceful."

Zane scoffed. "I don't doubt it. Dam' and Victor are both MIA. Seems like such a happy coincidence."

Sinohne agreed with Zane's sarcastic sentiment. He wondered whether Victor had survived the events back at the Pride faction. If not, Sinohne was anxious to unleash the monster the angels feared.

To both their surprise, his question was soon answered, as three portals opened in the middle of the floor.

Rylan stepped out on the far left, holding the end of a chain connected to a shackle around the throat of another demon. Maribel followed close behind them.

From the right, Dale and Carl emerged with gleeful grins.

The last to emerge, from the center, was Cyrus. He held a velvet bag, tied off with a string. Black liquid dripped out of the bottom. As nonchalantly as you please, Cyrus set the bag on the floor then took a seat at the table behind him. The portals vanished, and the room once again fell silent.

"I thought you said only your faction could open those," Zane whispered to Sinohne under his breath. "And, so much for no cell towers."

Sinohne's expression darkened, remembering the singer's earlier quip. He shook his head. "Two fucking peas."

Zane studied the demon on Rylan's chain.

The demon had forest green skin with glittering scales, which covered the softest parts of his body. His hair was a deep, golden blonde, long enough to run hands through. Two braids dangled at the nape of his neck. The demon had wings like a dragon, their tips trailing into sharp spikes. The demon's pointed ears were set beside a face with sharp, angular cheekbones. A dash of scales followed the lines of the demon's face, and pointed teeth poked out over his lips. His hands and feet were clawed, spines protruding from his ankles.

Seeing the demon, Sinohne sighed with relief. Then he gestured to Zane. "Don't look now. But there's our boy."

Zane blinked. "Victor...?"

He examined the demon again. His blue eyes sparkled like jewels, the pupils now reptilian slits. It took a moment, but he could see the similarities.

Victor noticed Sinohne and shifted toward him. Rylan jerked him backward on his chain, but the demon struggled against him in earnest. Rylan raised his hand.

"Don't!" Sinohne yelled.

Rylan froze and stared deliberately at Sinohne for a moment, then backhanded his prisoner, forcing him onto his knees.

Sinohne glared. He jumped from the stage, advancing toward Rylan.

"Ah, ah, ah," Cyrus spoke from his table across the room. "You haven't opened your present yet, *ambassador*."

Dale and Carl cackled, sending chills down Zane's spine.

Zane grabbed Sinohne's arm, pushing the demon behind him. "Let me."

Sinohne studied his face but then nodded, expression grim. "Go."

When Zane reached the bag, he knelt and pulled at the rope holding the bag shut. The material fell away. Zane gagged, the smell of burnt flesh assaulting his nose. He struggled to control his reaction, but couldn't stop himself and twisted away, dry retching. When Zane finally pulled himself together again, he clamped a hand over his nose, studying the bloodied flesh.

Half a severed head lay before him, the face still frozen in a confused state, the other half burned away at an angle. A short horn protruded from the temple, curling toward an ear, red hair matted against the skin. The eyes bothered him most; an odd but familiar emptiness.

Confused, Zane turned back to Sinohne, who gripped the stage with white knuckles, fury in his eyes. "Who is this?" Zane asked. But Sinohne was too busy glaring daggers at Cyrus.

Cyrus smirked and dropped his glamor. Rylan and Maribel took his cue, dropping their glamor as well.

"Whose head is this?" Zane repeated.

"Baelozar. Demon Lord of Pride," Sinohne announced, snarling at the others across the room. Zane's eyes widened in surprise.

Maribel giggled, a forked tongue flicking out between her fangs and lips. "Um! *Ex*-demon lord, babe."

The hair on Maribel's head had vanished, leaving her completely bald. Her ears had grown bat-like, and her skin had turned to pastel pink, a short covering of maroon fur dashed along her skin. A glittering chain wrapped around her body, held up by piercings through her nipples, belly button and settled on her hips.

Maribel placed a clawed hand on Victor's shoulder, and he winced. When she pulled away, black blood trickled out of the spots where she'd touched. Maribel brought her fingers to her lips, then licked them clean while sending the angel a flirtatious smile.

Zane made a disgusted face. "What the fuck?"

"Mirul is a succubus, a demon from Lust," Sinohne explained. "Her fingertips can drain the energy of anything she touches."

Beside her, Rylan lifted Mirul's hand and kissed her palm, pulling her against him. "Beautiful."

Zane looked away, revolted.

Rylan's body had grown even more massive, his muscles doubled in size. His skin was pitch-black, shiny, his hair slicked against his skull. Horns jutted out from his temples, twisting toward the ceiling, the tips sharp needle points, gleaming a stark, polished pearl white. Like the others, he had fangs, claws, pointed ears, and a tail with a dangerous-looking spine on the end.

At his side, Victor was leaning forward, head dropped, breathing heavily. Rylan lowered his bright, yellow eyes. He dug his claws into the already bleeding wounds Mirul had created, his sneer full of pure arrogance.

Victor cried out in pain, the sound causing a growl to erupt from behind Zane.

"Remove your hand, Rhaisur," Sinohne warned, murderous energy emanating from the demon.

Zane straightened, leaving the mutilated head on the floor.

Rhaisur's lips curled back into a maniacal grin, deliberately digging his claws in harder. Victor struggled, but he was too weak to do much more than bare his own fangs in rebellion.

"Barely a reaction when your master is killed…but the anger you're showing now? And about a mere servant?" Culzahr tapped his claws on the table, a consistent, slow drumming. "*Ambassador*, are you aware of what has happened? Your faction has been decimated…only a few remain. But they'll be hunted down. I'll personally see to it myself. And…once you are gone, we will march upon Lucifer."

"I'm unimportant. My death, and Pride's destruction, won't help you in your quest, Culzahr," Sinohne replied.

Culzahr stood, his horns gleaming under the lights. He reached inside his jacket. In his hand was a large stone, as blue as a sapphire.

Zane gasped. "What is that?" He glanced at Sinohne, who had stepped up beside him.

"Something impossible," Sinohne whispered. "Unless, of course, you were colluding with a general from Heaven." He gestured to the stone. "A soul vessel, I should've known. Dammit. You can contain millions of souls and harness their raw energy as a weapon. You saw what they're capable of at my faction's lair."

"Fuck."

Sinohne snorted. "About sums it."

Culzahr slammed the stone onto the table, refocusing their attention. "What are you two whispering over there? Do you really think I've been fooled? I've destroyed your faction! Yet your body was not among the dead, Sinohne!"

From their position near the edge of the stage, where they'd been observing the scene unfold, Carl and Dale retreated to a dark corner. Mirul gasped, taking a step behind her lover. Rhaisur's grin disappeared. He snatched his hand from Victor's shoulder.

Sinohne chuckled and kneeled toward Baelozar's severed head. He took in the shock frozen in Baelozar's remaining eye. Grabbing the head by the only horn left, he stood and dropped his glamor, the splashes of blood from earlier still covering his skin.

"The ironic thing is, Culzahr," Sinohne murmured, his tone low. "Without Baelozar, no one knows the King's location." He flung the head at the demon lord across the room.

Culzahr dodged, stepping to the side. Bloodied flesh slapped savagely into the wall behind him, leaving a trail of black liquid as it slid to the floor. Culzahr's rage was palpable. He ripped off his jacket, shredding the material of his shirt with his claws. "Not possible!"

The corners of Sinohne's lips turned up, a sly grin which only caused Culzahr's already furious expression to twist further. "Not even I know where he can be found. Baelozar was his favored and most-trusted minion." Sinohne gestured to the enemy before him. "For good reason."

Culzahr snarled. He seized the stone from the table, holding it in their direction. Malice flashed in his eyes. "If you're not useful, then you're just in my way."

Zane held up his hands. "Whoa. Hold on. We can work this out still — !"

"*Scriogelen!*"

The stone blazed a brilliant blue. A beam of light shot across the room, heading straight for Sinohne. Victor screamed. Zane tackled the demon beside him.

They landed in a heap on the floor, Sinohne's arms wrapping around him protectively. The stage exploded, pieces of wood and metal flying in all directions. Smoke filled the room, and Sinohne lifted a hand, his palm burning. Crimson blood mixed with black, the back of his hands charred from the blast.

Zane raised himself onto his arms and rolled off Sinohne. "Or not," Zane said as he coughed.

Sinohne sat forward, eyes wide. The silver demon watched his friend move away, shocked by his rescue. No one had ever saved his life — never sacrificed their own flesh, nor their own blood — for his safety.

But Sinohne knew why his palm ached now.

The angel's already mangled wing had been vaporized in the blast, the price of his rescue. The skin on the angel's right side was scorched, blistered and bleeding. Only remnants of the bandages which had bound the crippled wing to Zane's body were left. His shirt hung in tatters off his other shoulder, half-melted to flesh. Thankfully, the other wing was still intact.

The sound of rattling chains made Sinohne pause in his assessment. He glanced across the room to Victor, who was still struggling to reach them, pulling hard against his shackles.

"Sinohne!" Victor gnashed his teeth and snarled.

Rhaisur became fed up and tossed him onto a nearby table. The table gave way, breaking apart beneath him.

Culzahr snapped his fingers. Carl and Dale withdrew from the shadows and advanced toward Sinohne. Sinohne kneeled and hissed, his claws extending. The two strongmen stopped in their tracks.

A golden portal suddenly opened with a sharp electric crackle.

Culzahr sneered, his confidence returned.

Alatos stepped through the portal, dragging a bruised and bleeding Damaceous with him, his wrists shackled. The general left the unconscious angel's body splayed out in front of Culzahr, Damaceous's wings crumpled beneath him.

Culzahr laughed, throwing his head back, his victory now assured.

TWENTY-TWO

"The Council is ready to see you now."

General Remiel nodded and followed the attendant as he pushed open the entrance leading to the High Council meeting room. The general ran his hand along one of the heavy metal doors while he passed over the threshold, the intricate designs carved into the ancient golden entrance cool against his fingertips.

The doors depicted the long history of Heaven, from the times of the Atlantic Empire to the last Great War between demons and angels. The relief was a mixture of black and yellow gold, to distinguish between the species. The images were always a sight to behold and stood as a reminder of what all those who'd sat among the Council had witnessed. When Remiel had first taken his station, the general had been intimidated, unsure of himself. Now the doors were a calm, constant touchstone in an ever-changing world.

His steps echoed, sandaled feet slapping across the pearly-white marble floor, and he gazed at the golden dome above. He was able to see the stars beyond the delicate tapestry, a swirling design of vines and flowers some long-ago blacksmith had painstakingly created. He'd known the name once but now...Remiel couldn't seem to recall, his mind filled only with a sense of dread. The room before him curved, the walls decorated with paintings, statues, artifacts; a museum of their long-dead empire. In the center of the room was a round table made of thick stone, the center an inverted glass dome.

There were fifteen wooden chairs, twelve carved to tell the individual story of each member of the Council. The middle four chairs were taller, indicating the seats of the Seraphim, the highest order and most powerful angels of their society. Eight of the remaining chairs were for the lower Council members, the Cherubim. The three chairs left, plain and dark, were for the generals of the separate dominions; Virtues, Powers, and Warriors.

Only General Remiel chose to attend on a regular basis. Their chairs were meant as symbols for the generals; leadership wasn't comfortable. It was a lesson the general was still learning, even after ten thousand years.

The Seraphim were already seated per usual, each with a black cloth wrapped around their eyes. According to their mythology, after having spoken to the Creator, their eyes were burned away. Perhaps, their eyes shone too bright, or the Seraphim chose to suppress one of their senses to stave off madness. No one knew the truth.

Seated in the first of the taller chairs was Azrael, the Angel of Death, who aided all souls in their transition to the afterlife. His wings were the blackest of black, the darkest abyss, not even light reflecting off his feathers. He was unusually tall, rail thin, and had pale skin which glowed, barely containing the immense power held within his body. But his slicked-back hair was dyed a platinum blonde, and he wore the brightest clothing imaginable.

Today, he was clad in a bright neon-yellow shirt with a symbol of some cute yellow creature on the front. Remiel couldn't see what Azrael wore on his legs but assumed it was something just as cringe-worthy. The Angel of Death was very powerful yet seemed to hold a strange humor for bright fabrics found in the modern world of Earth.

The second Seraphim, Ariel, the Angel of Nature, was known as Mother Earth to some. She fulfilled the duty of preserving Earth's ecosystem and protecting its wildlife. It was she who inspired those who fought against animal abuse and the destruction of natural habitats. She, who inspired those who worked to preserve nature as it was intended—a battle which became harder with every passing day.

Ariel's complexion was dark, her hair a deep chestnut with vines and twigs woven into a decorative barrette she clipped to the side of her temple. Her tanned skin helped camouflage the adorable baby fox she cuddled in her arms; Remiel wouldn't have known it was there except she was scratching behind the creature's ear while the animal slept against her bosom. Her wings were the color of a romantic sunset; dark purples against shades of red and orange. She was dressed in a pale, purple gown, flounces cascading over her arms.

In contrast, Chamuel, the third Seraphim, had skin the color of alabaster. Her hair was pitch-black and cut short, sticking up in stylish spikes. The angel's body was thin, clothed in a light-gray suit with Capri pants. Her feet were encased in high heels, studded with diamonds. It was her version of a modern politician. Her wings were a sparkling white, glittering like diamonds, even in the smallest amount of light. Chamuel was the Angel of Peaceful Relations, tasked with inspiring love, harmony, and compromise, even among hated rivals. She was responsible for the specialized task force in the Virtues Dominion which dealt with global politics.

Last, but never least, Michael, the warrior, the protector, the Angel of Righteousness and Justice. He was the last of the Empire, the rest killed off during the wars with Lucifer, after his initial betrayal. He had dishwater-blonde hair and a strong, sculpted jaw covered by a short beard. His body was hardy and muscular, clad in a full set of bright, silver armor. Michael had thoroughly enjoyed the medieval era and styled his battle armor after the knights he'd favored. Small plating was set along the upper—and sturdiest—bones of his wings, whose feathers captured all the shades of blue; sapphire to sky, pastel to ocean.

Remiel entered the room, surprised to see one of the plain chairs occupied. The angel turned her head toward him at the sound of his footsteps and smiled a small smile not reflected in her eyes. Her expression was troubled as she stood to greet him, her wings giving off a dusting of gold with every movement.

"General."

"Commander Jophiel."

The general bowed with a hand over his chest, the other hand outstretched for hers. When she took his hand, he placed a chaste kiss on the back in respect and straightened.

Commander Jophiel was tall—taller than him—with voluptuous hips and dark, mocha skin. Her eyes were a molten gold, no pupil to be seen, glowing with power, matching the golden feathers of her wings. The commander's face was all soft curves, and her lips were full, complementing a narrow chin. Her brown curls were swept to the side and pinned by a gold, decorative barrette as they cascaded around her head. Her dress swayed, the sheer golden skirts slit to her waist on each side, not doing much to cover the details beneath. As the Angel of Beauty in Life, one only had to gaze upon her to see why.

Commander Jophiel was the leader of the Virtues Dominion. But she had relinquished her seat among the Seraphim to Ariel two hundred thousand years ago when Remiel had still been climbing the ranks of his dominion. Out of respect for her former position, Jophiel was referred to as Commander rather than General; the deciding vote among the three dominions.

She removed her hand from Remiel's, and both angels took their seats at the table.

The general peered around nervously. Of all the Council members, only the four Seraphim were seated. The rest were not in attendance.

"Where are the Cherubim?" the general whispered, leaning toward Jophiel. She shook her head, unsure herself.

"The Cherubim will not be joining us today."

Remiel winced, shocked to hear the voice of the Seraphim, Michael. In all his time attending their meetings, not once had the Seraphim uttered a single word in his presence.

The general licked his lips, his mouth dry. "May I..." He cleared his throat. "May I ask why not, Councilmen?"

Azrael turned his head in Remiel's direction as if his covered eyes were examining the general's soul. Perhaps they were. "The Cherubim are busy dealing with the duties we were asked to abandon for this *urgent* meeting. Do you think we, Seraphim, can drop everything and be at your beck and call? Are you so arrogant, general?"

Remiel bowed his head in deference. "No, Councilor. I apologize if the urgency of this meeting has inconvenienced you in any way." Azrael had a right to be annoyed. As the Angel of Death, his duties overshadowed all others. The angel was a rarity at High Council meetings. For him to show when asked indicated to Remiel the importance Azrael placed on the matter.

The general continued. "I hope we can resolve this issue quickly, in a way which will suit the atrocities committed. As you know, I called this meeting because the investigation my lieutenant carried out has led to disturbing and, now, *real* proof. We have witnesses who can give sworn statements and a file detailing all of it, written by General Alatos himself."

Azrael nodded. "The Cherubim brought out the records of the Fallen and those who Sleep for me to look over. The discrepancies you mentioned in your message are confirmed. In just the last three hundred years, eighty-one angels sent to the Warriors Dominion were reported to Sleep, or Fall, mere months after arriving."

He leaned forward on his elbows, his jaw muscles twitching. "The total count of human souls has barely diminished, but the number of missing is still in the high thousands. Do we know what General Alatos or this demon lord are doing with these souls?"

"No, but there is speculation," Remiel confirmed. "One of my investigators, unaware of this situation, found out the likely intention; killing Lucifer. But, General Alatos's ambition, ultimately, remains unclear."

Michael turned his head to the other three Seraphim then back to Remiel. "Is it true your investigator is in the custody of General Alatos, with permission from Lieutenant Ashliel? And due to your own orders ten years ago, Zhanerious was abandoned, then tortured at the hands of Lieutenant Khamael?"

Jophiel gasped. "Tell me it's not true!"

"I have no defense. But...I do have an explanation."

Remiel waited.

Chamuel nodded, gesturing for him to continue.

"Lieutenant Ashliel initially discovered the discrepancies in the reports General Alatos filed. I advised her to get close with him but not to reveal her intention. I was afraid he would destroy all evidence if he were caught...and a part of me hoped this wasn't true. He's a colleague and a great angel."

"For years, there was nothing more. Or at least nothing to connect him directly to. Then, one day, Zhanerious came to us. He approached Lieutenant Ashliel and professed to have seen for himself the torture and mutilation of younglings. He said he even had proof. Unfortunately, I was here, in a meeting. She left him to come fetch me."

Remiel paused. "But...on her way, General Alatos confronted her, having overheard the entire conversation between them. There was no way for Lieutenant Ashliel to stop the general from retrieving Zhanerious without revealing her intent. I had given her express orders which stated, under no circumstances was General Alatos to ever find out about the investigation. Had she known Zhanerious carried a written file, she would never have allowed him to be taken."

"Days later, we both went to the Warriors Dominion to rescue him and stop General Alatos. But Zhanerious had disappeared, then, later, registered as Sleeping. When I finally found him, he was living on Earth, surrounded by demons and…Lord Culzahr. Zhanerious had lost his memory. There was no way to know if he'd really seen anything."

Remiel rubbed his neck, the weight of his decisions heavier with expected. "Since then, I've posed as his neighbor, Remus. I kept watch, tried to protect him, just in case. Lieutenant Ashliel still wakes up with nightmares and I…cannot forgive myself. She believed in me, trusted me to keep them safe, and…I used her trust to create opportunities. But…I…have deep regrets. I *never* wanted this. I was arrogant…foolish."

Remiel stood then stepped back from the table. He bowed low, and extended his wings, kneeling on the floor. "I'm willing to give up my position as general and take whatever punishment you decree if it will satisfy the Council."

Chamuel waved away the suggestion. "Not necessary. You made *grave* errors in judgment. But you will rectify them."

Michael remained silent, but his disapproval was evident in the lines of his face and the purse of his lips. The Seraphim leaned back in his chair and crossed his arms over his chest, the metal guards on his forearms scraping against his heavy silver breastplate.

Ariel gestured in front of her. An image appeared in the glass dome before them. She quietly petted her fox as she watched the hologram brighten and snap into focus.

Zane and Sinohne, the silver demon of Pride, stood in the middle of a large room. They argued with several other demons in the room. The angels watched while the events on Earth played out in real time.

When Culzahr pulled out the stone, Azrael leapt to his feet. He slammed his hands on the table. "How does he have his hands on a soul vessel? They are locked in our vaults!"

All the angels watched, powerless to stop Culzahr when the piercing beam shot from the stone. But Remiel's heart sank most when Alatos appeared with Damaceous in tow, battered and bloodied.

The image froze on a three-dimensional hologram of Zane, hovering within the glass dome.

General Remiel gazed across the table to see Chamuel turning her wrist and cocking her head to the side, manipulating the image. She flicked a finger, and Zane's image moved closer to her. His right hand extended, exposing marks on his palm.

After examining the image, Chamuel waved her hand in dismissal. The hologram disappeared. "General Remiel. You are officially tasked with returning the angel, Zhanerious, to Heaven. By whatever means necessary, he is to return safely to our realm."

Ariel turned to her. "Chamuel?"

"Zhanerious has accomplished the act of establishing a peace treaty. A treaty none have negotiated since the age of the Atlantic empire. With not just any demon, but the new heir to the throne of Hell, Sinohne of Pride. It cannot be overlooked or ignored."

Azrael straightened from his brooding position. "I would like to propose a promotion." He retook his chair.

Commander Jophiel pursed her lips. "Such a trivial matter should wait."

"Yes, Commander. But in this case, I agree," Michael said. Remiel narrowed his eyes as the other Seraphim nodded.

Azrael smiled. "Zhanerious will be promoted to Thrones."

Remiel's eyes widened. "You can't! The power alone will drive him mad. He's too young!"

Ariel scratched the ear of the fox in her arms, the tiny creature mewing happily. "We can place a temporary compulsion to protect his mind. But even I can see...Zhanerious is special."

The general considered. A Thrones was the enforcer of High Council law, given the power to play judge, jury, and executioner, if warranted. Acting independently of the dominions, Thrones were more powerful than any general, their authority rivaling the Council.

Ages had passed without a need for a Thrones, and none had held the title since the wars.

"And what of Sinohne?" Remiel said, standing to leave.

Chamuel raised an eyebrow. "His safety is just as important, general. This treaty is worthless with his death. The method was flawed but without Lucifer...one day, there could be peace between our species. But only if Zhanerious and Sinohne live."

The general bowed to the Seraphim. "I will go and retrieve them, now."

TWENTY-THREE

Remiel stepped out of the room, and Ashliel looked up from where she leaned against the wall, eagerly waiting for him. She straightened, dressed for battle. Her armor was made of a hardened metal that was a silver color as much as it was blue. The general enjoyed seeing her in it. The color reminded him of her eyes, which in turn warmed his heart. Her forearms and shins were covered in armor plating, while leather encompassed her feet and hands. Her lower torso was enclosed in scaled armor, allowing for swift movement. A breastplate covered her sternum.

Her hips were clad in black leather, which she had set beneath her metal skirt. At her sides were two short swords, each blade gleaming from a recent polish and sharpening, the hilts wrapped in plain leather. The lieutenant's hair, which normally hung in a long braid, was now twisted into a plaited bun, poison needles stuck deep within. More hidden weapons were on her person, but the general knew they were better kept secret.

The armored lieutenant strode forward, her expression anxious and grim.

"Have you been waiting long?" The general brushed the back of his hand over the lieutenant's cheek, the pad of his thumb tracing her bottom lip.

Ashliel shook her head with a sigh, leaning into his hand. "No. What have they decided? Are you...are you still...?"

The tension in Remiel's neck released, happy Ashliel still cared for him enough to worry after their disagreement over Damaceous's capture.

Remiel kissed her forehead. "Yes, love. I have kept my position as general."

She blew out a breath in relief. Remiel frowned, the next moments on his mind. "General Alatos and Lord Culzahr are, at this very moment, in battle with Zhanerious and the demon, Sinohne. Damaceous is with them but in chains. I've been tasked with ensuring their safety."

Her eyes widened, but she nodded curtly.

They moved down the hall.

"What of Lieutenant Khamael?"

Remiel glanced at her while they walked. "When I return, we will take him into custody. He must answer for his crimes."

Ashliel bowed, fist over her heart. "With your permission, I will take him into custody while you are gone. When you return, you'll no doubt be too exhausted to enter another battle. I trust the contingent of guards I chose. Their abilities should be more than enough for me to subdue the lieutenant."

"No," Remiel replied. "Lieutenant Khamael is dangerous, even for me. Do not approach him until I return."

"But, I—!"

"That's an order, lieutenant."

Ashliel hesitated, stubborn to her core, but nodded. "Yes, general."

"Now…I should go. Time is running out."

Remiel stopped and closed his eyes to concentrate. An aura of gold surrounded him. When the aura disappeared, Remiel was dressed for war. His armor was platinum, similar in style to the cladding of both his lieutenant and the other leaders of the Powers Dominion.

His weapon of choice was a bow and arrow, but for close combat, he wielded two daggers, strapped to his thighs. Like Michael, the Seraphim, his wings were plated in armor, the practice of most angels in Heaven.

Remiel opened a portal to Earth, the energy crackling like static. Then he smiled at Ashliel. "I'll return soon."

Remiel stepped through.

"Be careful...I love you!" she called, but the portal had already closed—and he was gone.

Striding forward, Ashliel exited the Council building then took off from the platform. Her wings pumped, adrenaline coursing through her body. She was joined by eight other angels, male and female Powers, all clad in silver armor.

One of the angels saluted. "Lieutenant. Where is the general?"

"Earth," Ashliel replied. "Head for the Warriors compound. Lieutenant Khamael must not escape!"

"Come, little pet," Culzahr crooned at Sinohne, his smile wide.

Sinohne continued to hiss in warning, keeping Zane between him and the stage. The contract compelled him to protect the angel, and he did so, willingly. After Zane's bold rescue, he'd forever hold the angel in high esteem. Zane's body had paid the price for saving his life; even now his friend struggled to stand, his limbs shaking from blood loss. But the sight of Damaceous, shackled and unconscious, had lit a fire in the angel's eyes, and he was busy staring at General Alatos across the room.

Sinohne's lips curled back. "Fuck off, Culzahr, you filthy pest."

Culzahr snarled, taking a step forward, his claws extending. He flicked his head in Sinohne's direction. The bouncers quickly advanced. The fear they had displayed earlier was gone now they'd taken on their demonic forms; Drauxon from Wrath, and Caerum from Greed.

Drauxon's horns protruded forward from his head, his skin a grayish leather. His fingers had melded into two large digits with razor-sharp talons, which he used to support himself as he leaned forward, like an ape, scratching his nails into the floor. His eyes were bulging, having grown twice as large, their frenzied, crimson sclera surrounding reptilian pupils. Each eyeball darted around, the left eye moving in a different direction from the right, like a chameleon.

Caerum looked as wild as a starved wolfman. His limbs were long and spindly, his knees bent backward, and a snout shot out from his ugly face. The snout was filled with pointed teeth. His eyes were yellow, beady things, both laser-focused on Sinohne.

Drauxon jumped up to the height of the club's balcony, then dive-bombed through the air, screeching a high, dark whine from his shrunken mouth; a round hole filled with pale, rotating teeth. Sinohne dodged the demon with ease; both demons moved too slow to stop him.

Sinohne launched himself toward Drauxon and slashed at his back. The demon cried out, falling to the floor. The lieutenant struck Caerum when the second demon tried to attack from behind; his claws sliced away one of the minion's hands. Caerum howled, the sound echoing throughout the nightclub. Both demons bared their teeth but retreated, backing away.

"You made quick work of those guys, dude," Zane said. He shifted his gaze away from Alatos and moved to stand beside Sinohne. His mouth turned upward into a smirk, but Sinohne noticed the corners were white with strain.

"Simple enough for me, of course." Sinohne returned Zane's smile with his own toothy grin. He grabbed Zane's shoulder with a light squeeze. "You saved me earlier. I'm sorry for the price you paid. How're you holding up?"

Zane shook his head. "It sucks. What I can feel hurts like hell. But, mostly, thankfully, I'm numb. If we ever get out of this mess, I'll just make the assholes in Heaven fix me. Okay? No worries, brother."

Sinohne's admiration for the angel grew once more. He pressed their foreheads together in solidarity then turned to refocus on their opponents.

Culzahr appeared less than amused.

Zane snorted. "Hard to find good help these days?"

"Cocky brat," Culzahr spat.

Alatos had stood stoically across the room, watching the action unfold. Now the general chuckled, diverting all attention onto himself. The general's mirth made the hackles on Sinohne's neck rise.

Alatos knelt, his large wings brushing the ground, his robes pooling around his feet. He extended an arm and seized Damaceous's chin. In his free hand, he palmed a dagger. He flipped the hilt around his fingers several times then plunged the knife into Damaceous's shoulder.

Zane gasped and took a faltering step forward. Sinohne moved with Zane, supporting his friend by his waist when Zane took another step.

"Youngling, you have two choices," Alatos said. "Surrender yourself to me, and everyone lives, except the demon." He pointed to Sinohne. "Or...fight and die, including Damaceous."

Zane swallowed. He watched as Alatos reached for the knife, drawing it ever-so-slowly out of Damaceous's shoulder. The shackled angel groaned, even though he was still unconscious.

"Don't test my patience for too long, youngling." The general held the dagger up to the light, gory red fluid dripping onto Damaceous's brunette hair below. "The blood on this dagger is not from a false threat."

Zane clenched his teeth, his fists balling. He swayed, but Sinohne supported him. Sinohne grew worried when warm blood from Zane's back seeped onto his hands. Zane shook his head to clear some fuzziness, leaning harder against him. He took another step closer to Alatos. The general beamed, smiling as he touched the tip of his dagger to Damaceous's shoulder again, ready to pierce the angel's skin a second time.

A streaking arrow knocked the knife out of the general's hand.

The arrow rebounded off the hilt, and landed in the wall behind the general, the arrow's gleaming silver reflecting the lights above.

Alatos grasped his bleeding hand and stood, cursing in surprise.

"Still giving impossible choices in battle, Alatos?"

Sinohne turned. He saw a dark-skinned angel clad in sparkling silver armor approaching them. Remiel nodded to Zane, moving to stand next to the two allies.

Alatos glared. *"Remiel?"*

Remiel notched another arrow and trained it on his faithless colleague. "You have been found guilty of treasonous, disturbing crimes. I have collected evidence and brought it before the Council. You have all but damned yourself to Hell."

Alatos scoffed in denial. But with Remiel's arrival, Culzahr retrieved the stone from the table, pocketing the soul vessel. Rhaisur stepped toward the trio with Mirul at his side, waiting to attack.

"Do you really believe you can take me in for trial? That, between just the three of you, the battle will go in your favor?" Alatos spread his wings, straightening to his full height. "I am the general of Heaven's Army!"

He unsheathed his sword and pointed it at his foe. His expression contorted into pure outrage. The metal of his blade was a dark onyx, reflecting the bloodred rubies twisting out and around the hilt. The blade curved, the edge sharp enough to cut paper.

"Could've fooled me," Zane murmured under his breath.

Remiel glanced at him, his lips pursed, but then he refocused on Alatos.

"Are you really so arrogant you believe you're above our laws? Was torturing angels for some backward strategy worth it? For what? To obtain more power? Your pride and greed are your downfall, Alatos." He spread his own wings in challenge.

Sinohne stepped beside Remiel and extended his claws. He roared, a deafening wave of sound which caused Zane, Rhaisur, and Mirul to cover their ears. "I am now Lord of Pride...the heir to all of Hell. I gladly enter battle beside this general. You will all pay for the deed wrought against my own, dearly."

Culzahr chuckled, returning to his seat. He waved a hand dismissively. "The dramatics of Pride. Give it up."

The ground trembled, the whole building starting to shake. A light fixture plummeted from the ceiling. The three allies jumped apart to avoid the impact as glass and metal shattered on the dance floor.

Zane stumbled, weak, unable to keep his balance. He leaned onto what was left of the stage, the wood still smoldering mere inches away.

"Zane!" Sinohne started to move close again to help him—

Intense thunder erupted above, and the ceiling split open with the light of a golden portal.

Lightning bolts exploded into the room, crackling with electricity. The bolts burst closer and closer to Zane, herding him into a narrow space until he was surrounded. Outside the circle, the light became so bright, Sinohne and everyone else in the room had to shield their eyes as Zane was engulfed in lightning.

For the first time in ages, Sinohne experienced fear. He had never seen the process for himself—the cacophony of lightning, the empowering of an angel—but he remembered the result. Now he backed away, the ground still trembling beneath his feet. Sinohne had personally fought one of the last to hold the legendary title. He had come out of the fight barely alive. To this day, Thrones were the only angels he truly feared.

Everyone watched in wonder as the blinding light faded, though Zane remained engulfed by a cylindrical beam. A final concussive wave of power knocked them all on their asses. And then…the beam disappeared.

No one moved. Gradually, Zane's form came back into focus. He knelt, but he had risen onto the balls of his feet, steam rising quietly from his body, his hair hiding his face.

His remaining wing had been completely restored, not a scratch to be seen. Bright blues and dark greens glowed with a vibrancy absorbed from the lightning, small sparks dancing among his feathers, the colors amplified by his untamed power…a power which throbbed in waves, crashing over them all, even from where he knelt across the room. The other wing was still missing. But the shadow of the appendage crackled, lightning and charged air manifested in its place.

In his hands, Zane held two curved daggers made of blackened steel, spells engraved along the edge, the hilts wrapped in dark leather; simple but deadly weapons. His armor reflected the same style, blackened metal over black leather. The angel's breastplate, angled outward, an image of white wings spread out over his chest, jeweled swords crossing a flame rising within a circle; the symbol of the Thrones. His shoulder plates were pointed, his arms encompassed by scaled gauntlets, his gloved hand encased in armored claws.

Metal plating set along the upper bridge of his wing scraped when he straightened. His boots were dark leather, but bracers protected his shins and calves. Only his thighs had been left bare, his lower body covered by an armored skirt, reminiscent of ancient Roman soldiers.

Zane raised his chin, his expression unreadable. His eyes glowed, the green and blue so vivid Sinohne was forced to lower his gaze as he swallowed anxiously.

"No!" Alatos bellowed from behind them, startling the rest of the room. "It's not possible!" He advanced toward the newly empowered angel, springing upward, taking flight.

Remiel dashed across his path, their weapons clashing.

Zane remained still, his eyes evaluating the battle before him. Without warning, he was gone — then instantly reappeared before Rhaisur, slashing a dagger across his chest before the demon was able to react. Mirul cried out in rage. She attacked — but Zane kicked her backward. Rhaisur hissed, swiping out with a clawed hand. Zane shifted too quickly; the demon struck nothing but thin air.

Victor grunted and sat up from the table where Rhaisur had tossed him, the battle before him mesmerizing. He just hoped all of Zane's newfound energy wouldn't be directed at him because — *Holy shit!* — he was making Rhaisur, the lieutenant of Greed, look like a newbie in training...!

Not seconds after the thought crossed his mind, Zane stood before him like a dark omen. Victor backed away fearfully, pushing against the wall behind the tables. Zane advanced. When he was close enough, the angel squeezed Victor's chains. The chains around the demon's body shattered, and Victor was left dumbfounded as Zane flicked away.

Sinohne launched himself at the two minions, who cowered in the corner. A few seconds of the silver demon's wrath…then Drauxon and Caerum stared out at the room with glassy eyes, death quickly overtaking them.

Mirul screeched from across the room, her frustration and fear evident, but the battle against Zane was useless. Victor watched as Zane smirked and drove his dagger through Raiser's stomach. The angel twisted the blade, and the demon coughed black blood.

"No!" Mirul yelped when Rhaisur stumbled backward. "You can't kill him! Please!"

Zane hesitated, his blade already at the demon's throat. Rhaisur snarled and grabbed his wrist, twisting away while Zane was distracted by Mirul's plea. The angel remained motionless as the two demons opened a portal. Mirul dragged Rhaisur inside, the lieutenant holding his own guts in his hands.

Mirul shot Zane one last glare. "This isn't finished, you buzzard! If he dies, I will come for you."

Victor raised his middle finger when the portal closed around them. "No one gives two dicks, drama queen." He smiled at Zane. The angel ignored him and flicked away to another part of the battle.

TWENTY-FOUR

When he came to, everything hurt. His muscles ached, his wounds stung from hours of torture. Warm lips touched his, energy pouring into his body and reviving his senses. Then, Damaceous moaned. He reached for more of the same but realized his hands were bound. The chains rattled, chafing his already tender skin. The angel opened his eyes, his vision blurry. Blinking, Zane's face came into focus, his midnight hair tickling the wounded angel's cheeks.

"Zane…"

Damaceous's voice was scratchy from disuse, his mouth dry. Zane smiled, reaching for his shackles. Damaceous's chains shattered, to his surprise. Elated, he embraced the singer, renewing — then deepening — their kiss. Energy flowed into him, like nothing he had ever encountered before. His wounds disappeared one by one until he was fully restored.

To his left, someone cleared their throat. Damaceous jerked his head to see a black demon staring at them with disgust.

"Am I going to have to watch you two make out the whole time? Or just until I decide to kill you?" Culzahr growled, baring his fangs.

Damaceous's eyes narrowed. "What?"

The chaos around him came into sudden focus. Above, the two generals—Remiel and Alatos—each breathed heavily, neither one winning the fight. His attention was redirected back to Zane when the angel stood. Damaceous shifted to his feet, Culzahr still in his sights. Sinohne nodded to him from his position across the room.

"What's happening?" Damaceous asked Zane.

The younger angel didn't respond, but power vibrated off his body, and he held out a weapon. Damaceous accepted, happy to have his blade returned. But, when he noticed the symbol on Zane's breastplate, he gasped and took an involuntary step backward.

"Hmph. You're not the only one who's surprised." Unimpressed, Culzahr drummed his fingers on the table behind them.

Zane turned to the demon lord. Culzahr stood, his eyes full of suspicion. Zane advanced toward him, one deliberate step at a time.

Culzahr snarled, his claws extending. "You want to die today? After all I've done for you, you ungrateful buzzard? That's fine by me."

Damaceous shouted in warning as Culzahr lunged forward—but Zane disappeared. The Thrones materialized moments later, a dagger ripping a hole in Culzahr's pants pocket, the stone falling out. Zane grabbed the soul vessel midair and flicked away, faster than anyone could see.

Culzahr howled, grabbing at his pants. *"Where is it!"*

Zane smirked, hovering above them. He held out his hand, the stone resting in his palm, lightning surging out, shooting into the awaiting portal above.

The stone disappeared, and the portal closed.

Culzahr fell to his knees, his mouth hanging open in disbelief. "Where is the stone?"

"The High Council," Zane replied. "Where the souls inside can be safely recovered without further damage." His expression was calm. As if he didn't notice how such a simple act had thwarted a plan decades in the making.

His own plans for the stone now accomplished, the Thrones turned his attention to the generals.

Culzahr's expression contorted, giving off an aura of evil. His shoulders moved with his heavy breathing as he stalked toward the angel. The demon charged, raising an arm, attempting to slash Zane's wing.

Sinohne grabbed his wrist and snarled, stopping him just in time. The greed demon jerked loose, crouching on the balls of his feet, his hair flying around him. Zane moved toward the generals, not paying the others any mind.

"Now, we can finish this, Culzahr." Sinohne took a defensive stance.

Culzahr chuckled. "Even without the soul vessel, you're no match for me, Sinohne."

Damaceous moved to the pride demon's side. "He's not alone."

"One little angel will make no difference."

"Then, let's go!"

Sinohne flashed toward Culzahr, a streak of silver. They collided in a mix of black and silver skin, their claws clashing together. Damaceous launched forward, aiming his blade for Culzahr's side. The demon lord dodged, striking the angel's arm. Damaceous grunted in pain.

Sinohne used the opportunity to come from behind, slashing the other demon's back.

"You damn rat!" Culzahr gnashed his teeth and refocused his attack on Sinohne. He struck quickly, but the silver demon matched him, blow for blow. Sparks flew between their claws. Culzahr bit into Sinohne's shoulder, ripping out flesh.

"Fuck…" Sinohne jumped away, grabbing his arm as blood spilled from the wound.

Damaceous swung downward. He left a gash in Culzahr's upper back, then twisted around and plunged his blade into the demon's side. The opportunity cost him. Culzahr dug his claws into Damaceous's wing, tearing away feathers. "Die, angel!"

Pain lanced through Damaceous's body. He jerked away, taking his blade with him.

Blood gushed out of the wound on Culzahr's side. "I'll kill you both for this!" He hissed, fangs bared, and held his ribs.

"You murdered my people!" Sinohne launched another attack. Dropping at the last moment, Sinohne kicked upward, into his chest, sending the demon lord crashing into a table, smashing the furniture to pieces, then smacking against the wall. They both advanced, but Culzahr chuckled. He was gone in an instant.

He reappeared behind them, slicing into muscle and spine on Sinohne, whose knees buckled.

Victor appeared, joining the battle, and jumped on the demon lord's back, clawing at his eyes. "Screw you, fuckface!" He bit into the lord's neck, tearing at his jugular.

Culzahr roared, snatching the demon off his back and launched him into a pile of debris nearby. But the potent venom from Victor's bite worked its magic — the black demon listed to the side, unsteady on his feet. Sinohne and Damaceous tackled him against the wall, holding down his arms. Sinohne plunged his free hand into Culzahr's chest and gripped the bastard's heart in his claws.

Culzahr growled, the sound muffled by the blood flowing over his lips. "Filth!"

Sinohne sneered, moving his face closer. "You are everything Lucifer made us. Evil, vile, and less than the dirt beneath my claws." Sinohne started to pull out the organ.

"Sinohne, wait," Damaceous warned.

The silver demon paused, his gaze sliding toward the angel, revenge pumping through his veins. "Why?"

"We need him."

Culzahr cackled, blood splattering onto Sinohne's face and neck. The silver demon growled, squeezing the demon lord's heart.

"I want him dead."

"No," Damaceous barked, struggling to hold the greed demon against the wall. "He has knowledge. Answers we need. As a Powers, I can't just let him die."

"What's there to know?" Sinohne argued. "He killed my faction, my *family*. He deserves to rot right alongside all the corpses he's made."

Damaceous shifted, snapping Culzahr's neck with his hands. Culzahr stilled, the lack of blood to his brain sending the demon into a death state until he could regenerate. The angel released his body, forcing Sinohne to do the same. Culzahr fell forward, body slumping to the ground.

Bloody claws grabbed Damaceous around the neck. "Why?" Sinohne seethed.

Damaceous's eyes narrowed, but he chose his next words carefully. "When my dominion finishes extracting every minute bit of information from him, you can make the kill. I promise."

Sinohne studied his features then shoved the angel away. Damaceous rubbed his neck.

The silver demon bent over, grabbing one of Culzahr's horns between his fists. With a loud grunt, the bone snapped in two, leaving the demon lord with a short stump protruding from his temple. Sinohne repeated the action with the second horn.

The silver demon straightened, eyeing Damaceous in challenge.

The angel nodded. With this action, Culzahr would never hold rank in Hell again and be shunned by the factions if he ever returned.

When Sinohne walked away, Damaceous used the chains strewn around the area to secure the demon lord. He enchanted them; the chains wouldn't break no matter how hard the demon struggled.

Sinohne wasted no time. He rushed to Victor's side, his feet skidding on the floor. The injured demon leaned against the wall, his breathing ragged. His wings lay folded protectively over his chest, but Sinohne could see the tip of a silver arrow sticking out from his stomach.

"Vic'!"

Sinohne brushed aside the demon's wings to assess the damage. Victor had landed on one of Remiel's arrows. Blood trickled out of the wound, but the deadly runes from the arrow were already eating away at his skin.

Sinohne tried to pull out the offending object, but Victor stopped him. "There is nothing you can do," he whispered. "I can feel it, the decay…in my heart. It's too late." Sinohne's throat closed in on itself, choking his emotions. He gently removed the arrow, breaking off the head. Victor smiled at him, his eyes filled with pain.

Sinohne brought a knuckle to his lips, trying to soothe his fears. "I'm so sorry. I should have protected you."

Victor tried to laugh but grimaced. "It was my turn this time. You and me...I was happy."

Sinohne's heart broke. He gathered his beloved into his arms, letting Victor lean against him. "No," Sinohne said. "You're not going anywhere."

"Shut up. Just...let me die a hero, okay?" Victor's lips curved up, but his smile faltered, fear entering his eyes.

Sinohne blinked away his tears as Victor kissed him, using the last of his strength. Victor released his lips and buried his face against Sinohne's neck. "Sin'...I-I'm scared..." he whispered.

"I know. I'm right here, right here." The silver demon held him close, rocking the blonde until he felt the last breath leave his body. The brightness in Victor's eyes faded, and with his death, Sinohne roared, a long, sorrowful moan that echoed throughout the room.

Damaceous watched the ordeal, his own heart twisting. The green demon had been feisty but good-natured.

He sighed. The fight was not over yet. He turned his gaze and watched as the battle between Alatos, Remiel, and Zane continued.

TWENTY-FIVE

Zane walked toward the generals, battle breaking out behind him, his demeanor eerily calm. He ignored Remiel, his glowing eyes fixated on his enemy, Alatos.

Seeing Zane approach, the traitorous general sneered, breaking away from Remiel. He spread his wings in challenge.

Remiel frowned. Zane may have immense power, but he'd had no time to hone his abilities, unlike his shameful colleague. It might be the only edge the twisted angel needed. Remiel sheathed his swords, drawing his bow.

"You have two choices," Zane spoke, throwing the general's words back at him. The power of a thousand Virtues filled his voice, a hypnotic churning until his own voice was lost in the mix.

Alatos struggled to resist the hypnosis, gritting his teeth, jaw clenched.

"Surrender to me and stand trial. Or, die and forsake reincarnation."

Remiel had forgotten that tidbit. His eyes widened, but he held his bow steady, trained on the rival general.

Thrones were dangerous, not just for their immense power, but for what happened if they killed their victim; the soul was decimated, ceasing to exist. There were no more chances, no more lives...nothing.

Alatos spun his sword around his hand a couple of times, frowning while he weighed his decision. "I have never surrendered to anyone. What makes you think I'll do so now, to a sniveling, wingless buzzard like you?"

"Is that your final answer?"

Alatos growled and launched an attack upon the Thrones, his robes flying around him. Zane dodged, his armor whining imperceptibly at the swift movement, the breeze of the attack ruffling his hair. A thin cut appeared on his cheek, his gaze still glued to the general, his head tilted to the side.

Alatos chuckled as blood trickled down the younger angel's cheek. He had drawn first blood. His blade was poised inches from Zane's face, his arm still outstretched. "Witness the glory of Heaven's wrath, Zhanerious!" Hot flames engulfed the general's arm, snaking along his blade, flaring toward the other angel.

Zane twisted away, the rushing air generated by his flickering wing blowing the flames aside. Once steady again, Zane charged straight on, his weapons poised for attack. But, at the last moment, he jumped into the air. He spun, landing behind the general.

The general had anticipated the move, raising his sword to block Zane's blades from behind. Across from him, Remiel let loose an arrow. Alatos spun out of its way, and the arrow flew passed, just grazing his arm.

Zane flew, lightning sparking from his hands. Alatos shot his own flames back at Zane, neutralizing the attack, the dueling elements dissipating against each other.

Remiel exploited the distraction, throwing a dagger across the room, aiming for the general's chest.

But Alatos wasn't fazed. He twirled his sword, and the dagger pinged away, useless.

Alatos launched into the air, swinging his sword at Zane's head.

Zane deflected with his blades, but his assailant spewed fire at his unprotected face, catching the angel off guard. The blast sent Zane to the floor, flames licking his feathers. But the Thrones glanced up to see Alatos's sword aimed for his chest. He rolled, but the edge of his wing caught on the blade.

Alatos cackled, his blood singing.

The Thrones jerked his wing loose, muscles tearing, several feathers falling out as he tumbled away.

Kneeling, Zane inhaled large gulps of air, his lungs heaving.

Remiel moved closer, nocking another arrow.

Zane turned just in time to see Culzahr's body fall to the ground, heightening the tension in the already charged room. He cast a glance at Remiel, and they nodded to each other.

As one, Remiel and Zane attacked from both sides. Alatos dodged with superhuman speed, spewing flames to form a protective circle around him. Zane pushed through the flaming barrier, his electricity sending sparks in all directions, protecting him from the fire. He jabbed forward, but Alatos countered, sending the Thrones' blade out of reach.

Remiel was cut off, trapped beyond the circle as the flames rose around the other two fighters. Without an elemental ability in the general's arsenal, Zane was on his own.

Heat rose like a suffocating blanket, and Zane's breathing became heavier. Alatos grinned while they circled each other. Electricity protected Zane, but it wouldn't last, the oxygen in the enclosed area dwindling fast. Sweat poured down each fighter's face, Zane's hair sticking to his forehead. He swiped at the strands with his free hand, pushing the hair out his face.

Zane's calm demeanor was cracking before Alatos's eyes, and the general relished every moment. "Something the matter, youngling?"

Zane flicked away, just as suddenly reappearing before him, his armored claws slashing across the general's face.

The general caught Zane's arm before he made contact, twisting the angel around. His blade plunged into Zane's lower back, the pointed end passing entirely through his stomach. "Were you actually human, Zhanerious, this would've been fatal," he whispered into Zane's ear, the angel choking on his own blood. "Fortunately, for you, I missed your heart." He propped a foot on Zane's back and shoved him off the sword.

The Thrones crumbled in a heap on the floor. Alatos laughed, watching Zane gasp for breath. With great effort, Zane made it to one knee, using his weapon as a prop.

"Give it up, youngling. You'll never win."

Zane bared his teeth and launched upward at the general. But he was too slow, the injuries having taken their toll. The general merely shifted out of the way, pummeling Zane in the back with the hilt of his sword.

Zane fell at the general's feet. Alatos took great pleasure as he kicked Zane over, placing a heavy, sandaled foot atop the singer's chest. Zane grabbed the general's foot, transmitting electricity through his leg.

Alatos jerked his shin away and kicked Zane in the face. "Any last words?" He raised his sword, ready to plunge the dark blade downward for the final blow. The circle of flames dropped. As if he wanted the others in the room to see what was happening and to bask in the glory of their misery.

The barrier gone, Damaceous launched forward, crying out in dismay.

"Alatos!" Remiel bellowed, his bow poised.

When the general turned his head, Remiel let the arrow fly. Alatos swung his sword. The arrow bounced off the blade, heading in another direction. But it didn't matter. Zane took advantage of the distraction, linking their legs, tumbling his assailant to the floor and rolling on top of him. Alatos struck out, letting the momentum sink his sword into Zane's shoulder, piercing the leather, muscle, and bone.

"Fuck!" Pain exploded behind Zane's eyes, his shoulder burning as though it was dipped in acid. Zane growled, using the last of his strength to raise his fist, striking the angel beneath him with full force. The hidden blade in his gauntlet sprung forward, directly into Alatos's heart.

The general grasped at him, hands gripping his neck. "No!" he shouted, voice hoarse.

Zane twisted the blade, finishing the job. The general's eyes bulged, his neck straining. His mouth guppied like a fish, searching for air. His fingernails dug into Zane's skin, tearing at his hair. Zane pushed the blade harder, leaning onto his wrist as the life drained from the general's eyes, his hands falling to the ground.

Zane rolled off the dead general, lying on the charred surface of the dance floor. He coughed, blood splattering out of his mouth, covering his chin. Damaceous appeared beside him, removing the sword still stuck in Zane's shoulder. He gathered the Thrones into his arms, pulling the angel onto his lap. Sinohne approached them, cradling Victor's body.

Remiel knelt beside his rival, closing the lids of his eyes. "Goodbye, old friend." He frowned, noticing where Alatos's robes had ripped down the front. Leaning forward, he pulled the material apart, exposing the deceased angel's chest — and he gasped. A black pallor had spread inside his skin and veins in all directions. Pulling the cloth farther down, the origin of the vile blackness appeared to be an old, scarred-over wound on his side.

Remiel reached out to touch the skin, but Sinohne growled.

"Stop."

The general snatched his hand away. "What is it? I've never seen the like before."

Sinohne shook his head. "It smells rotten. Like his insides were already dying."

Remiel pursed his lips. "Perhaps the Council members will have more insight. I will have his body retrieved once we return." He glanced at Zane, whose eyes fluttered as he struggled to stay awake. "He needs to see the healers."

Damaceous clutched Zane tight against him. Zane dragged his face close, capturing his lips. Damaceous sighed into Zane's mouth, pouring energy into the angel in his arms, the tangy taste of blood on his tongue. The Powers kept on, until he weakened and pulled his mouth away, his breath now coming in heavy pants.

Zane brushed hair back behind Damaceous's ear, several pieces of the brunette locks having fallen out of his hair tie. He smiled at Damaceous through sleepy eyes while his wounds healed. Then the Thrones sat forward, one arm around Damaceous's shoulder. He turned to Sinohne, who still clung to Victor, and beckoned the demon closer.

Sinohne knelt beside them, and Zane ran a hand through Victor's blonde hair, gently smoothing the locks. "How?"

Sinohne's chin trembled, his grief seeping into the air as if to become a tangible marker of his loss. A deep pain pierced the coldness hovering over Zane's mind, and his palm twinged. But there was nothing anyone could do.

Victor — *Victor* — was gone.

Damaceous squeezed Zane's shoulder to comfort him. "Your friend helped distract Culzahr long enough to stop him. But he was thrown backward during the fight. And he...landed on a stray arrow. It was sticking out of the debris. The angelic runes...on the arrow. He might've survived the wound but...."

"I understand," Zane said. "I'm sorry, Sinohne, we both loved him."

Sinohne refused to return his gaze.

Remiel cleared his throat. "I'm sorry about your friend. But we need to hasten back to Heaven. There are still more battles to be won."

Zane narrowed his eyes. "Khamael." The power of his voice filled the room as his expression darkened.

"Correct. General Alatos did not work alone," Remiel replied. "I am truly sorry about your friend, but Lieutenant Ashliel waits for us. She's standing by to help take him down."

Damaceous scoffed.

The general sighed, his face turning haggard. "I know you're angry, Damaceous, but the lieutenant was only doing as ordered. Everything was a part of *my* plan. I urge you not to hold it against her. The things she's done have haunted her. Please...try to forgive her."

Damaceous's eyes widened, a vein in his forehead popping. "It was you?" With jerky movements, he set Zane aside and stood. He stalked toward Remiel, murderous intent behind his eyes.

"You bastard."

Damaceous grabbed the general by his breastplate and snarled in his face. "I trusted you. They could have killed me. I was...*tortured* for days. Khamael...he...for a fucking *investigation*?"

Damaceous released the general with a hard shove. "Whatever happens now, we are done. I'm finished. I want nothing more to do with the Powers Dominion." He turned around to regain control. Remiel reached out, but Damaceous slapped his hand away. He levelled his gaze on the general. "It was your arrow that killed their friend. Haven't you done enough?"

The general's brows knit together. "Yes, and I am...truly, truly sorry for their loss."

Sinohne lifted his gaze, the aura of grief turning ominous.

Zane stood and placed a hand on Sinohne's chest. "It won't bring him back." The anger left Sinohne's face, his eyes going empty as the truth rang through him like a gong. His head dropped forward, his lips brushing against Victor's cheek.

Remiel squeezed the bridge of his nose, sighing deeply. "I was tasked with bringing Zhanerious back to Heaven safely. It seems he established a peace treaty with you, Sinohne."

Sinohne raised an eyebrow. "It's a protection contract," the demon said, a hollowness in his voice.

"Semantics." Remiel waved a hand, and a portal opened behind him. "Zhanerious, Damaceous. Enter. We must return and finish this business with Lieutenant Khamael."

Zane brushed off his armor, still covered in ash from the fire. He pointed to Sinohne. "He must come with us."

The general balked at the idea. "Demons are not allowed in Heaven!"

"Sinohne is no ordinary demon. He is royalty. More importantly, without his presence, I won't set foot in Heaven. He's coming. You will bring Alatos's body, and Damaceous can grab Culzahr."

Remiel opened his mouth to reply but stopped. The power in the angel's voice compelled him to obey. Before he realized what he was doing, he'd picked up the body of the dead general.

Damaceous crossed to the demon lord, throwing Culzahr over a shoulder without care. Zane gestured to Sinohne to enter the portal. Sinohne's glamor reappeared as he stepped through, carrying Victor with him. Zane followed, Damaceous at his side. Remiel was the last to enter.

The portal closed behind them.

TWENTY-SIX

They emerged in front of the compound for the Warriors Dominion. A crowd of angels had gathered outside the entrance, talking in hushed whispers. Many angels stared at them as the group strode forward.

A youngling screamed. "Demons!"

"Demons?" The crowd grew restless, some beginning to panic. "We're under attack!"

One pointed to Remiel. "The general's dead!"

Zane led the pack. "Move," he ordered. Immediately, a path opened before him.

Expressions of shock and fear laced the crowd when Sinohne passed. "Filthy scum!" someone shouted.

Zane stopped short on the top step and his wing brushed the ground as he twisted to face the crowd, rustling up a cloud of dust. His armor caught the light, the frightening symbol on his chest covered in a layer of ash and blood. The Thrones glowered, eyeing each face in the crowd, his expression commanding silence. "Disperse…now."

The angels glanced at each other but then scrambled to leave. Sinohne didn't notice the attention, his eyes distant. Zane continued into the compound.

Remiel frowned, confused. He had expected Ashliel to join them, to be waiting in the area. A knot formed in his stomach when they opened the gate and stepped through the entryway leading into the main courtyard.

The general dropped the body of his traitorous rival, Alatos, and rushed forward when he saw the carnage.

Weapons were scattered upon the grass, bloodied and battered, headless bodies clad in silver armor lying in all different directions. Farther along, spears protruded from the ground. The heads of eight Powers were impaled, blood dripping down the wooden shafts.

Broken and lifeless, a pair of blue wings were shredded, feathers strewn across the courtyard. Pieces of armor had been laid out in front of them, covered in blood. Next to the armor, a braid of golden red hair lay pinned to the ground by a bloodied dagger. But there was no body.

Remiel cried out, running to the braid. "Why didn't you listen? Why didn't you wait for me?" He was broken, the sight of Ashliel's wings among the dead forever burned into his mind. His own became soaked in blood as he knelt, running his fingers through the soft, blue feathers. The general's chin trembled, everything else falling away to make room for the rage darkening his heart.

Damaceous winced, even as he carried Culzahr. Remiel's low wailing formed a lump in his own throat. He'd never wished this upon Ashliel. He had spent enough time under Khamael's torture to know what she would endure.

Zane stood among the mutilated heads, his expression somber.

Damaceous stepped closer. "What is it?"

"Lieutenant Khamael has fled. I cannot sense his presence here."

Damaceous cursed. "The High Council might know if he's gone to Earth. I assume he would. After committing such a public atrocity...he wouldn't dare stay in this realm."

Zane glanced at Remiel with a frown. "We should leave him and the bodies. We'll head to the High Council." Zane closed the doors of the compound, blocking out the public's view of the gruesome scene.

Sinohne found a clean patch of grass as far from the massacre as he could get and laid

Victor down. He crossed his arms, tucked his wings in. Sinohne bent over, placing a gentle kiss on the demon's brow. Victor's scales sparkled in the sunlight, the green shimmering against the grass. Zane and Damaceous approached him from behind.

Zane knelt next to Sinohne. "We should go now. No one will disturb him here."

"Surely I'm not welcome."

"They will treat you with respect, upon my honor," Damaceous replied.

Zane gently removed the demon's hands from Victor's body then grabbed Sinohne around the waist. He lifted off, his good wing beating against the air, the other crackling with lightning. Damaceous followed, still carrying the shackled demon lord. The group was quite a spectacle, and angels of all ages came out of their homes to watch them ascend. As they flew up the side of the mountain, the Council building appeared, nestled at the peak.

"Whoa..." Sinohne gasped.

He hadn't seen architecture like the Council building in thousands of years, the sight of the golden dome dazzling his mind. White stone walls stood tall, a monument to an ancient empire, clouds misting the air.

Victor will never see this, he thought.

Zane landed on the ledge and released Sinohne's waist. When Damaceous touched down, they entered the building together.

Damaceous gazed around. "How do you know where to go? I've never been allowed to come here before."

Zane cocked his head, his eyes narrowing. "The knowledge is there...as if I've always known the way."

Damaceous shook his head, sloughing off the thrall of Zane's voice and following behind him. The group continued down the hall, two large doors with carved images growing closer.

An attendant angel squeaked in surprise when she noticed their approach. She rambled about the demons and how they polluted the purity of the air, twisting her white robes between her fingers. Zane glowered again. The angel fell silent, then bowed and moved out of their path.

Zane pushed open the doors to the High Council's chambers.

Seated around a massive table were four angels, their eyes covered by a cloth. An angel closest to them turned in her chair and smiled, her great, golden wings sparkling in the light. Commander Jophiel came forward, holding her arms out to Zane.

Zane kneeled before her, his head bowed. The commander dropped her arms, her expression filled with a mixture of remorse and happiness.

Jophiel used a finger to lift Zane's chin. "Hello, my darling. Why do you bow before me?

I, who let you go to General Alatos…and to a terrible fate."

Zane returned her smile, covering her hand with his. "Jophiel…Commander. It has been too long. But nothing that happened to me was ever your fault. You could not have known what the general was capable of."

"Such power in your voice." She shivered. "We will speak on it later."

Jophiel stood with him, and, taking his arm, presented Zane to the High Council's Seraphim.

Damaceous set Culzahr by the threshold then bowed low, fist against his chest.

Sinohne ignored them, studying a portrait of Lucifer on the wall nearby. The ancient painting must have been preserved by magic, and Sinohne imagined the artwork had been finished long before the initial betrayal. Lucifer's aura of darkness was missing, and the angel glowed with an inner light. He assumed this was why the Dark King was once known as the Morning Star.

In the portrait, Lucifer's hair was a platinum blonde, waves falling to his chin. His eyes were full of mirth, one corner of his mouth curled up, as if he mocked the viewer. His facial bones were slender, but his nose was angular, his lips thin. The devil's wings were a stark white, a rare trait among the angelic species.

Sinohne shivered when he gazed into the icy blue stare. Lucifer's portrait alone held its own presence. He had encountered the Dark King twice and knowing he'd have to be in his presence again left Sinohne uneasy.

"Your Thrones, Councilmen."

Jophiel urged Zane forward, and he moved to kneel again.

"Rise, Zhanerious." Michael's voice echoed around the room. "General Alatos has been defeated, along with the demon lord, Culzahr. You've even established a peace treaty with the demon who will one day rule Hell. Well done."

"What of Lieutenant Khamael?" Ariel asked.

Damaceous's eyebrows knit together. Straightening his shoulders, he stepped forward. "Your Esteemed Councilors, Lieutenant Khamael has escaped. We aren't sure if he is still in our realm."

Chamuel cocked her head to the side. "Where is General Remiel? He was tasked to bring you back to us himself."

When the investigator did not immediately answer, Michael's expression darkened. "Well?"

Damaceous's mouth went dry. Zane discreetly laid a hand on his lower back, and his nerves settled. It wasn't every day an angel with his status addressed a Seraphim. "My Lady Councilor, we believe Lieutenant Khamael has taken the Power's lieutenant. He killed the guard contingent with her. When we found the aftermath, General Remiel became…distraught. We left the body of General Alatos in the courtyard. Although our battle was successful…we've endured a significant number of casualties today. Zane and Sinohne, they lost someone very dear to them."

"I…I'm so sorry," Chamuel said with a sniff, brushing quickly at her cheeks. She stood from the table, turning away.

Azrael watched her leave. "This is…upsetting." He lifted his hand and snapped his fingers. The attendant they'd encountered before entered the room, walking to his side, head bowed. "Have someone collect the bodies of the victims. They deserve a proper burial. Also, notify the Powers to retrieve the prisoner. Speak with him." Azrael pointed to Damaceous. "He will tell you where to find the dead."

The attendant nodded, pulling Damaceous aside.

Zane stepped closer to the table. "Also. We noticed a strange blackness on General Alatos after his death."

Jophiel gasped, a hand rising to her mouth. "Not possible." She glanced toward Michael.

"It was Lucifer, wasn't it?" Sinohne questioned from the portrait, not turning to them.

Michael's eyebrow raised. "How would you know of this?"

Sinohne shrugged. "He corrupts. It's one of Lucifer's powers. One of the reasons he was banished from the Empire, correct? Playing with the Dark Arts? He likes to experiment these days. I remember him mentioning it the last time he spoke to Baelozar…his experiments. We all know how he created demons."

Ariel frowned, the fingers she used to pet the baby fox going still. "If Lucifer somehow used his power to prey upon General Alatos's weaknesses, then all of this could have been his plan from the beginning; destroy us from within. He wants to use our own against us." Michael nodded in agreement.

Chamuel approached the portrait and stood close to Sinohne. Closer than he deemed safe for any angel. The assurance of her own power left him nervous, and he cleared his throat.

"Such a beautiful portrait, wouldn't you say?" she asked, her face gazing at the canvas. Though, how she saw through the cloth over her eyes left him baffled.

"Yes."

Chamuel chuckled and crossed her arms. "Do you know why you were brought here when so many of your kind have been denied or simply slaughtered?"

Sinohne kept his gaze firmly on the portrait. "No, I don't."

"Can you not guess?" Chamuel turned to him, an amused smile on her face. When he remained silent, she chuckled again. "You have formed the first peace treaty since the age of the Atlantic Empire. Were you aware of this?"

He frowned. "It's temporary. And, only as a protection contract. How is that a peace treaty?"

Chamuel chuckled. "Tomato, tomahto. The contract can be extended for however long you and Zhanerious remain on good terms. It is a contract of your allegiance to one another, your bond, is it not? Having the heir, the new Crown Prince, as an ally for our new Thrones is a good thing."

He turned to her, his frown deepening. "My friendship and allegiance to Zane has nothing to do with Heaven itself."

Chamuel was undeterred. "But we can offer safe harbor for you here. Baelozar was not well liked by the other factions, and with the royal faction diminished, there are few left to ask for help. Hell will be in chaos. Our protection and support may come in handy when you are faced with the other demon lords. And…we can arrange a proper burial for your friend." Sinohne's jaw unclenched at her last words, but he didn't get the chance to reply; Chamuel headed back to the table, rejoining the Seraphim.

"Zhanerious," Michael called.

Zane stepped closer, waiting.

"You've proven yourself," Michael said. "But you also have a decision to make. As a Thrones, you will be called upon to enforce the laws and rulings of the High Council. Plainly speaking, you are enormously more powerful than the generals of each dominion and will be treated with the same regard the Council receives. But this power comes with a cost. At your young age, your mind and body may not be able to withstand the strain, and when released from the compulsion we placed, you may go mad. The compulsion has protected your mind by suppressing your emotions, leaving you with pure logic and instinct alone."

"You have another option," Ariel continued. "This promotion was meant to be temporary because we were aware of the risks. You can return to your original state and live a peaceful life in the Virtues Dominion. Eventually, when you are ready, you will be allowed to take on the Thrones title and powers again if you wish. If you decide to keep your title, we do have a mission ready to assign you."

Azrael picked up the explanation. "Roughly seventy percent of the human souls in the soul vessel have been accounted for, according to the Cherubim. But the angels who Fell during General Alatos's campaign cannot be located. None of their souls were within the vessel. But their Fall corresponds with the discrepancies. We need someone to find these Fallen and offer to return their status if they wish it. Their seals will be removed, and their power restored. Any faults they may have committed will be pardoned, and they can return with a fresh slate."

"This is your choice alone, Zhanerious," Chamuel finished. "The risks of your power are significant, but Heaven needs a champion in a time when our dominions falter. Please, choose what will make you happiest."

Damaceous stepped beside Zane, grabbing his elbow and then turned to the Council. "If he can't access his emotion, how can he choose? And, if he stays a Thrones, will Zane ever be himself again?"

Ariel smiled. "Of course. But…it is the heaviest of responsibilities, and we've avoided bestowing this title since the wars ended. They are our swords and, until now, we didn't need one."

"I would like to experience my power with my full senses before I choose," Zane said.

Michael shook himself before answering.

The power in Zane's voice even affected the Seraphim? Sinohne tucked the information away for later use.

Michael regained his footing. "We can't release you from your compulsion without a decision. Your mind may break, and it would be too late."

Zane turned to Sinohne. "You've known me the longest, and you're my closest friend. What do you think?"

Sinohne sighed. "I don't know the answer. I don't think…V—" He choked on the demon's name. "Victor wouldn't know, either. I know he'd want you to be careful. He'd have some stupid joke…we'd all laugh. But, yeah. He'd say to be careful."

Zane considered his words. He glanced to Damaceous, who appeared lost deep in thought, and placed a hand over the one on his arm. The investigator jerked, startled at the contact.

"You're intimate with me…"

Damaceous blushed, a red flush creeping into his cheeks. "Zane!" He hesitated and glanced at the Council before drawing the Thrones into a tight hug, the smaller angel's armor poking at his skin. Zane allowed Damaceous to gather his thoughts, but he did not return the embrace.

Soon, Damaceous pulled back enough to see his face. "You should do what will make you happy. I don't want to lose you. I'll stay with you, even in your madness, if that's the case. Or I will gladly spend my days frolicking among the flowers in the Virtues Dominion." Damaceous stared into Zane's mismatched eyes then pressed their foreheads together. "I have strong feelings for you, Zane. I want more time to…explore them and to know you more. But I can't help you with this decision." He released Zane, but still held his hand.

Zane nodded and finally gazed back at the Seraphim, who waited patiently. "I know the High Council could find someone else to find the missing Fallen. But I wouldn't be able to find peace, knowing there are others out there, alone, who may have faced the same horrors. I will take the title of Thrones, permanently."

Damaceous linked their fingers and squeezed, offering a worried smile. The Powers glowed with pride at the bravery his lover showed, but a deep fear of the outcome rooted inside his mind.

Michael remained grim. "Are you sure? Do not make this decision lightly. You cannot take it back."

"Yes, I'm positive."

Azrael sighed. "This could get...messy."

Damaceous chewed on his inner lip, his eyebrows knitting together.

Ariel stood from her chair, gazing at the ancient artifacts in the room with concern. "Perhaps we should do this...outside?"

Chamuel agreed. "Yes. We will head to the colosseum. Leave Sinohne. For now, he is safer away from the community."

Michael frowned. "Not a chance."

Jophiel stood from her seat. "I will stay with him if this will satisfy you, Councilor?"

Michael sighed, his frown deepening.

Sinohne crossed his arms, scowling. "I'll be fine to wait. But, Damaceous?"

The angel twisted around at his name. "Yes?"

"Keep him safe."

"Always."

TWENTY-SEVEN

The four Seraphim stood on the platform of the High Council building, facing the city below. The two suns had begun to set, bright streams of light reflecting off Chamuel's wings, the brilliance of each feather like a diamond. Ariel's feathers reflected the color of the clouds as the suns dipped, the sky turning different shades of red and purple.

But, for Damaceous, the real beauty stood beside him. His only wing glistened an iridescent gold among feathers of blues and greens, taking away his breath from the mere sight. Even the crackle of Zane's shadow wing was magnificent. Damaceous reached out, a light fingertip brushing along the nearest feather. Zane shivered, glancing at Damaceous in curiosity. Damaceous returned Zane's gaze with heat, and he could've sworn the Thrones blushed; it was impossible to tell with the sun setting behind them. The Seraphim took off from the platform at the same time, startling Damaceous out of his fixation. Zane cleared his throat and followed.

All six flew across the sky, down the mountain, and over the city, heading for the small colosseum, the same place Zane had performed years ago. Angels all over the capital pointed, some in awe, some in fear. They fell to their knees, bowing in respect as the Seraphim flew overhead.

After they passed, the citizens launched into the air, filling the sky behind them, following the entourage. A public appearance of the Seraphim was a rare occurrence; unannounced, it was unheard of.

The group landed in the middle of the ring, and the citizens who had followed took the surrounding seats.

Damaceous's brows scrunched, eyes darting to the crowd. He had not prepared for such a public display. There was a tense silence while the Seraphim surveyed their surroundings, nodding to the citizens.

"Sir? Uh…Councilor?" Damaceous whispered to Azrael, who stood closest.

Azrael's lips thinned, his arms crossed. "Yes?"

"Should we really allow so many to be here for this? Zhanerious's fate is still uncertain."

Azrael frowned, his expression grim. "You're right, of course. But most have never seen one of his title, and...with the recent tragedies, they will need reassurances from their High Council. If Zhanerious truly goes mad, and he cannot be saved, he will be put down."

Damaceous paled. The possibility of losing Zane had not occurred to him.

Azrael laid a hand on his shoulder, squeezing gently. "Should he survive, the citizens can rally around their new protector. Zhanerious may carry out our laws and missions, but Thrones have always been the ones who seek out injustice. Our younglings read about them, worshipping the Thrones of the past as heroes. We want Zhanerious to survive, young one. Have no doubt, his loss would bring a great blow to us all."

Azrael released his grip. Damaceous was still concerned, but he was honored the Seraphim had tried to comfort him. He bowed, a fist against his chest. Azrael dipped his head in acknowledgment. Damaceous licked his lips, his mouth drying out again, while he watched Michael direct Zane to stand in the middle of the arena.

Michael turned to the crowd, holding up his hands to catch their attention. "Angels of Heaven." His voice carried on the wind, reaching every ear within the colosseum without having to raise his voice, wielding the ability to control the air and the wind. "Today, we gather to speak of the tragedy among our own. Your High Council knows what you've seen in the Warriors Dominion. Alatos...the general of the Warriors...aided by his lieutenant, Khamael, started a conspiracy against our own kind, against our younglings...his trainees. While this is no excuse, we believe Lucifer caused this with his ties to the darker arts. He corrupted the general...and used his weakness...twisting Alatos and Khamael to destroy Heaven from within."

Michael paused. Zane spread his wing and kneeled, bowing to the audience.

"With help from this Powers investigator...Zhanerious was able to bring the former general, Alatos, to justice. General Alatos was executed for his crimes, and Lieutenant Khamael is still free. Zhanerious, as well as many other younglings like him, suffered at Alatos's hands...due to Lucifer's corruption. He has agreed to help find those who suffered and bring them home, willing to sacrifice his own happiness...just to bring peace to others. He is the first among us...to establish a treaty with a demon, the new heir to the throne of Hell. This type of character and honor...has not been seen since the age of the Atlantic Empire. With great risk to his mind, Zhanerious had chosen to take on the title of Thrones, the first since the Great War."

Michael paused, scanning the audience. "What say you!"

The crowd burst to their feet, cheering and screaming their praise. Many angels flew into the air, shouting with joy. He let them go on for a little while but soon waved for them to settle. When the excitement was over, his expression became serious. He turned to his fellow Seraphim, and they backed away from Zhanerious, creating a wide box. Azrael pulled Damaceous with him, putting the younger angel behind his back.

"Are you ready, Zhanerious?" Michael asked.

Zane looked at Damaceous, holding his gaze as he nodded. "Yes."

"Zhanerious...your mission is complete. You are released."

The key turned on Zane's mind like a fog had been lifted from his senses. Everyone around him waited for something, anything, to happen, holding their breath. Zane grabbed his chest...ran his fingers through his hair. Everything seemed about as normal as possible. He lifted his gaze to Damaceous and smiled. But Zane's peaceful moment did not last long.

A wave of emotions crashed into him, from horror to pain to amusement to anger, every sensation he should have experienced in those moments following his rise to Thrones. Within seconds, another wave roared through his body, his vision going white. He screamed, but no sound came out, a loud static taking over his hearing. His body bowed painfully backward, the weight of his power sending him to his knees.

He clawed at his head, unable to control his thoughts, flashes of memories scattering here and there, distorting reality. Lightning crackled across his skin, sparks shooting out in all directions. He was losing control, the power building under his skin, burning at his mind, erasing his memory, turning him into nothing but energy. And he was helpless to stop it, any control he'd had cut from his thin grasp.

Damaceous watched in horror as lightning shot from Zane's body into the sky. The lightning created a dangerous arch of energy, swirling around him, searing the ground, scorch marks striking within inches from where Damaceous and Azrael stood. Everyone backed away, their faces grim. The angels in the stands panicked, screaming, a few retreating in fear. White light shone out of Zane's eyes, his body contorting backward.

"We have to do something!" Damaceous shouted to Azrael.

The Seraphim shook his head. "This is what we feared might happen! There is nothing we can do for him now!"

Damaceous grabbed Azrael by the front of his shirt. "I'm not going to let him die like this!"

Azrael's nostrils flared angrily. "There is nothing you can do!"

"I don't believe that!"

Damaceous rushed forward, but Azrael hauled him backward, holding him. "Are you stupid? You'll be killed if you try to get closer!"

"He needs me! I won't let this happen!" With the back of his fist, Damaceous coldcocked the Seraphim in the nose.

"Shit!" Azrael grabbed his face, in pain and shock, his reflexes forcing him to release Damaceous. Before Azrael could stop him again, he launched forward, twisting and ducking around the lightning. "Damaceous! No!"

Damaceous was determined to reach his lover. An arch of energy burst out of Zane's body, straight at Damaceous, leaving him no way to avoid it. He was wrenched backward from the impact, his chest scorched and bleeding. Undeterred, he continued desperately toward Zane.

After two more attempts, Damaceous snaked an arm around Zane's waist, shocks of electricity burning into him. Damaceous gritted his teeth against the pain and did the only thing he could think of. He dragged Zane's mouth to his, pressing their lips together, a hand cradling Zane's head.

Damaceous pulled energy out of Zane, extracting as much power as he could. Lightning danced across his own skin, singeing his hair, his feathers, the smell of burning flesh wafted to his nose. He pressed harder, drawing Zane's immense power inside of himself. Zane's hands gripped his arms, responding to him. The Seraphim gawked, struck with wonder. A static arch of lightning and energy surrounded the two angels like a force field, sparks dancing over them.

An explosion erupted, a deafening blast which caused everyone to grab their ears in pain. When Azrael raised his head, the lightning had dissipated. Damaceous lay splayed out on his back, still. His hair was singed, his feathers burned away. Scorch marks covered his body, steam rising from his skin. Zane lay in the opposite direction, in similar condition, both angels unconscious. The Seraphim acknowledged each other, unsure of what action to take. The remaining audience stayed mute. Not even the wind dared to ruffle the scattered feathers on the ground.

Azrael went to Damaceous's side and placed a finger on his neck. He heaved a sigh when he found a pulse. "This one lives." Taking his cue, the four Seraphim moved toward Zane.

Michael checked his pulse. He frowned, and Azrael's stomach sank. Michael's expression was unreadable.

"Is he alive?" Ariel asked, beating Azrael to the punch.

Michael narrowed his eyes and nodded. "Yes, Zhanerious is alive. But how it's possible…" His voice drifted off, lost in thought.

Chamuel sighed and turned, her expression filling with happiness. "Angels of Heaven, Zhanerious lives!"

The audience cheered.

Chamuel turned back to the Seraphim. "We must get those two to the healers, or my statement will not remain the truth. I will fetch them myself. Today is a historic moment. It will not be said I did nothing."

Chamuel took off in the direction of the Virtues Dominion.

Azrael chuckled at her excitement, watching her leave. "A historic day, indeed."

Zane gasped and shot forward on the bed, startling the attendant who kept watch. Zane stared in confusion, his throat parched, his lips dry. Glancing down, he realized he wasn't clothed — instead covered in just the white sheets on the bed, and he blushed.

The attendant was posted in a wicker chair by the bed. He'd grabbed his chest as if afraid he was going to have a heart attack, and he let out a long breath. He wore a white robe, sleeves tied at the shoulders, a sash of bright green cinching his waist. The attendant had brown hair, parted to the side, and gray eyes with a boyish face. His wings were the color of honey, a deep, golden amber.

The angel smiled. "I'm glad you're awake."

Zane tried to respond but sputtered into a coughing fit. The attendant handed him a glass of water.

Zane took the glass, emptying the contents in seconds. "Thanks." He set the glass back on the table. "Um...what — uh...what happened?"

The attendant angel's expression turned into a look of adoration, beaming at him with a brilliant smile. Zane cringed, opting to check his chest and legs for injuries rather than face such a bright smile. He found no signs of trauma or illness.

"In my lifetime of sixty thousand years, I'm honored to attend the first Thrones since the empire," the attendant whispered, his voice filled with awe.

Zane blanched; the angel looked no older than seventeen. "Uh…Thank you? But, really, I don't remember what happened. And, I have no idea who you are."

"Yes, my apologies. My name is Gadriel." The angel bowed his head in respect. "I am your personal attendant from this moment forward. I will take care of all your needs, platonically, as you act as an enforcer of Council Law."

"And, I am where? A hospital?"

"Of sorts. You were brought here, to the Virtues Dominion, to heal and recuperate. Michael released you from compulsion. As I understand, from his account, you were unable to hold the power on your own. An angel, Damaceous, drew your power from you, saving your life and helping your body balance your energy. This was seven months ago."

Zane's jaw dropped. "*Seven months?* But I don't understand. What happened? Where's Damaceous? Sinohne? Victor?"

Gadriel pointed to his immediate left. Zane let out a sigh of relief. Sinohne was asleep in a chair in the corner of the room, arms crossed, chin resting on his chest.

"He called me here today. It's as if he knew you'd finally wake," Gadriel said. "I didn't believe it but…Sinohne was right."

On another bed beside his, Damaceous was fast asleep. Like Zane, his body was covered in only a sheet, his wings splayed out beneath him. Feathers had regrown, and his hair was spread loose over a pillow underneath his head. There were no visible injuries Zane could see from where he was positioned.

"Did I wake up first?"

Gadriel nodded. "He hasn't woken since that evening. We only know he is comatose, just like you were until now. We've tried everything, but no remedy has been found. The fact you have woken is a mystery in itself."

Zane bit the inside of his cheek then slid toward the other bed.

Gadriel caught his elbow. "You should not move. We don't yet know what condition you're in, mentally, or physically."

Zane shrugged him off.

"Gadriel," a gravelly voice said from across the room.

Zane turned to see Sinohne yawn. The demon leaned forward onto his elbows. "Give us a moment, alone. I'll find you later."

Gadriel huffed but bowed to Zane. The attendant left, closing the door behind him.

"You're finally awake!"

Sinohne rushed over, embracing the angel tightly to his chest. It was a display of emotion Zane wasn't used to seeing from him.

Zane patted his companion's shoulder. "Yup. Very awake. What are you doing here? What happened? Why the fuck are we in Heaven? Where's Victor?"

"Whoa! Slow down." Sinohne released his hold and settled onto the mattress beside him. "You don't...remember?"

Zane's brow scrunched. His eyes landed on a green scale dangling from a chain around Sinohne's neck. His stomach dropped.

Zane pointed to the necklace. "What is this?"

Sinohne's eyes flashed with pain. "This is one of Victor's scales. The angels made them for us before we buried him. I thought you might want something of his, too." Sinohne laid a similar necklace in his palm and closed Zane's fist over it.

Zane shook his head. "I don't...I don't understand."

"He died, Zane. Victor is...dead." Sinohne's voice cracked on the last word.

"But...we won. I...I beat Alatos, right? We're alive, so we must've won!" Zane protested, his voice rising.

Sinohne's grabbed the angel, hands on either side of his head. "I know. But Victor died. Nothing you say will change the past."

He forced Zane's eyes to focus on him. Zane started to blink, tears threatening to fall.

"It's okay," Sinohne said.

Those two words broke whatever dam Zane held back, big sobs racking his body. Sinohne hugged him close and buried his face in

Zane's hair, blinking fast while hot tears splashed onto his chest.

Together, they mourned.

A while later, Sinohne went to retrieve Gadriel, leaving Zane to check on Damaceous. Zane stood from his bed, then climbed under the sheet with the other angel. He laid himself against Damaceous's side, reveled in the warmth burning off his body. Zane put his ear to his chest, listening to the steady heartbeat, and closed his eyes.

Damaceous had saved his life, but had he sacrificed his own? Zane pushed his midnight locks back from his eyes, sighing, unsure of how to fix the problem. He tried to recall that night, unable to recover more than quick snippets of the events. His memory shorted out after Culzahr tried to kill them with a soul vessel. From what he gathered, they'd taken down Culzahr and Zane had killed Alatos, but the crucial details were blank.

Zane wrapped an arm around Damaceous's waist and snuggled closer, squeezing the angel like a giant teddy bear. He had nothing to fear, his greatest enemies were vanquished. But without Damaceous's kindness, his warm eyes, his dry sense of humor, his...everything. His throated constricted as Zane fought off another wave of sadness.

Propping himself on his elbows, Zane gazed at the investigator's face. His lashes were dark, and curling at the ends, dusting a shadow across his cheeks. Zane reached over, and he cradled Damaceous's head. He pressed his lips to his unconscious lover's mouth, pouring a jolt of power into the angel. If it had worked to save himself, perhaps, it might reawaken Damaceous.

He paused, searching for a sign, a twitch, anything.

To his dismay, Damaceous remained still. "Damn it..."

Zane twisted away, sitting on the edge of the bed. He dropped his head into his hands, defeated. If the others couldn't find a solution, how would he? What was the point of all his power if he couldn't save the ones who meant the most to him?

"Gadriel!"

Zane paced the room, his wing scraping along the floor. The door creaked with Gadriel's return to the room. The angel bowed in respect, causing Zane to frown. "Please, don't bow for me. It's weird."

Gadriel straightened. "Of course."

"I need clothes. Can you...?"

Gadriel chuckled. "Follow me. But you might want to grab the sheet."

Zane blushed, wrapping a sheet from the bed around himself like a towel after a shower. He glanced toward Damaceous.

"I'll be back soon. I promise."

About the Author

R.J. Benson has been writing urban fantasy, supernatural and romance since she was a young girl. She studies at the Cleveland Institute of Art, pursuing a BFA in Game Design with a minor in Creative Writing.

Her childhood was spent among the northern hills in the bluegrass state and some with the Huskies up north. For a time, her soul was under contract to the government. But she has seen the world, meeting peoples of many lands and cultures.

Benson enjoys spending her days with her puppers, reading novels and comics or, playing video games. She often spends a great deal of time creating original stories or, sometimes, fanfiction just for fun.

If you enjoyed this story, please follow R.J. Benson on all social media platforms under the tag-name; @therealrjbenson.

Find more fantastic authors with her publisher by visiting; ATBOSH.com.